PUBLICATIONS PRESENTS

GHOSTS OF THE BX

5 Star Publications
PO Box 471570
Forestville, MD

Ghosts of the BX

ISBN -13: 978-09832473-4-0
ISBN-10: 0-98324734X
Library of Congress Control Number: 2011933373
First Printing: January 2012

Printed in the United States

www.5starpublications.net
www.tljbookstore.com
authoradonis@icon5star.com

Acknowledgments

Not to many kept it real so my shout outs won't be long. First, all praises due to the most high with out your love and support none of this would be possible, you've continued to love me more, even when I didn't deserve to be loved. Never once have you closed the door on me or turned your back, I love you. Mrs. Trivia Jones, my mother. Deborah Occena, I will always love you. Jerry L. Reed, my brother. Winston Shim, my father, rest in everlasting peace. My uncle, Thaddeus Suazo, I know I've made it hard for us to be as tight as we should've been, but if I turn out to be 25% of the man you are, I'll be good. Ms. Lorraine Alcimas, and Cynthia McCormack and family. To my sisters Bonita Giles, Thank you, every time I was hungry you cooked. Serina Sampson, Francine Curry, Sherelle, Lolita, and Jasmine Gray. Latoya Clay it's been years but you always told me I'd make it. Marjorie Adolfe, Thank you for showing me how to love. Rosette James, you already know. Shaunta Fireston, Denise Brown love you both, we all we got. Leslie Brown, my best friend, thank you for everything and understanding. Latisha Deshommes my ride or die. Chuckie and Tiffany, friends till the end. Kisha Warren ain't no future without you. My brother's Andre Teal, Jamie Giles, Sai Giddy, Blam and the Blam nation. Ray Wellington thanks dawg you taught me so much. Kevin (K.G.) Gene love you. Jeremy Knok Poole, my second favorite white boy, sorry dawg Howard Stern came first. Shawn Valentine and the 5 Star staff, thanks for the opportunity. Harvey Banga Mitchell, Rashid Evans, James T. Berekley, Rome Lucky Daniel, The GOD Garner and Jamaal Coleson, James Scoop Bethea Sadot Yancey we here now!!!!

Dedication

This is dedicated to Danice Washington, you inspired me to do this, without your words of encouragement, I might still be playing those hot blocks. Thank you for being there since I was a foolish kid to give me words of wisdom... I Love you like a fat kid loves cake. Also, to the mother of my children, your hatred, your lack of faith and love, have been the greatest inspiration.....

GHOSTS

OF THE

BX

Chapter 1

CoCo just laid there. Although her body was there, her mind was distant as Hard White pumped away at her as if he were killing it. Every now and then, she'd moan as if in agony just to stroke his ego. Asshole! This is what had become of her life.

"You love me mami," he asked.

"Oh yeah daddy," she moaned trying not to laugh.

Love him? Ughh! She felt like throwing up, but managed to nod through the nausea. Love? Was he crazy? This had nothing to do with love, but somehow this had become her livelihood. Love? The word even sounded ridiculous to her. After all the shit she did, she doubted that she even deserved to be loved. To hell with love! Love was just some illusion painted by some chick so blinded that she refused to believe she was some man's whore.

It didn't matter if she considered him her man or her husband, because regardless of what a broad believed, she still used her body for money. CoCo faced reality that love didn't pay bills, pussy did. Better yet, arrogant, ignorant imbeciles, such as the man lying on top of her breathing like some out of shape baboon did. Everything about him turned her off, except his money. For the past month, Hard White was getting it more. He had been generously feeding CoCo and her best friend Sincerely. Thank God her brother was supposed to be back tomorrow.

"Oh shit ma… I'm about to cum."

"Get it daddy," she called out as if she was about to as well, but all she could think was *please hurry up so I can get the hell outta here.*

His cell phone was chirping simultaneously, as he began to thrust harder while trying to force the nut out of his little prick. She almost laughed, but then she finally felt him inside of her. "Damn daddy, answer your phone."

"Shit," he called out as he pulled out of her. "Damn this pussy is too good," he said while rolling over and answering his phone.

She just rolled her eyes, wishing she could say the same about his dick, but she couldn't, so she just decided to get dressed. She wanted badly to wash his nasty, wet dog fur smelling sweat off her body, but she wanted more to just to get out of his apartment.

"Tior, what's up baby boy?" Tior was a Guyanese cat from Washington Avenue Projects, which was up the street from where CoCo lived. He was Hard's business partner and they had 170th and 3rd Ave on lock. CoCo knew Tior well. She even went out with him a few times, but ultimately ended it when her brother found out. Her brother was another reason she knew she'd never really experience love or being loved. He would never allow it, especially if she was dealing with any kind of man who was getting money. Fully dressed, she sat on the edge of Hard's king size bed, patiently waiting on payment for her services, but now she would have to wait for these two assholes to converse.

Tior had always been the muscle of the operation. If anyone dared to violate their hood, Tior never hesitated to let his gun negotiate, and that earned him the nickname The Wild Indian (Appache) or Crazy Horse. Hard White on the other hand was the brain of the operation. He was a punk white kid from Throgs Neck, who was now said to be sitting on six digits. They laughed.

"So what's the deal with my second favorite white boy," Tior asked.

"Second? Who's the first," Hard asked.

"Howard Stern."

"You're an Asshole."

'*You got that right,*' CoCo thought to herself.

"So what's up, you hittin' the Savoy tomorrow night?"

"Hell no Apache! What's the purpose of making money if you spend it making other niggas rich?"

CoCo hated to hear this white boy use the word 'nigger' and could never figure out how the black guys he ran with allowed it.

"What's the purpose? Son, to live it up," Tior replied.

"I'm livin' it up right now," Hard said squeezing CoCo's ass. She turned her head the other way so he couldn't see her roll her eyes.

"Oh word? Who you with?"

"The sexy CoCo."

Tior sucked his teeth, "Dog, that bitch is trouble."

"Nah man this is my baby. She good."

"Yeah I heard. You better stay protected."

"I'm always strapped up," Hard White shot back.

"I ain't talking 'bout condoms. I'm talking about her grimy ass brother. Fuck around and have to kill both they asses."

"Nah she ain't on it like that."

She hated sitting there listening to him talk about her and not knowing what was being said on the other end. There was no telling what faggot ass Tior was filling Hard's head with. She knew he would do whatever to get with her or get his man away from her, because most men were like that. She huffed and puffed, and Hard finally got the hint.

"Yo, Apache let me holla back at you. I got a little business to take care of."

"Yeah man, just watch that bitch, she's no good."

"I got you," Hard said hanging up. "Now what's your problem," he asked.

She sucked her teeth. "You said you'd give me the three hundred and fifty to pay my rent."

Now he sucked his teeth, digging through his pants pocket. Three hundred and fifty dollars wasn't a thing to him. He'd blown four or five times that on ceelo games in the projects that his team controlled. He handed her an even five hundred and told her to keep the change, and that brought a smile to her face.

*****

The white Acura Integra flashed its headlights to alert the green Dodge Caravan that it was pulling off the exit ramp. The driver of the green Caravan blew the horn in response. Blast looked into his rearview as he exited the Major Deagan Expressway on 161st street and smiled to himself. Do Dem Boys had done it again. That was the name of his crew of West Indians that wore gold, iced out chains with a DDB pendant hanging from it. Blast started the vicious arm robbery crew over four years ago and they made their living robbing drug dealers. Now their name rang bells up and down the East Coast, after years of terrorizing the Bronx and Manhattan.

Blast couldn't wait to see his older sister Chanel, better known as CoCo. CoCo was only two years older than him, but since the

death of their mother, Blast took care of her. He had been gone almost four weeks, in which time DDB hit NC, GA, VA and made three hundred and seventy-five thousand dollars that they split six ways. Blast smiled at himself in the mirror. *'Sixty-two grand? Not bad for less than a month's worth of tax free money.'* The smile quickly changed. No one knew about the fifteen keys he had in the trunk that he managed to hide from the rest of the team. The biggest problem that presented itself was that he was a stick up kid who didn't know shit about selling drugs.

While the kids in his tenements were starting to save money to buy half ounces of weed, he started saving to buy his first .25 automatic. His mother always thought something was wrong with him because he never played with the other boys in the building. He hated them, that's why. However, they loved CoCo, because she was a dark skin, pretty, and well developed girl by the age of fourteen. They always teased him and beat him up. When they started selling drugs, he watched them from the roof and spotted their stashes, and by seventeen he was a full fledged stick up kid. Now, he had fifteen keys and nothing to do with them because none of the local hustlers would deal with him; and this was something that he knew for sure.

He turned on to Webster Avenue where he could see his building from the distance. Damn it felt good to be home. Just then, it came to him as he smiled to himself. He was a genius, nah a criminal mastermind. Not only would he be able to make the money, but he'd be able to get a little revenge for all the years they terrorized him. He pulled into the back parking lot at 1240 Webster Ave and was home. As he got out of his car, he scoped the area. Blast knew he could never be too safe because he'd done a lot of dirt and never knew when karma could be creeping up around the corner.

He couldn't wait to see CoCo, but for the past month, all he could really think about was Sincerely. Sincerely, or Sin for short, was his girl now. She had been his sister's best friend since they were kids, and now she was two months pregnant with his child. He walked into the 7th floor apartment that used to belong to their mother in the past. Even though she moved down to Tennessee, Sincerely still had her grandmother's apartment. CoCo and Sin both sat on the sofa watching re-runs of Friends and didn't see Blast walk in. CoCo was about to hand Sin a small blunt, but was rudely interrupted when Blast yelled, "I'll break your fuckin' neck if you give her that weed." CoCo jumped because she was startled and Sin jumped out of total fear.

"Cornell, hey baby," Sin said as she jumped to her feet to hug and kiss him.

"Ill, you two disgust me," CoCo said as she mashed up her face.

"Stop hatin' CoCo. You just mad 'cause you ain't got no man!"

"What? I got a man," CoCo stopped in mid-sentence.

"You got a what," questioned Blast as he raised his voice.

"Nothing Cornell! Damn Sin you talk too fuckin' much. God!"

"Let me find out you fuckin' with one of these niggas around here and his ass is out!"

Coco said nothing.

"You hear me?"

"Yes, Cornell," she finally answered while rolling her eyes at Sin.

"So listen. I want you to do something…" Blast went on to explain his little plan. Although CoCo didn't like it, she really didn't have a choice, because there was no way she could tell Blast no.

*****

Lawson "Lace" Anderson stood in the full length mirror admiring himself. He looked at his four year old daughter Latisha. "Baby, is daddy laced," he asked as the little girl just smiled. He looked at his Movado. It was almost time to go meet Marisol at the train station. She got off work at eight and the train would be dropping her off on 225th St. and White Plains Road by nine pm. She hated walking home late by herself through the drug infested area. Although Lace made a name for himself in the hood and the local thugs knew who Marisol was, nonetheless it was still dangerous. Lace took little Tisha downstairs to the landlady's, Ms. Maddy, house.

Even though both of their mothers were alive, she often baby sat for Marisol and Lace as well as did other things. Ms. Maddy treated them like her own children, even though hers were grown and much older. Ms. Maddy loved having them around. As Lace took the three block walk to the 225th Street train station, every local spoke to him and every thug gave him a pound. Lace was early, because he didn't want any reason for Marisol to argue. He knew he would already have problems, because he was going out to the club later with his cousins Mark and Maurice, so an argument over being late was not in his forecast.

Lace was getting money on his block that he controlled with a small, loyal three man crew. Mark and Maurice were hustlers for real. While Lace and his crew hit and Rich moved dimes off base, Mark and Maurice moved heavy weight. On several occasions

Maurice, known as Moe Money, offered Lace bricks on consignment, but Lace refused the offer. He was content with his five ounces a week, although at any moment he could have turned it up. He felt the more drugs he tried to move, the more attention he would get from the police, so he decided to keep it simple.

His cousins were the men to know, especially Moe. Moe pushed a candy apple red six hundred, while Mark pushed a simple Acura Legend. He could've definitely afforded something bigger, but rule number one was, never try to out shine the boss. So, Mark laid back while Maurice flossed through the hood. Since he was planning on going out with his cousins, and not Rich and Hitz from his little Bronxwood crew, Marisol wouldn't really beef too much. He saw her coming down the station steps long before she saw him. Damn she was fine, Rosario Dawson sexy. At first his mom and sister, Lynette, were mad he was dealing with a Puerto Rican girl and not a black woman, but once she had Latisha his mother fell in love with her.

"Mami, you look so tired."

"I am baby," she said, while handing him her bag, as she looked his outfit up and down. "Oh that's why you here on time tonight," she said rolling her eyes.

"Why you say that baby?"

"Don't baby me. You're going out with your cousins tonight, so you rushed down here to butter me up."

He smiled at her statement as they started walking home, but he knew not to say anything, because all she wanted was an argument, so she could throw a little fit to keep him from going out.

"So you plan on staying out all night?"

"No Madi," he replied.

"So you just gonna drink all night, so that I have to worry about taking care of your daughter in the morning?"

He still wouldn't give her the satisfaction of an argument.

They stopped by Ms. Maddy's to get baby girl before they went upstairs. Lace took Tisha into her bedroom and laid her sleeping body in her Dora the Explorer bed sheets. He kissed her forehead as he tucked her in. When he walked back into the living room, Marisol was standing there with her arms folded, tapping her foot.

"What do you want," questioned Lace.

"I want to know when do I get a break?"

"Madi don't start!"

"Don't start? I never get to go out Lawson…"

"What are you talking about? We just went out last weekend!"

"Oh, wow! I got to go to the circus and smell elephant shit. That was beautiful!"

He laughed and she couldn't help but laugh too.

"I'm serious Lawson," she said jokingly shoving him.

"I know… that's the funny part. Listen, next weekend you can have your own little ladies night out."

"Oh wonderful," she said sarcastically. "That means I'll get to hang out with your mother."

"It ain't my fault you ain't got no friends."

"Fuck you Lawson," she said again laughing. Just then there was a knock on the door. She opened the door and it was Mark.

"Marisol, hey babe," he said kissing her on the cheek. She just looked at him with a blank expression. "Okay what'd you do now," Mark asked Lace.

"Nothin' she's crazy!"

"I'm not fuckin' crazy! You just don't have him drinking all night Mark or you'll be up here cleaning up after him."

They all laughed.

"I won't. Where is baby girl," questioned Mark.

"She's sleep and your not gonna wake her up either," shot Marisol.

"Let's get outta here Mark before she changes her mind."

Again Mark kissed her cheek, followed by a long passionate kiss on her lips by Lace. Then they quickly headed out, jumped in Mark's Acura, and quickly pulled off.

"Shit," Lace called out.

"What happened," Mark asked.

"Dammit man," he replied. "I left my keys." He pulled out his cell phone and dialed the number. It rang twice.

"Yes, Lawson? What you miss me already," Marisol asked.

"You know I do, but listen, I forgot my keys."

"So come back and get them."

"You crazy!"

"C'mon Lawson. I'm tired and I want to go to bed."

"So go to bed. I'll call before I come home," Lace said.

She sucked her teeth. "Dammit Lawson I…"

Click. Lace hung up.

"Did you hang up on Maddie," asked Mark.

"Yeah and it's Madi."

"No nigga, it's Mad-dee!"

They both laughed.

"So how is business up here in the suburbs of the Bronx," questioned Mark.

"Suburbs? Shit, this is as much the hood as the South Bronx."

"Yeah, whatever!"

"Shit, you not in the hood no more."

"Man, fuck the hood, the haters, the gold diggers, the wannabe ballas, and them grimy ass esse's."

Mark was different from his cousin and his brother Moe. Lace and Moe did it all. Smoked weed, drank, everything. They would be partying, but Mark most likely would be sipping on ginger ale and orange juice tonight. His thoughts were, that all extra activities cost too much, because it was extra money that could be stacked.

Lace wanted to smoke a cigarette so bad, but he knew Mark would have a fit. He looked over at him, "Yo Mark, you ever miss Webster?"

"What? The projects?" Mark paused, then gave a half smile. "Sometimes. You know there were a lot of memories, but that's what they are, when you gonna step up to the big leagues?"

"Big leagues…," Lace repeated.

"Yeah motherfucker, the big leagues. You know whatever you want Moe and I will hit you with."

Lace looked out his passenger side window at the views of the Bronx skyline, while shaking his head. "Nah I'm good." Lace was content with the money he made. His bills stayed paid, he and Madi lived fairly well, and although he loved the life, he didn't want all the attention. That was a part of the reason he moved his girl out of the South Bronx when she got pregnant. Even his mom and two sisters Lynette, twenty-seven, and Elise, seventeen, moved out the projects and were now living in Park Towers.

"You good? Man you're a fool, that's what you are! Lynette told me Henny done opened up a beauty salon upstate," stated Mark.

Henny, or Henry, had been Lace's best friend since they were in daycare and they grew up together. Lace lived in 1240 on the 5th floor and Henny lived in the building directly behind him, 1250 on the 9th floor. It was Henny that introduced Lace to the game. Henny hustled with Webster Avenue legends and was getting Moe good money by age seventeen. He took over the block when his boss was gunned down in a so called robbery in the mid 90's, and now at twenty-six he was living the life in upstate New York. He came down every now and then and kicked it with Lace, but since he met Carol the visits definitely slowed down.

"Yeah, he's out there doing his thing in Rockland County," Lace shared.

"See what I mean? That should be you."

Lace had nothing to say when Henny decided he didn't want to deal with the city anymore. He asked Lace to make the move with him, but he turned it down. Lace couldn't do what Henny did. Henny literally turned his back on everything and everyone, including his girl, and she definitely hadn't been the same since he left. Lace just didn't have it in his heart to walk away, and it has been five years now.

Jerome Avenue looked like an auto show as Mark and Laced pulled up to the club. Cats were out in full effect representing their hoods. Patterson P Jays, Edenwald, Melrose, Soundview Boston Secon, and Monroe were all present. It looked as if the party was outside on the street rather than inside the Bronx night club. Mark began to wonder to himself how many guns were out there, or if this had been a good idea at all. Laid back in the cut were the D.D. Boys, just watching every thing.

Blast couldn't help but smile when he saw the two neighborhood superstars step out of the Acura. '*Maybe tonight*,' he thought to himself, as Sin and CoCo sat in his Integra. CoCo was smoking a blunt and every now and then sneaking Sin a pull.

Moe, Mark, and Lace gave respectful nods, pounds, and bro

hugs. They noticed that the inside of the club was more alive than the outside. Mark lived on the fact that he tried very hard not to stick out. He didn't wear any jewelry or flashy clothes, and even those that thought they recognized him from the hood weren't really sure. Both Lace and Mark knew that Moe would be as far in the back as possible with his back against a wall, and that's right where they found him. He had the biggest Kool-Aid smile on his face as he watched the two women sitting with him French kiss.

"Oh my God, dogs," he said standing up over the table, with ten bottles of Moet and two bottles of Cristal. "Dogs, let me introduce you to Asia and India." The two women stopped kissing to smile at Lace and Mark. Lace smiled, nodding his head anxiously, as Mark just shook his head in disbelief at all the liquor on the table.

"Moe, what is all this shit," Mark asked gesturing to the table.

"It's a party man. Just enjoy yourself for once."

"Yo, this is too much," he said looking around to see if anyone was watching them.

"Man, will you relax! Asia this is my older brother. Show him something nice." As Moe said it, Asia picked up a Heineken bottle and deep throated it, nearly taking in the entire bottle.

Now Mark smiled. "That's... that's very nice."

"Yeah," Moe added. "Now can we enjoy the night? Sorry Lace. I didn't think Mad-dee was gonna let you out, but there is plenty of pussy in here, if she'll let you stay out tonight."

"Man listen...," Lace replied, picking up a bottle of Moet. "I came to party and then I'm going home." He placed the bottle to his lips and took a long swallow.

*****

It was after 12:30 a.m. when Henny pulled into the parking lot of his condominium home in Nanuet, New York. Normandy Village was a mixed neighborhood of mostly middle class and retired white folks. There were a few asians here, blacks there, and middle eastern indians over there. Henny and Carol were able to fit in as small business owners of a beauty salon on Middletown Road in Nanuet. Not only was it unisex, but Carol also hired older white women as stylists to give it an even more suburban atmosphere. They all loved Henny, although none of them really knew what he did for a living. Even their neighbors spoke so kindly of him. He just had a people person aura to him.

He met Carol two and a half years ago, but the love wasn't there immediately, at least not for him. She was intelligent and business savvy which he found attractive, and although this business plan had been an idea he and another had years ago, he decided to keep the dream alive. One thing he learned long ago from a man that didn't practice what he preached was never shit where you sleep. Since he was now sleeping in Rockland County, he was shitting in a small town in Orange County called Highland Falls, New York. Out there, he nicely set up two spots and a three bedroom house to sleep safely.

Carol knew what he did and argued a lot about him quitting, but the salon wasn't bringing in enough to support their living expenses, as well as her lavish lifestyle yet. Sometimes on days like this, he'd drive out to Highland Falls just to get away from Carol, and while silently thinking, he concluded that he chose the wrong woman.

The apartment was dark and quiet when he walked in. It was obvious Carol was sleep and he had no intentions of waking her up, so he slid off his shoes, jacket, and laid on the sofa in the darkness. If he turned on the television, it might wake Carol up, so he just stared into the darkness thinking about Webster Projects, the memories, the ghosts, and the things he left behind, including his heart.

*****

By 1:30 a.m., Lace and Moe were twisted. Lace decided to wobble out to the dance floor to mingle because Moe and Mark had their hands full with Asia and India, and he felt like the third wheel. He honestly wasn't out looking for any women. He just came out to get drunk and enjoy the weekend, because with a family to take care of, he didn't get to do this a lot. Lace wasn't an angel, as he cheated on Marisol in the past, but these days it just didn't make sense. He walked past a few half naked chicken heads and found it amazing the extent some women went in order to trap a baller. Finally, a hand grabbed him and Lace gave a drunken smile to the familiar face. This was a face he had also grown up with.

"Chanel, what's up baby," Lace said as he smirked.

"Baby? Lawson are you drunk," Chanel questioned.

Lace just smiled.

"Yeah, you're drunk!"

"Come on ma lets dance," Lace said while grabbing her hand.

"Dance? Where is your little Mexican girlfriend," Chanel sarcastically questioned.

"She ain't Mexican," he started to laugh; "she's Puerto Rican. Shit, where's your asshole brother?"

"Cornell never did nothing to you!"

"You're right... I apologize. Still, where is he," Lace asked looking around.

"He's probably with his baby momma," Chanel remarked.

"Baby momma? He ain't gay?"

"That's enough… I'm out!" She turned away, but he quickly grabbed her wrist.

"Chill, Chanel. Wait, I'm sorry! Dance with me."

She took a deep breath and relaxed in his hands as they walked out and danced to *'Just in Case' by Jaheim.* They laughed while reminiscing about the old neighborhood, which she still belonged to. "So how old is your baby girl now," she asked as she rubbed his body.

"You remember my daughter?"

"Of course! You brought her to my mother's funeral," Chanel answered. It was then that Lace realized how long it had been since he'd seen Chanel, over two years. "I never got a chance to thank you for coming," she added.

"I loved your moms. We all did," Lace remarked, as Chanel smiled at his statement. "She's four now and bad as hell though."

"Um, so I guess you and that yellow girl are still together?"

"How 'bout you and the beige kid," Lace countered, knowing she would know who he was talking about, Tior.

"Ugh," she sighed, giving Lace the sour lemon face.

Just then the D.J. slowed it down to *Lauryn Hill and D'Angelo's 'Nothing Even Matters'.* "I love this song," Chanel said while taking a deep breath.

"Me too," Lace replied pulling her closer to him.

She smiled because it actually felt good being in his arms. She wanted to be there so many times when they were younger, but Lace always chose the light skin or Spanish chicks who were the total opposite of her dark, mocha complexion. This song gave her more of the opportunity to feel his body as he held her tightly against him.

"So, who do your brother got a baby with?"

That question brought her back to the reality that this was business. Chanel almost lost herself in the moment, but she knew this was just play time away from his family and it meant nothing to him to dance with her. "Let's not talk about my brother please," she reluctantly responded.

"Alright," he answered pulling her tighter to him.

She couldn't help it because he smelled so good. She took a deep breath of him as she rested her head in the crevice of his neck, while he caressed her body with his strong hands. He began to ask himself why he never chose to get with her when they were younger. Lace always liked her but he couldn't stand her brother. Her body was so soft and her complexion was as beautiful as it had always been. Lace ran his hand down to her lower back and just then, he felt her breath on his neck. He leaned back just a little and kissed her forehead. It took her by surprise as she looked up to stare straight into his brown eyes. She was lost again for a moment, until he kissed her. At first she tried to fight it, but it was a losing battle because maybe she wanted it just as much as he did.

His hands drifted down her back to a softly, cushioned apple bottom and she moaned as the kiss seemed to become more passionate. He felt his manhood rising and started to pull away, but the strength in her arms now matched what his had been all along. It all came to a halt when she abruptly backed up, as it stabbed her in the mid-section.

"Oh my God, Lawson! What are we doing," she said backing away.

He held her hands while pulling her back towards him.

"Something we should have been done!" "Please Lawson, your drunk," Chanel shot at him.

"I know what I'm doing!"

Chanel shook her head. "No you don't. You have a baby and damn near a wife at home and I don't want to come between that," she said as she again tried pulling away from him.

"Wait Chanel…"

Again she shook her head. "No, it was nice seeing you Lawson. Maybe you should come by sometime… I'm still in the same apartment," she countered and quickly walked away, disappearing into the crowd.

Lace looked at his watch and then his protruding sweat pants. He couldn't believe how long they had been dancing or how excited she made him. It was almost 3 a.m. He needed to get home, so he made his way to the back of the club in the opposite direction Chanel went. Mark and Moe were still hugged up with Asia and India. "Yo, Moe take me home," Lace slurred.

"What? Nigga you crazy! You better take a cab or something," Moe said laughing.

"I need to bounce…," slurred Lace again.

"Nah nigga," Moe began, "you need a car," he said still laughing.

"I'll take you home," Mark said.

"What? Nigga do you see these two bitches here," Moe snarled.

"Yeah I see them, but I'm taking my cousin home first. I'll meet ya'll at the Castle Hill Diner…" "That's what's up," Moe added.

"…Then the Hotel," Mark finished.

Chanel made it back to their table. Sin sat on Blast's lap and they were tongue kissing, while D.D.B. seemed to be standing guard. "You guys are disgusting. Why don't ya'll get a room or something?"

"Stop hatin'," Sin replied.

Blast's face was dead serious. "What's up," he asked.

"He's here with Mark and Maurice," Chanel said giving up the information.

"Faggot ass niggas," Blast replied.

"He's not driving and he's not strapped."

Blast smiled because he knew he taught his sister well. The dance had been part of the plan. She could dance with Lace only to frisk him from head to toe without him realizing it. Blast didn't know that now she seemed to be regretting it, because she knew her brother's plan. "Yo Take, take Sin and Chanel home," he said to one of his boys.

Sin sucked her teeth. "Damn, baby can we chill for a little while," she whined, but his facial expression quickly silenced her. She also knew what Blast was doing and she was upset with CoCo. They grew up with Lawson, Mark, and Maurice. What Blast was going to do was wrong, but she didn't dare say a word about her feelings, for fear that he would flip. D.D.B's small entourage exited the club, with Take following the instructions to take Chanel and Sin home. Drama and Blast hopped into the Integra and waited as Take went for the green Caravan.

Lace was drunk as hell, which was apparent from him stumbling out of the Savoy. "Yo, Lace you gotta get a whip man. I'm serious."

Lace didn't answer. He just plopped down into the passenger seat.

Damn motherfucker, watch my leather!"

Still Lace said nothing as he pushed his seat all the way back, and before Mark hit the Major Deagan Expressway he was snoring. Mark couldn't lie, he was kind of anxious to get back to India and Asia, and bringing Lace home made him pissed about leaving them. Still, it was only a ten or fifteen minute ride. As soon as he hit the 233rd street exit, he called Marisol.

The phone rang about four or five times before Marisol answered in a raspy, dry voice. "Hello?"

"Mad-dee? I mean Marisol," Mark said into the receiver.

She knew all of Lace's family made jokes about his nickname for her because of her attitude. "What Mark?"

"We'll be there in about five minutes."

"Is he drunk?"

"You know he is!" Mark heard her curse in the background.

"Let me speak to him," Marisol said.

Mark tried to hand him the phone. "Yo, your girl is on the phone."

"Madi," Lace yelled out loud ignoring the phone. "I love you Madi!"

"Take the phone," Mark said solemnly.

"Madi, I'm comin' baby," Lace called out again.

"Yo this asshole is trippin'! Just look out the window," Mark said, growing tired of Lace's charades.

"Alright, but if he throws up I'm calling you to clean it up."

Marisol checked in on Latisha before going to stand up in the living room window, which was two stories up and looked right onto 224th street. She loved living uptown. She left her old friends in the South Bronx and now looked down upon them, and that was her problem. Marisol began to think she was too good for those she'd grown up with and that was the reason no one liked her anymore. She didn't give a damn because she had her man, they had money, and they had a beautiful daughter. When she saw Mark's Acura pull up in front of the house, she turned to go open the door for him, but she was tired and wasn't gonna rush. His drunk ass could wait a minute.

"Go head with your drunk ass," Mark said.

"I'm home?"

"Yeah you home! Hurry up, I got something sweet waiting for me man. Go head!"

Lace got out and stretched.

"Yo I'll call you tomorrow so we could talk business," Mark said a little eager to get back to the sisters that were waiting with his brother.

As Lace began to walk towards his front steps, Mark blew the horn and pulled off. Lace's stomach was spinning just as bad as his head was. When he started feeling a little nauseous, he quickly bent over to avoid throwing up on his uptowns.

Just as he stopped, an Integra came to a halt. Lace's back was to the car and as the window rolled down, Blast pulled his black hoody over his head. He cocked back on a chrome forty-five and aimed it directly at Lace. "Yo Lawson," Blast shouted. Lace turned to the call of his name.

Marisol froze for a second, because the sound literally echoed through her body. It couldn't have been what she thought, but the following boom told her it was. She began to run down the stairs after she heard five shots and the Integra speed off. As she burst through the door, Lace lay on the ground rolling in his own blood.

"Oh my God, Lawson!" Lights began to pop on throughout the block as neighbors began to wake from their beds. "Call an ambulance," Marisol screamed as Lace cried in pain. Ms. Maddy had her cordless phone in hand and 9-11 was already on the line.

Police were the first on the scene. It took the ambulance over forty-five minutes to get there and rush him to the ER. Mrs. Anderson, Lynette, and Elise tried their best to calm Marisol, but she couldn't stop crying, and the more she cried the more Latisha cried. It was 6 a.m. and Lace had been in the ICU for over two hours, but no one said a word about how he was doing. Lynette paced back and forth, cursing out everyone in scrubs. Elise finally got Latisha to sleep at about 7:30 a.m., and shortly after, Mark and Maurice came storming into the ER waiting room.

Maurice was strapped and steaming as he asked, "What the fuck happened?"

"Watch your mouth boy!"

"Sorry Auntie, but what happened?"

Marisol stood up with her eyes red and puffy from crying. "Mark why'd you leave him," she asked while sobbing.

"Sorry Marisol. Did you see anything?"

She shook her head to Mark's question.

"I don't know what happened, but somebody better tell me something about my fucking brother," Lynette chimed in.

"Lynette," Mrs. Anderson yelled.

"Sorry mommy, but we been here for hours and ain't nobody said shit! I mean nothing…"

Mrs. Anderson stood up taking Maurice's hand in hers. "Maurice?"

"Yes, Auntie?"

"You promise me you all won't do nothing stupid."

"I can't promise that Auntie," he answered.

"Yes we can Auntie," Mark replied.

She looked at him and nodded, "I swear you've always been

the brains between the three of you Mark."

Just then a doctor came out wiping his hands on a towel. "Mrs. Anderson," the doctor said in the direction of Marisol, but Lynette jumped up.

"Yes?"

"Are you Lawson's wife?"

"No, my brother is not married. We've been sitting in this stink ass hospital for hours! Now, how is my brother?"

"Lynette let the man be. Sorry doctor, I'm Lawson's mother," said Mrs. Anderson.

The doctor now extended his hand to Mrs. Anderson. "Mrs. Anderson," he said, more as a question.

"Yes," she nodded slightly.

"My name is Dr. Morton. We've done everything for your son. He's a very strong young man."

"What does that mean," Lynette yelled.

"Lynette please…," said Mrs. Anderson.

"It's alright Mrs. Anderson. I understand her concern for her brother. Yes, he's fine," he said while nodding. "He's definitely a fighter and I can honestly say that had it took the ambulance forty seconds longer we might have lost him, but he's fine now."

"Can we see him," Marisol asked.

"Not yet. We'll be moving him shortly, but he'll be unconscious for a while. When we move his room, you all will be able to go in and see him. I apologize," he said, while looking at Lynette, "for taking so long to inform you, but I had to make sure he was fine. I must admit it was very much a miracle." He spoke a little more before leaving to tend to another patient that was rushed into the ER.

It had definitely been a miracle that Lace was still a part of this world. He was shot five times, but none of them hit his bones and all of them went straight through. He was hit twice in his shoulder, twice in the arm, and once in the back. One of the shots in the arm hit an artery and the second shot in the back hit his lung, causing it to collapse. They were the two worst ones, but luckily they ricocheted and came out under his underarm and no bones were hit. It was truly divine intervention.

Chapter 2

Henny was barely awake and Carol was at it already. "Why didn't you wake me up when you came in," she asked with her arms folded across her chest.

"It was late Carol."

"You could have woke me up. I was worried sick." He took a deep breath, rubbing the cold from his eyes with his thumb and index finger. "So me caring about you is a problem now?"

"Carol, can I brush my teeth or something before you start your bullshit?"

"My bullshit? Now my feelings are just bullshit?"

Henny got up off the sofa and went to their bedroom with her right behind him running her mouth about him being so inconsiderate. He pulled out some boxers, a t-shirt, and went into the bathroom. He started to lock the door but knew if he did, she'd just yell and have the neighbors involved with her argument. So, as she babbled, he jumped in the shower.

"Henny, don't you realize I love you? Why do you just shun my feelings?"

"Can you pass my toothbrush," Henny said.

Sucking her teeth, Carol replied, "Sometimes I swear you're just a heartless bastard!"

"Can you pass me the mouthwash?"

"Mouthwash?"

"Yes, that bottle with the green liquid inside of it," Henny said very matter of fact.

She huffed, puffed, and stomped out of the bathroom. He laughed, because to him they were the perfect example that opposites attracting was bullshit. She was definitely Lisa Raye type bad in her Diamond from the Player's Club days, but Carol's suburban upbringing turned him off.

She was really stuck in the white picket fence fairy tales, and Henny just wasn't. He got out of the shower and threw on a pair of blue jeans. When he came out of the bedroom, Carol was in the kitchen scrambling eggs, but to spite her, he grabbed a bowl, a box of cereal, and the milk, and headed for the living room. When she sucked her teeth, he had to bite his lip not to laugh out loud. He sat on the couch and turned on the television to his Sunday morning modern day show, Degrassi. He could see she was pissed about him eating cereal.

"You do these things on purpose don't you," she asked and he smiled as he nodded. "Why?"

"Cause you're so cute when your mad."

"I can't stand you sometimes. You know that?"

Again he nodded. "What time are you opening the salon today," he asked.

"Monica opened it this morning at nine."

One Sunday a month Carol opened the salon, and that's the reason Henny made sure to come home because he knew today was that Sunday. Monica was one of her trifling friends. Henny couldn't stand the girl, but she could do hair and kept her chair in the salon filled. So, because of that Henny kept his feelings for Monica between him and Carol. Henny sucked his teeth.

"Why do you hate Monica so much?"

He couldn't just come out and say that every time Carol turned her back, Monica was throwing the pussy at him, and luckily just as he was thinking of a lie to tell her, his cellular phone rang. "I'll just answer that," he replied.

"Oh, don't worry this is not finished," Carol said.

He smiled as he answered his phone, "Yo, who this?"

"Yo, Henny it's Hitz!"

"Who the fuck is Hitz," Henny shot.

"Lace's man."

"What's up, why you callin' my phone?"

"Lace always told me if anything happened to call you," Hitz just stopped.

Henny shook his head, as he thought how stupid dudes were. "So," he replied, "what the fuck happened," he added.

"Oh yeah, Lace got hit up last night."

"What you mean hit up?"

"Somebody hit 'em up in front of the crib last night!"

"What? Is he okay," Henny asked with a concerned tone.

"I don't know man…"

"Where's he at?"

"The hospital," said Hitz casually.

"I know that asshole. What hospital?"

"Oh, Our Lady of Mercy on 233rd."

Henny just hit the end button. He was already dressed so he grabbed the keys to his Lexus and his knapsack out the hall closet.

"Henny where are you going," Carol called as she ran behind him to the door. "Henny?"

"Yo, I'll be back!" He jumped in the car and pulled off.

She slammed the door sulking. Henny was the best thing to happen to her life, and it was like he answered all her prayers. This had been the best two years of her life, and he just didn't understand that he didn't need the streets, as they had at least a hundred thousand in the salon safe. She picked up the television remote, and that's when she saw his Nextel on the table. In the two years they been together, that phone never left his side. Now she began to worry that something had to be wrong, because he would never leave the house without his Nextel.

*****

Blast paced back and forth cursing. "Baby relax," Sin said, trying to calm him down.

"Relax how I'm a relax and this nigga ain't dead?" Blast didn't know if his car had been identified or what, but he did know he hit Lace at least three times.

"Maybe it can still work," CoCo offered.

Sin just looked at her in disgust, because she couldn't believe how much CoCo was really into this. They all grew up together, but now she helped her brother try to murder one of their closest friends.

"Tell me how it can work Chanel," Blast yelled.

Sin didn't understand how Blast thought his plan would work in the first place! Now CoCo sat there with a stupid look on her face, and Sin could see Blast getting more and more frustrated. She knew if he was mad, it would be her to suffer the consequences of his rage, not CoCo.

"Maybe you could just have CoCo run a little game on Lawson," Sin offered as her remedy.

"What," CoCo replied screwing up her face.

"I mean," Sin began, "we all know the boys been open off you since junior high school."

CoCo just rolled her eyes. As much as the thought aggravated Blast, he knew it was the truth. He stood there silent at first deep in thought, but it made more sense than his own plan. He never thought his own plan out. He just thought of a way to get a little revenge, and now this would really work.

"That's what you gonna do Chanel," Blast stated.

"What?"

"You heard me. You gonna get in this nigga head!"

She was lost. "How? I mean he has a girl," she started, but Blast interrupted her.

"Fuck that bitch. She could die too!"

CoCo said nothing, because she knew her brother meant what he said.

"Might even be able to get that other bitch ass nigga too," Blast added.

Neither woman said a thing, because they both knew who Blast was talking about, but now Sin hated herself for giving him the idea. She should have known that would be part of Blast's plan anyway. Since they'd been together, Blast always made comments about him, because he was always jealous of him. As she and CoCo began calling the hospitals to find out where Lawson was, Sin couldn't keep her mind off of him. She had his cell number, because it hadn't changed in five years. What would she say to him? Did he even deserve a warning?

Once they found out Lawson was in Our Lady of Mercy, Blast left as he said he needed to check a few people. CoCo had the nerve to be mad at Sin for getting her even further into Blast's bullshit. Sin couldn't understand her anger, because CoCo played the biggest part in the murder gone wrong. Once CoCo left and went downstairs, Sin held the phone in her hand just staring at it. He did her so wrong and was the reason she was in this fucked up, abusive relationship now. Still, she couldn't lie. She still loved him, but he moved on and forgot her. Now CoCo and Blast were all she had. Blast literally saved her life, but he was her everything at one time. He even gave her a choice and promised that if she didn't come, he'd come back for her. She took a deep breath and dialed the number. It went straight to his voice mail, but she didn't leave a message.

*****

It was after 12:30 p.m. on Sunday afternoon. Lace had been in his own room since Saturday night but still hadn't woke up. Marisol hadn't slept yet, and Mrs. Anderson, Lynette and Elise napped in his room on chairs. Lynette was pissed that her mother wouldn't go home and get some rest. Moe and Mark came and went because they still had business to handle. Tisha laid in the bed with her daddy, as they all prayed for him to wake up soon.

Lynette stood up to stretch. "I gotta get out of here for a minute," she said as she yawned.

"Where you going," Elise asked.

"Just to go stretch my legs," Nette answered.

Mrs. Anderson sucked her teeth and shook her head. "It don't make no sense," she said.

"What mommy," Nette asked.

"You think I don't know you going to smoke them filthy cigarettes?"

"Mommy I'm twenty-eight years old. I'll be back!" She left the room and stood waiting for the elevator.

The pearl white Lexus pulled into the hospital parking lot and Henny sat there for a minute. He hated hospitals because they reminded him of losing his parents ten years ago. They passed when he was sixteen, leaving him with his sickly grandmother that died a year later and forced him to take care of himself. Losing everyone in his life at such an early age made it seem as if the crack game was heaven sent. The controlled substance literally fed him when he was starving and clothed him when he was cold. The drug had been his mother and father at one time. It gave him a chance at life, and now it was his livelihood.

When he had her, everything was complete. They were all they had. Why couldn't she understand he had to leave? It hurt him as much as it hurt her, but he had to force himself to ignore those ghosts and haunting memories. That was one of the reasons he avoided the Bronx. Henny got out of the car and as he approached the hospital, he shook off the thoughts of her.

"Henny?" He turned to see Nette running towards him. Her face brought a smile to his, as she jumped in his arms, and began hugging and kissing him. "Damn baby I miss you," she said.

"I miss you too. How is he doing?"

"Doctors say he'll be alright, but he hasn't woken up yet."

He could see the tears forming in her eyes. He took her by the hands, and looked her up and down. "Damn mama you looking real good," he said.

She smiled and blushed a little.

Henny's plan worked, as he just wanted to cheer her up, although she did look good. "Ain't nobody put no baby in that ass yet," he added.

"You know I'm waitin' on you. Come on lets go upstairs!" She took his hand and led the way. When they got to the elevator doors

★ ★ ★ ★

he stopped in his tracks. She sucked her teeth, "don't tell me you still scared of elevators!"

He nodded, because it had been a phobia since he was nine years old. He, Lawson, and Little Chris were playing elevator tag and Chris fell down the elevator shaft. Since then, he never liked riding them.

Even living in the projects on the fourteenth floor, he used the stairs except when his mother forced him, and as a child he hated his mom for that. Still as a grown man some habits were still impossible to break. Nette sucked her teeth as they made their way to the stairs. She slowed him down, and was huffing and puffing, as they reached the seventh floor. Henny hadn't lost his breath, and as they entered the room, Elise jumped up and ran to hug him. Then he hugged and kissed Mrs. Anderson.

"Hey mom," he warmly said.

"Boy, I'm so glad to see you and in one piece," she said as she looked him up and down.

"It's good to see you too mom. Ah senorita como esta," Henny said turning to Marisol.

"Tu tambien?"

"I guess," he answered not really understanding Spanish. "Mad-dee how you really doing?"

She shook her head, as she looked back at Lace lying in the bed unconscious. Henny was the only one of Lace's family and friends that called her Mad-dee, and she didn't mind, because she knew he was sincere in his feelings towards her. However, she knew Lace's family only showed her respect because of Tisha.

"There's my girl," Henny said to little Tisha.

She smiled and raised her arms to her godfather, "hi Henny!" It made him smile the way she always said his name. With that smile, a tear ran down his cheek seeing his man laid up in the hospital bed.

*****

It was after 11:30 p.m. when the six hundred Benz pulled up on 169th and Boston Road. Maurice was driving, Mark rode shotgun, and Henny was in the back. The thugs watched carefully as the Benz parked.

"I hate these cats," Mark replied to their stares.

"If anything goes down in the hood, Genocide knows about it. Let me holla at him and see what he knows."

Genocide and his little brother Baby Homicide were local terrorists, who were well respected throughout the Bronx and Harlem. As Moe stepped out the ride, so did Henny. The boys stopped rolling dice and were all prepared to pull out if any trouble came from the foreign car. It was easy to see they all were packing, but still Henny stepped up with no fear and the desert eagle on his waist.

"Geno, what's good," Moe said with his hands in the air showing he came in peace.

"Oh shit, balling ass Moe. It's all good," he said to his crew, calming the tension.

"So what brings you to the hood," Genocide asked.

"I need to holla at you about something," Moe answered.

Genocide didn't say a word, so Moe knew what it was. Nothing in the hood was free, so he quickly pulled out five crispy benjamins.

"So let's holla," Geno now invited him to the side street. Henny slowly followed. "What's up with your man," Geno asked, as his brother Homicide also followed.

"I know you heard about my little cousin."

"Yeah man, Lil Lace. How he doin'?"

"He's alright. Anyways, that's his best friend. He just as eager to find out some info as I am."

Geno nodded. "I feel him. Peace God," Geno said to Henny as he nodded his head to show respect. "Nigga look familiar. Where he from?"

"Web," Moe answered. "That's Henny."

"Starsky's lil man," Geno asked.

"Yeah!"

The entire hood had respect for the dearly departed Starsky.

"So talk to me Money Moe."

"You heard anything about who hit my cousin," Moe said matter of factly.

"Nah, dog. Nothing. Shit crazy, 'cause I got a couple of goons uptown and nobody knows nothing!"

"You know any beef the nigga had," Moe asked, trying to dig deeper.

Geno leaned back on his Q45 Infiniti with his hand on his chin, as if in deep thought. It was abruptly broken by his brother's voice.

"Yo son why the fuck you ice grillin' my brother," he yelled in the direction of Henny.

"What nigga," Henny replied not backing down.

"Yo, I don't trust these niggas Geno," Homo spoke.

"Nigga, I don't trust you either," Henny shot back.

"So what you saying," Homicide said pulling out his four fifth.

Henny responded by pulling out his desert eagle. "Yo chill Henny," Moe called out.

"Yeah, tell your man be easy," Geno replied.

"Fuck that! Tell this nigga be easy," said Henny. "Yo look, we just came to get a little info man. We ain't come for no bullshit," Henny replied.

"Then put the ratchet down," Homo said.

"You first," Henny said.

"Fuck that," Homo said cocking his weapon and getting it ready for war.

Now all of his boys began to approach with their weapons drawn. Mark jumped out holding a mac ten. "What the fuck is goin' on," he said pointing the mac at Baby Homicide.

Genocide began to laugh. "Yo this is a funny ass situation. For some reason I think ya'll should just put the gats away before somebody gets hurt." Nobody moved. "Homicide it's good. You and the boys go back to what ya'll was doin'. Everything is straight."

Homo looked at his brother, and although he didn't want to, he obeyed his older brother's orders. He stared Henny down as he passed and watched as he tucked the desert in his waist. Mark did the same with the mac.

"Yo, Geno. Man, you know I'd never disrespect. I just need to find out what went down with my cousin, that's all. I don't want no problems with you and your boys."

Genocide knew Moe was no clown or lame, and knew better than to take his words for weakness. Maurice Brown had paper and loyal soldiers that would ride against anybody. "Wild Appache," Geno replied. "The Indian."

"Yeah, I heard a few months ago they had a little beef. I don't know why, but I never trusted that little Guyanese bastard." Moe knew "The Indian" well. He was from up the block in Washington Projects and had a reputation as a gun man in the hood. His actions spoke louder than the words said about him. "Yo, Geno. Man I appreciate it. If you hear anything else just give me a call."

"You know it God, and give ya cousin my blessing."

After giving each other pounds and the exchanging of several bone chilling stares between Homicide and Henny, Mark, Henny, and Moe were back in the six hundred. Moe explained what he heard from Genocide.

"I remember that," Mark replied.

"Do you know what it was about," Moe asked.

"Nah."

"So we gonna get Tior," Henny asked.

"Maybe we should wait to see what Lace knows," Mark replied.

"Fuck that," Henny started.

"I say we ride on this nigga now," Moe responded.

"That's what I'm saying," Henny added.

Mark just shook his head. Sometimes he wondered how these two managed to be as successful in the drug game as they were.

"What's all the shaking your head about," his brother asked.

"Do you motherfuckers ever think? I mean, don't get me wrong. I'm ready to ride but do ya'll think? Ya'll just ready to run around like vigilantes and don't know if Lace knows anything. Come on!"

Both men were quiet because Mark had a point. Tior was from the South Bronx, and Lace got shot way uptown. Very few people even knew where he relocated to.

"So what you wanna do," Moe asked.

"I say we get something to eat and lay low. God willing Lace will be up tomorrow and we'll know what's up!"

"That's what's up. I feel like Spanish," Moe offered.

They drove over to Coochie Fritos on 167th Street and Morris.

Carol spent hours of her Sunday in the beauty salon being ridiculed by Monica's rants. All she heard was, "Oh the nigga ain't shit. She needs to find a good man, one that loves her." Carol sat on the sofa in their living room staring at Henry's cell phone because it hadn't rung in over an hour. She had ignored it all day. Maybe Heather, one of the white women that worked in her shop, was right. Carol had a good man so she didn't need to jump to conclusions. Still, Monica countered with Heather not knowing anything about black men. "It doesn't matter what you do for them. Cook, clean, wait on them hand and foot... a woman could even suck dick like a certified pro. These sorry ass black men would still find some bullshit reason to do a good woman dirty!"

That wasn't Henry, because he wasn't sorry. He was the best man she'd ever dealt with, but so much changed in two years. She could still hear Monica's voice in her head, "We spend twenty-four hours a day and seven days a week trying to look glamorous and be beauty queens, and the next thing you know some broke, grimy, nappy headed hood booger is riding shotgun in his forty thousand Lexus, in her name." Henny also purchased a beauty salon for her, once he found out how much she loved doing hair. Not many men would just go out and spend sixty thousand dollars on their girlfriend's dreams.

Then the phone finally rang again. Carol looked at the time and it was almost 1 a.m. He still hadn't come home or even called her to let her know he was alright. She was tempted to answer it and tried to reason with herself why she should and also why she shouldn't. She definitely didn't want to violate his trust. She looked at the screen. It was the same number, (718) 555-1234. She saw that same number at least eighteen times that day. Maybe it was him! Carol wondered if he thought he lost his phone, or maybe something had happened. *'Duh,'* she thought, *'of course something happened.'* He left in such a hurry and only grabbed that knapsack out of the closet, and Carol knew it contained his gun. He rushed out of the house, left his phone, and took his gun. This caused her to wonder.

Anger was now being replaced by worry, fear, and curiosity because it had been over an hour since the last call. Her heart was pounding and her hands became clammy. Fear told her to answer it, and terror told her not to. What if something happened to him? Carol was almost in tears with that thought! It was on its fifth ring, and one more it would be forwarded to his voice mail. Whoever it was hadn't left a message yet, and she didn't have the code to check it anyway. What would Monica do? Fuck that! What would Heather do? Heather would have faith in her man! She would understand that there would be consequences for answering it, but she would also need to know her man was alright.

Ring number six. Carol hit the symbol of the ringing phone. Her throat was so dry, she couldn't even say hello.

"Henry, baby," the female voice on the other end said.

The words shattered Carol's heart. She swallowed the knot in her throat while fighting her body to let the words out. "Henry baby? Who the fuck is this?"

"Oh," the female voice said in shock. "I'm sorry. I thought this was Henny's number!" Click!

Whoever it was hung up. There was no longer any fear. There was just rage and anger, as tears ran down her cheeks, as she clutched the phone. Carol needed to talk to this woman. She needed to know what was going on with this mystery woman and Henry.

She didn't need to check because she memorized the number hours ago. She dialed it. On the first ring the woman answered as alert and fearful as Carol had been at first.

"Hel... Hello," she asked in almost a whisper.

"Who the fuck is this," Carol yelled.

"Why are you calling my house," she asked Carol.

"Because you callin' my man and I want to know who the fuck you are!" Click again. She hung up. '*This Bitch*,' Carol thought to herself as she dialed the number again. The first ring barely finished, when the woman answered with a little more anger in her voice.

"Hello," she said, still just a little over a whisper.

"Are you fucking him," Carol asked.

The other woman chuckled and it crushed Carol.

"Listen Carol," said the woman.

Carol couldn't believe what she had just heard. "How the fuck do you know my name? Who are you?"

The other woman took a deep breath. "I'm just an old friend that cares about Henny, and if you do, please tell him to please stay away from the Bronx."

Now all other emotions had been replaced by confusion. "Stay out of the Bronx, why?"

"It's not safe. Lawson got shot Friday night."

Carol knew who Lawson was. Lace was Henry's best friend, and even though she never met him Henny always talked about him. "What does that have to do with Henry, and is Lawson alright," she asked, now understanding why Henry left like he had.

"Yes he's alright. Just tell Henry to stay away from the Bronx, especially Webster!"

"Who is this," Carol now asked.

"That's not important; just give him the message please!"

"Why wouldn't he tell me about Lawson," Carol asked out loud, but really asking herself.

Again the woman on the other end laughed. "Maybe you're not as important as you think. Goodbye!"

The woman's words stung, like salt on an open wound. "Wait, wait, please! What's your name," Carol pled.

There was a brief moment of silence, as if the woman was debating if she should tell her name. "Ceily. Please don't call my phone again," the woman said hanging up again.

Who was this Ceily? How did she know her name? Carol sat there in tears, as she thought of this Ceily woman's words. "Maybe you're not as important as you think.

*****

After eating Moe decided they should all find a spot to crash. Henny said several times that he didn't want to go anywhere near Webster Projects.

"Let me find out you forgot where you came from," Moe stated.

Henny looked out at the Bronx skyline. "Nah, how could I?"

"So what's wrong with the Pec'z? You too good for them now," Moe now asked.

"I just don't want to go there. Is that a problem?"

★ ★ ★ ★ 40

Moe just let out a breath and shook his head as he made a left onto College Avenue. 1343 was a six story tenement that Moe pulled up to and parked.

"This where you decided to go," Mark asked in a depressing tone.

"Why not? It's a low spot," Moe answered.

"Who lives here," Henny asked as they all got out the car.

Mark sucked his teeth as he answered, "Tamika Shaw."

Henny nodded to himself. He was surprised to hear that out of all the chicks he could remember from the old hood, Tamika was one that escaped. He loved his birth neighborhood, but it just felt like a curse sometimes, that once you settled there it was almost impossible to get out. Out of all of them, he was the first one to get out and he never turned back. He left so much behind, that it hurt his heart to even see the place. They walked up the stairs to the fourth floor, and Tamika answered the door after the third knock.

"Oh shit, Maurice! Why didn't you call and tell me you was comin' over," she said as she turned her back letting them in. Tamika was a bad almond complexion, about five foot six, one hundred and forty pounds, with an ass like Buffy the Body, especially in the spandex she wore. She hadn't noticed Maurice wasn't by himself yet, but they all enjoyed the view of the jello jiggling. "Shit, my house is a mess," she said turning to face him. "Oh shit, Mark! What's up my nigga?"

"What's up ma," Mark answered.

"Get the fuck out of here," she yelled, as she finally recognized Henny. "I think I'm seeing a ghost. Henny Rock," she said in a sexy tone biting her bottom lip. "What's up baby," she said hugging him, while pressing her mid-section against his and squeezing him tight.

⋆ ⋆ ⋆ ⋆ 41

"Mika, what's good?"

"You," she answered. "What brings you to the hood," she asked.

Henny didn't answer, because he didn't know what she heard or knew, but if they had to ride he didn't need anyone mentioning him being around.

"Ya'll niggas hungry," she asked.

"Nah, we just left Coochie Fritos," Moe answered.

"And you ain't bring me nothing?"

Moe tossed her a Dutch Master and a bag of weed.

"That's what I'm talkin' 'bout. I hope this is that Elliot."

As everyone smoked except Mark, they all kicked it about old times. They had some good laughs until it came out that Lace got shot the night before. The mood took a drastic change, so trying to change the topic, Tamika asked a question that made things even worse, at least for Henny.

"So Henny... you seen your girl lately?"

They all knew who she was talking about, but Henny just shook his head.

"You know she's pregnant?"

"Word," Moe questioned from the side.

"Yep," Mika sternly stated.

"By who?" Henny asked, out of anger more than curiosity.

She smiled, "Your best friend Cornell."

"Blast," Mark responded.

"Yep," she answered.

"Get the fuck outta here," Moe replied.

"I thought the nigga was a faggot!"

"Shittt, Blast is far from a homo trust me."

They all looked at Henny. "I don't give a fuck," he said.

"You shouldn't. For years I've been trying to give you this pussy and because of her you ignored me," said Mika copping an attitude.

"Trust me Mika," Mark now spoke, "it wasn't because of her that he ignored you!"

"Why you say that," she asked.

"Shit who didn't you try to give that pussy to," Moe asked.

"Fuck you! You got it," she replied.

"Yeah, me and half of Web," Moe responded with a chuckle.

"Fuck you," she said again with a smile. "Ya'll need some covers or something?"

"Nah we good," Moe quickly answered.

"Well, if ya'll need anything just call me," she said walking to her bedroom door. "And Henny… my door will be open if you get cold or lonely," she smiled.

"I rather not," he responded.

"Whatever," she replied closing her door.

Both Henny and Mark laid back in the two lounge chairs, as Moe stretched out on the couch. Henny couldn't believe what Tamika just told them about Blast and Sincerely. She really played herself, because she could've been with anybody. Why Blast? '*Fuck her,*' he thought as he closed his eyes, trying to get some much needed rest. Hopefully Lace would be awake in the morning.

*****

Mrs. Anderson, Marisol, Nette, Elise, and Tisha had been in Lace's room since 7 a.m. and he still hadn't opened his eyes. They all sat there patiently and also a little anxious. He groaned and they all jumped to their feet, but the painful sound was all they got, because his eyes still didn't open.

"Fuck this," Nette said walking to his side.

"Nette what you 'bout to do," her mother asked.

"I'm about to wake my brother up!"

"Nette leave that boy alone," Mrs. Anderson said.

"Chill ma. I ain't gonna do nothing to him," she said, while shaking him.

"Don't tell me to cold nothing," Mrs. Anderson yelled back causing Elise to laugh. "I said leave him alone."

Nette still shook him.

"Don't hurt him," Marisol whined.

"Ain't nobody gonna hurt him Mad-dee," Nette responded.

"Don't call me that!"

"Yeah Auntie Nette, don't call my mommy dat," said Tisha in her best serious voice.

They all laughed at Tisha, as Nette continued to shake him.

"Aghh," he grunted.

"Wake up Lawson," Nette pled and his eyes opened. "He's up mommy," Nette called out, as they all rushed to his bed side.

"Shittttt," he groaned.

"Boy, don't make me pop you in your lips," Mrs. Anderson said, causing Tisha to laugh.

"You laughin' at your daddy," Lace asked through the pain.

"Uh huh!"

"Come here baby," he said in a dry, raspy voice, as his daughter jumped up in his arms which caused him to wince in pain.

"Ooh, you look like Pookie in New Jack City," Nette laughed.

"Yeah... funny," Lace replied in a painful laugh.

★ ★ ★ ★ ★ 44

"It wasn't a joke," she responded back.

"So what happened to me," Lace asked while looking around at his situation.

"We were hoping you knew," Nette said.

Marisol tried to get to his side, but his family seemed to be blocking her from getting close.

"Guess who's in the Bx," Elise said.

"Who?"

"Henny!"

"Word? Where is he," Lace questioned.

"I gave him your keys so he could stay at the house."

"Madi, come here baby," Lace softly said while looking in her direction.

She stepped toward him but Nette stepped right in front of her. "Excuse me Lynette," she said, with an attitude.

Nette sucked her teeth. "I'm going to call Maurice and Mark. Henny said he was gonna stay with them last night." Nette stepped out of the room.

Lace knew if his cousins and best friend were all together, it was drama. Truthfully, he was just happy to be alive. He didn't want any type of war, and besides he had no idea who tried to end him. He was in such pain, but still he tried to fake it just for his mother's sake, because he could see the worry in her eyes.

*****

It was just after 9:30 a.m. when Moe's cell phone began to ring, and Mark and Henny both jumped up at the sound. Maurice wasn't on the sofa, but Tamika's 6 year old daughter was.

"Hi Mark!"

"Hey, Mecca. Where's my brother," Mark asked.

"In the room with my mommy. What's your name," she said looking at Henny.

"Henny, Mecca. You don't remember me?"

"No," she said rolling her eyes and jerking her neck as if she were grown.

"Well, last time I saw you, you were about three," Henny said.

"Um," she sighed.

"Yo, Moe your phone ringing," Mark called out.

Maurice came out the room fixing his clothes.

"Um… Um… Um…," little Mecca uttered at Moe, as he exited her mother's bedroom. She had seen many men come and go.

Moe answered his phone. Seconds later, Tamika came out in a t-shirt that was barely long enough to cover the top of her ass cheeks. She walked past the men sitting in her living room, exposing more than just her black panties.

Mecca rolled her eyes. "Will you cover yourself," she said in disgust at her mother.

"Will you get a job," Tamika uttered back.

To himself, Henny shook his head and said a silent prayer for this young girl. God willing she'd make it out of this ghost town and be a better woman than her mother.

"Yo, Lace is up lets get out of here," Moe shouted.

The men prepared themselves to leave.

"So Henny… when you gonna stop by and see me," Tamika asked.

Mecca just sucked her teeth.

"It was good seeing you Tamika. You too Mecca."

"Whatever," Mecca replied.

As they walked out the door, Henny found himself feeling sorry for the little girl and what her mother was exposing her to.

It took them no time to reach the hospital. They burst into the room like the police and were all eager to see Lace. They all exchanged hugs and pounds.

"So who did this," Maurice asked.

Lace just shook his head, because he honestly didn't know.

"We heard you had some drama with Tior," Moe added.

Lace just looked at him and then at Marisol, who just rolled her eyes. He couldn't answer in front of her.

The look on her face made Henny change the topic. "So how you really feeling?"

"Horrible," he answered, pulling the piss bag out from under his bed sheets.

"It could be worse," Mark replied.

"How," Lace sarcastically asked.

"You could have a shit bag," Mark added.

Tisha laughed.

"Will ya'll stop cussin in front of my grandbaby!"

Now Nette sucked her teeth, as she sat on Henny's lap. "Mom you want me to take you to work?"

"Yeah I guess," Mrs. Anderson replied.

"I'll take her," Elise volunteered.

Nette really didn't want to leave because she wanted to know what was going on, so she tossed the keys to her broken down Camry to Elise. "Come on Tisha. You might as well let me take you to work Marisol."

"I want to stay," said Madi, in a concerned tone.

"Don't worry Madi, I'm good."

"Yeah Mad-dee," Nette started, "he's good. Carry yo ass to work!"

Marisol sucked her teeth as she leaned down to kiss him, "You sure?"

"Go head."

"Who's gonna meet me at the train station," she asked.

"Henny will," Lace said.

"Go. We need that money."

The love had been gone for months between Lace and Marisol. Lace found himself wondering if there had ever been any or if it was just Tisha that kept him in the relationship.

With them gone, Mark now got down to it. "What happened?"

Lace told the story, but honestly couldn't give any info about who shot him. Not only had he been drunk, but it had all happened so fast.

"What about The Indian," Moe asked.

Lace was confused. "Tior?"

"Yeah."

"Nothing! We deaded that months ago!"

"So what happened," Henny asked trying to get to the point.

Lace began to tell the story. He had been hitting this chick from Washington Projects named Tia and would use her crib to bag up, because he didn't want to do it in the crib with his own daughter. One night while he was there laid up, Tior showed up. "Come to find out he was hitting shorty and paying her bills. He came up in the crib barking and shit! Then he stepped to me, so I backed out the Smith and Wesson on him..."

Lace paused to sip some water. "After I pulled out, he calmed down a little and I explained that I didn't know shorty had a man.

We still exchanged a few words, but I packed up my shit and got up out of there!"

"So how you know it was dead," Moe asked trying to dig deeper into the story.

"That was the last I heard about it."

"Tior still running with the white boy," Henny asked.

Mark nodded, because he supplied the white boy a few times.

"Well I want to holla at Tior," Moe said pulling out his cell phone and dialing numbers. After a few seconds he spoke. "Sha Asiatic, what's good God? Yo, I need you to do something for me God."

Sha was from 168th and Webster, and he and his boys were the definition of gangsters. They were the boys you called for beef or if you needed someone to just disappear. Moe quickly gave Asiatic all the info he knew from other resources about Tior and seconds later he hung up. "We'll have Tior tonight. Listen, I gotta take care of some business. You too Mark. So Henny you staying out here?"

"Yeah, I'll be at Lace's."

"Alright... Yo, we gonna handle this. Don't sweat it."

Mark and Moe left leaving Henny, Nette, and Lace to kick it. Although Henny sat there phoneless with Nette draped over him, Carol wasn't even on his mind. All he could think about was his nemesis having a baby with his ex-girl, no his ex-life.

*****

Moe had a delivery to make in Brooklyn. First he stopped by his stash house in the Mott Haven section of the Bronx, but he didn't go in he just switched cars. Everything he needed was in the trunk of the 2001 Honda Accord, which he called one of his throw away cars. While he was taking care of his financial business, his personal business was also being taken care. Sha Asiatic told him what he wanted would be done by 9 p.m., and Sha's word was his bond.

The cat he was going to meet in Crown Heights, Brooklyn was dangerous and Moe knew he had to be careful. He hated driving with drugs and guns, but the forty-five was most necessary for this trip. A twenty-five thousand dollar brick was a loss he couldn't live with. He would literally ride or die for his. Moe was very observant as he watched every mirror like a hawk. He looked four and five cars ahead, and seven and eight behind. It took him about forty-five minutes to hit the block Underhill and then he parked. When he got out he looked around everywhere, while walking to his trunk.

He pulled out his Nextel and chirped Grits, the Trini cat he came to meet. Grits was a grimy, Brooklyn kid and word on the streets was he murdered his own cousin to take over the block Underhill, the same block Moe was now parked on.

"Yo," Grits answered on the walkie talkie.

"Yo, G. I'm here," Moe replied.

"I see you… You know where I'm at."

Moe looked up into the sun and saw Grits in the usual spot which always made him uncomfortable. Moe slammed the trunk, threw the Jan Sport over his left shoulder, and headed into the building. Once inside the elevator he checked the fifth making sure the safety was off and that one was in the chamber. He got off at the last floor, then took the stairs up to the roof. Business as usual.

*****

It was just after 3 p.m. Nette had been sitting on Henny's lap for hours, even though all the other chairs were empty.

"What's up with you two," Lace asked, as his sister wrapped her arms around Henny's neck. She began kissing his cheeks and neck. "What? You ain't know? Henny has been my baby for years and I don't care who he's with! He'll always be my first," Nette replied very matter of factly.

"Your first," Lace said in surprise, wincing as he sat up too fast.

"Yes, my first," Nette answered.

Henny just shook his head with a guilty smile on his face.

"Hen, you was boning my sister?"

"No comment," Henny replied.

"Shit I ain't ashamed," Nette started without hesitation. "Damn near every time he spent the night at the house," she added.

"I don't believe ya'll," Lace said now trying to front as if he was upset.

"Yep, baby bro. Until he started messing with the chick upstairs…," she said rolling her eyes.

Her statement conjured up the thought of what he had just learned the night before. "Yo, you knew she was pregnant by Blast?"

"What," Lace replied, sitting up too fast, while grabbing his stomach in pain.

"Yeah, that's what I heard last night," Henny replied. "CoCo told me he was with his baby moms, but shit I thought she was playing! I always thought the nigga was a fag."

"Ha," Nette laughed out loud, while both men looked at her shrugging her shoulders.

"You was fucking Cornell too," Lace asked.

She just smiled.

"I'm starting to think my sister is a hoe!"

"Fuck you Lawson," she shot back.

"I'm saying, the proof is in the pudding."

Henny wanted to ask when was the last time he saw CoCo and Blast, but just then there was a knock on the door, and simultaneously it opened. Two black men appeared in cheap suits. Right away Henny recognized the first one as Officer Hobbs. It was obvious to Henny, that Hobbs was no longer a flat foot beat cop. He would soon find out he was now a Homicide Detective. More importantly, Henny wondered if the man recognized him.

As Hobbs flashed his badge, Nette quickly jumped to her feet. "We don't mean to disturb you Mister ah…" The other cop paused, flipping through his note pad. "…Mr. Lawson Anderson. We just have a few questions to ask you," he finished.

With an attitude Nette stepped between her brother's bed and the detectives. "What kind of questions," she asked.

Hobbs looked at her and pulled out his note pad and pen. "Questions about the shooting Miss… What's your name?"

"Lynette Anderson, and yours," she asked, while still displaying her attitude.

"I'm Detective Hobbs and this is Detective Mason," he answered, handing her his department business card.

She looked at it in disgust. "Well I hope ya'll find whoever did this to my brother!"

"That's why we're here Mrs. Anderson," Mason said jotting her name in his note pad. "So your Mr. Lawson's sister?"

Lynette nodded.

"And your name sir," Mason now asked Henny.

"Steve Jackson," Henny replied, noticing the slight smile on Hobbs' face. Henny was almost positive that Hobbs didn't remember him.

"And what's your relationship to the victim," Mason asked.

"He's my husband," Nette answered.

Hobbs grew up in the Bronx, not far from Webster Avenue, with some of the biggest and most dangerous drug dealers in the neighborhoods. He even went to high school with Lawrence Davis. There were times he wondered why he, himself didn't chose the other side of the law. It was because he wanted to make a difference in the neighborhood, but it was a difficult task.

Hobbs then looked at Henny with a smirk, but then focused his attention to Lace. "Mr. Anderson, can you please tell me anything you remember about Friday?"

"He got shot," Nette responded sarcastically.

"Excuse me ma'am, I'm speaking to MR. Lawson," Hobbs replied, with emphasis on mister.

"Well," Lace began, "we went to a party…"

"Who's we," Mason interrupted.

"My cousin Mark," Nette said.

Lace, Henny, and both detectives all looked at her at the same time. Lace had no intentions of giving Mark's name, after all the man was a known drug dealer. After the looks, Nette realized what she had done and shrugged her shoulders feeling a little ashamed.

"Alright, Mark your cousin. Please continue," Hobbs said writing in his pad again.

"Yeah, well I was pretty drunk so my cousin dropped me off in front of my house. Somebody called my name and I turned around. That's all I remember."

"Was the shooter on foot?"

"No it was a car. I think it was gray, but I don't know what kind it was." It was simple. He told the exact same story to his family, best friend, and now the police.

Hobbs nodded, as he continued to write in his pad. "Did you have any confrontations in the club?"

"No."

"Maybe you stepped on someone's shoes. You know how the homies get over their Jordans," Mason replied.

It was a derogatory statement, so stereotypical that Lace chose to ignore it.

"Maybe you were dancing with someone's girlfriend," Hobbs asked.

Lace just shook his head.

"How 'bout problems in the neighborhood," Hobbs suggested.

"No. None."

"Mr. Anderson," Mason spoke, "are you gang affiliated?"

"What," Nette yelled. "What type of fuckin' question is that?"

"Mrs. Anderson relax yourself," Hobbs ordered.

"No, why would he ask that?"

"It's a question that I have to ask Mrs. Anderson!"

Nette sucked her teeth. "Why 'cause he's black and from the hood," she replied and said 'hood' sarcastically. "I bet you wouldn't ask a white boy no shit like that!" She was now yelling at the top of her lungs.

"Yo, Mr. Jackson," Hobbs said with a smile, "please control your wife."

Henny pulled her closer to him.

"No, he ain't got to control me. You motherfuckers need to be out there finding the person who tried to kill my brother."

The door opened and a curious nurse poked her head in. "Is everything alright?"

"Listen Mrs. Anderson, that's what we want to do," Mason said.

"We'll then you need to be out there and not in here asking stupid ass questions!"

Mason just shook his head.

Hobbs smiled as he handed another card to Lace. "Lawson, here's my card. Please give me a call if you can think of anything that could help us."

Lace nodded as the detectives turned to head out of the room.

Hobbs turned and faced Henny. "So Mr. Charles, I mean Mr. Jackson…" It took Hobbs a minute to remember his name, but now that he did he had to let Henny know. "How long will you be in town?"

Henny just frowned.

"Well I'm sure you've seen for yourself that the neighborhood is not the same. These young boys lack morals and principles. I guess it's due to a lack of role models. It's good to see you. I know you can't like the hood anymore," Hobbs said, as he walked out and closed the door behind him.

Henny sat back trying to calm his nerves, but it wouldn't last long because Hobbs was right. He didn't like the neighborhood anymore.

"Oh shit," Blast said grabbing his sister's arm and pulling her towards the vending machines.

"Ow, Cornell! My arm," CoCo groaned.

"Shut up," Blast whispered. He saw the detectives stop at the nurse's station and wondered if they saw him. He put a dollar in

the machine every now and then while looking over his shoulder to watch the cops.

"What's wrong with you?"

"Nothing. Here," he said handing her the ice cold, bottled water. "Just drink this," he added.

"I'm not thirsty."

"Just drink the fuckin' water," he said through clenched teeth.

CoCo did as her brother told her. He continued to glance at the officers from the corner of his eye as they were walking down the corridor towards the elevators.

"Wait a second," Hobbs said to his partner.

"What?"

"I know the little motherfucker saw me," he added.

"What the hell are you talkin' about," Mason questioned.

"Don't make it obvious, but look back towards Anderson's room."

Mason did as his partner said just in time to see the man and woman slipping into the hospital room. "Who's that," Mason asked again.

Hobbs pulled out his pen and pad and wrote down a few things. "That's Cornell Winston!"

"And?"

"The shit just doesn't make sense," Hobbs said as the bell dinged and the elevator doors opened. "Talk to me Hobbs…"

"Alright, let's get to the car." As they stepped inside and the elevator began to descend, Hobbs began to explain. "Here we go," he began looking at his note pad. "Here's the deal. We've got Lawson Anderson A.K.A. Lace, a small time hustler not known by any of my CI's, but his cousin is Mark Brown…"

"So who is Mark Brown," Mason asked, interrupting the story.

With a huge smile on his face, Hobbs flipped back a few pages. "Mark Brown is Maurice Brown's little brother."

Deep in thought, Mason rubbed his chin with his thumb and index finger. "Why does that name sound so familiar," Mason asked.

"Maurice Brown A.K.A. Moe Money."

As soon as Mason heard the A.K.A. he knew who Maurice Brown was. "Donald's is supposed to be bringing him in any day now," Mason said.

Hobbs nodded, and then turned the page of his note pad and jotted down something else. "Exactly! We got Anderson, a small time unknown. This kid has gotta be somebody Mason, I swear!"

"Why you say that?"

"Out of no where Steve Jackson pops up."

"So who's he," Mason asked seriously, not knowing any of the mentioned names.

"Steve Jackson, A.K.A. Henry Charles, used to be a runner for a big timer in Webster Projects. When the big man got gunned down in the courtyard of his building, Henry Charles took over. You remember when the feds did that big raid in 2005?"

Mason nodded his remembrance of the raid.

Hobbs continued, "Well Mr. Charles just up and disappeared, and now he's back in town."

"So where does the Winston cat fit in?"

"That's just it. He doesn't," Hobbs replied.

They arrived at the unmarked police car and Hobbs tossed the keys to Mason, "You drive!"

"So talk to me... What's on your mind," Mason asked.

"Here it is. You have two major drug dealers, Maurice Brown and Henry Charles, and then there is Lawson Anderson who we believe is a petty dealer."

"Alright, but where does Winston come in?"

Hobbs smiled, "Winston is a notorious stick up kid," he replied.

"Notorious?"

"Yeah. You ever heard of the West Indian crew, Do Dem boys?"

Mason laughed, but quickly stopped when he realized his partner wasn't joking. "You mean to tell me this crew is real?"

Hobbs nodded.

Mason had heard of the DDB many times in hearsay, but always figured it was a crew of urban legend. Several unsolved murders throughout the city were blamed on the crew, but there had never been any arrests made, so he never thought anymore of the name. "Maybe this Anderson kid is bigger than we think," Mason added.

"Yeah," Hobbs started. "That's what I'm thinking. You got Donald's' cell phone number," he asked as they pulled out of the hospital's small parking lot.

Chapter 3

Nerves just began to settle when the door opened, and CoCo and Blast walked in. Henny almost threw Nette to the floor trying to jump to his feet, because the last face he ever wanted to see was staring right at him.

"What the fuck are you doin' here," Nette took the words right out of Henny's mouth, although she was talking to CoCo. Her face was twisted in disgust, as she addressed her one time neighbor.

"Not to see you," CoCo replied, exchanging the same look of disgust.

Blast stood there with his muscles tense, as he felt like grabbing the concealed weapon on his waist. He and Henny stood there staring each other in the eyes. The hate between them was so strong, that neither could speak a word.

CoCo approached Lace's bed. "Lawson, how are you," she asked.

"I'm in a lot of pain, word!"

"I'm so glad you're alright," she replied.

"Why," Nette asked, with her face still twisted in disgust.

CoCo just ignored her. "Do you need anything?"

"No, he don't need shit from you," Nette snarled.

"Nette, would you grow the fuck up!" CoCo's words offended her and also caught her off guard.

"What bitch?"

"Nette chill," Lace winced through the pain. At that moment he was really glad to see her. He also found himself wishing Nette and Henny weren't there at the moment.

"Lawson, why is she here," Nette asked almost confused.

"I heard what happened and I just wanted to see you Lawson. Why does it even matter to you," she finished up saying by looking at Nette.

"Bitch, fuck you!"

"Fuck you Nette."

Henny and Blast stood silently, as if each man was waiting for the moment to attack. Henny must've felt the negative energy coming from Blast, so he finally spoke. "What the fuck you wanna do?"

"Whatever," Blast answered, as both men took steps towards each other.

"Please," CoCo now begged.

"Fuck him," Blast said through clenched teeth.

Henny smiled at Blast's anger. "Ain't shit changed Cornell. I'll still beat the shit out of you!"

"Nah pussy, a lot changed," Blast replied with a straight face.

Henny swung his fist and knocked over the small table by his side trying to get to Blast who didn't flinch. He did notice the Lexus car keys fall on the floor, as Nette threw herself in front of him.

"Henny! No!"

"You better listen," Blast said with a smile.

"What's wrong with ya'll? Won't ya'll grow up," CoCo said shaking her head. "Ya'll adults now. Ya'll ain't sixteen years old no more," she added.

"She's right," Lace said struggling to sit up. CoCo helped him and during it, he got a good smell of her perfume. It made him smile. "We all grew up together," he continued. "What happened when we were kids is over. Let bygones be bygones... I'm sitting in here with holes and tubes all over my body and ya'll arguing over childhood grudges!"

Blast looked at Lace. "You alright man? Chanel wanted to see you, so I brought her. I didn't know this asshole would be here."

"Bitch ass nigga," Henny spit back.

"Henny, chill please," Lace said.

"Cornell, thanks," Blast nodded, still looking at Henny.

"Maybe we should go," CoCo said, seeing how her brother and Henny continued to stare at each other. That's when she realized that Lace had been holding her hand, and she found herself not wanting him to let go. CoCo quickly shook the thought out of her head because this was business, and besides she and Lace were total opposites. Even when they were kids, she knew it would never have worked. She pulled away and picked up the pen that was next to his bed. She ripped a small piece of paper and wrote down her cellular number. "Here is my number Lawson. Please call me."

He took the paper and looked at it. Below her number there was a little note saying, *'I really miss you'*. He smiled and in response said, "I will. I promise."

She turned and rolled her eyes at Nette, who in return did the same. CoCo now looked at Henny whose smile was truly genuine. She almost apologized to him for showing up, but she knew what his being in the Bronx meant. "Henny, it was so good to see you." She wanted so badly to mention her girl but knew better. "I just wish you and Cornell would leave the past where it is," she added.

"It was good to see you too Chanel," Henny motioned and he truly meant what he said. Seeing Chanel made him think about her. If Blast hadn't been there he would have asked about her, but instead he chose to pick with him. "Cornell... fuck seeing you," he added for the road.

Coco sucked her teeth, Nette just laughed, and Lace rolled his eyes and shook his head.

"Don't worry son, I'll see you again real soon," Blast replied in a promising way.

"Yeah, and just like old times your sister will be there to protect you."

Blast shook his head patting at his waistline. Henny of course knew the meaning of the gesture, so he returned the gesture by patting his, even though he didn't have his gun on him because it was sitting under the driver seat of his Lexus. CoCo and Blast exited the room, and as they walked down the corridor headed to the elevator, Blast's heart pounded. It wasn't out of fear, but from excitement. He couldn't have asked for more, because this was the kind of hit he'd been waiting for, for years. He plotted on Henny, but when he was ready to move on his childhood enemy, Henny left the neighborhood and hadn't been seen in years. As he dialed the number, he thought about the Lexus keys he saw fall on the floor and now knew what to look for.

"Yeah, Yeah," Drama answered. Drama was Blast's right hand man.

"Yo, get down to Our Lady of Mercy hospital. Pussy boy Henry in town and I wanna know his every move. You hear me?"

"Yeah, I'm on my way right now," Drama responded as he hung up.

At this point, Lace didn't even matter, because the only thing Blast cared about was Henny dying, and by the look in his eyes, CoCo knew what her brother was thinking. "Cornell, please. You promised," she pled.

"Yo, you just worry about what you have to do."

There were several Lexus' parked in the lot, but it was easy for Blast to spot Henny's because doctors didn't tint their windows or put big rims on their cars. Blast just smiled as he and his sister jumped into the Integra.

*****

8 p.m. and it was dark outside. The dark blue Ford Explorer sat outside of the two story apartments on Third Avenue, which was right beside the Bronx State Correctional Facility Fulton Work Release. The truck had been parked outside the apartments for almost two hours, and Sha Asiatic and his team were just waiting for the sun to go down. Their target had been there since four that afternoon and now was the time to make their move. The three men got out of the truck and quietly entered the complex.

"You ready," Sha asked Bond.

"Yeah," he said pulling his ski mask down over his face and cocking back the fifty caliber.

"You Gotti?"

Gotti nodded doing the same and placing a bullet into the chamber of his nine millimeter. Finally, Sha pulled down his ski mask and checked his sawed off twelve gauge. With all of them loaded and masked down, Sha knocked on the door. Seconds later there was a "Who is it?" It was an elderly woman, who after doing his homework, Sha knew was his victim's grandmother. When

Maurice called him, it was for one reason. Sha and his team were ruthless, heartless men.

"Ma'am," Bond said in a childish voice, "somebody just hit Tior's car."

"Oh Lord," The Wild Indian's grandmother said, as the men prepared themselves.

They heard the security chain being unlatched on the door, and just as the bolt snapped open butt first, Sha crashed through smashing the elderly woman in the face with the butt of the shotgun. Blood was gushing from her head, as she fell silently to the floor. She was just knocked out, but she would survive. The three men quickly swept through the apartment.

"Grandma, who is it," Tior screamed through the door.

Sha had to bite his lip not to laugh. What a shame, they rushed in on the so called Wild Indian while he was on the shitter. He couldn't even respond, because he was caught so off guard. Three big guns held by three huge, masked men pointed at him. He pled for the men to allow him to wipe his ass, but there was no chance. The three men pistol whipped him brutally, but they knew better than to kill him. They would be paid thirty grand for delivering the man to the designated spot. With Tior badly beaten, they duck taped him completely and got him to the truck.

*****

It was 9:30 p.m. when Marisol got off the train, and she didn't expect anyone to be there as she headed down the subway stairs. She found herself sad. She knew Lace wouldn't be there, because most nights he was late anyway. Marisol gave him so much drama lately because he refused to leave the streets alone. They were far from rich, but Lace put away almost thirty five thousand dollars. Marisol felt that was enough for him to now get a little job and they could live comfortably. If he listened to her, he wouldn't be laying in that hospital bed now.

She was about to head down the block when the horn blew. Marisol looked to see the white Lexus parked about three cars behind her. She smiled, because Henny always did what he said, and that is a quality she wished Lace shared with his best friend. He got out and opened the door for her, which was another characteristic Lace lacked, except for dealing with his mother and sisters. Marisol got in the car, sat comfortably in the passenger seat, and exhaled. It was easy to see why all the women around him loved Henry. He went around and got into the driver seat, and before she knew it, she was at the house. Henny parked and they sat there for a minute. The ride had been silent the entire time. Marisol sighed.

"What's wrong Mad-dee," Henny asked.

"You know I hate that name," Marisol said as she smiled.

"I don't mean anything by it, but you know you got that hot Latina blood in you."

Now Marisol laughed. "So how is he," she asked.

"He's good, just complaining about that piss bag shoved in him."

"It's a catheter, she responded."

"Same shit!"

"So you think he's done?"

He knew what she meant. All women dealing with drug dealers always wanted their man to quit, but they loved the money. "Done with what," he asked, pretending to not know what she was talking about.

She just gave him a smirk.

"Only he knows that…," Henny replied anyway.

"Maybe you can talk to him?"

"And say what," Henry questioned.

"Tell him to leave the streets Henry! Tisha almost lost her dad!"

That topic was a little too sensitive for Henny, because he hated the thought of a child without a father. Since she lost their child years ago, he never tried to have a baby again. It was something Carol always talked about, but the business he was in was too hectic to have children. He treated Tisha, his goddaughter, as if she were his child and the thought of her losing her father sent chills down his spine. "Yo, let's go upstairs."

It was after 11 p.m., Henny expected to hear from Mark or Moe by then, but he masked his anxiety by exchanging laughter and jokes with Marisol. He nearly jumped out his Timberlands when the knock at the door came. It was Mark, and Miss Maddy went downstairs to let him in. He walked through the door carrying a bucket of KFC and sat the chicken down. "You hungry," he asked Henny.

"What the fuck is this man," Henny asked.

"It's chicken," Mark answered very frankly.

"What the fuck, my nigga is laid up in a hospital bed and you runnin' around playing Benson. I don't want no fuckin' chicken. I wanna know who hit my man!" Henny didn't realize he was yelling.

"Relax Henry," Marisol said in calming voice.

"Word, relax Henry," Mark said sarcastically.

★ ★ ★ ★

"Everything is taken care of. Moe's on his way, so just eat some food and calm your nerves," Mark added sitting back on the sofa, eating a piece of original recipe.

After while, Henny did the same, as he grabbed a drumstick and sat down on the recliner. Not only was he tired, but he was also hungry as hell, and angry that he'd left his phone.

*****

Most nights, Blast slept upstairs at Sincerely's apartment unless he was mad at her, which he usually was. He'd been gone for a minute and CoCo finally had the chance to go holler at Sin about who she saw today. They sat in her bedroom, CoCo in a chair smoking a blunt while Sin sat Indian style on her bed. Her belly was finally beginning to protrude at four months of pregnancy. Not wanting to excite her too much, CoCo slowly worked her way up to telling Sin. After an hour or so of idle chat, she finally told Sin she saw Henry.

"Oh my God CoCo! How did he look?"

"Fine as hell girl, but you know that bitch Nette was all over him."

Nette had been one of the problems in their relationship for years. They talked about her for a few minutes and called her every kind of bitch they could think of while laughing after every name.

Then Sin's face quickly grew serious. "What did Cornell say?"

"They had words you know that. Here take a couple of pulls," CoCo said handing Sin the blunt.

She took a few quick pulls, then handed it right back. Since being pregnant, it didn't take much for her to get high. That was how she had found out she was pregnant, smoking weed and then feeling extremely light headed. She went to the doctor and found out she was two months along. Blast had been so sweet at first, but after his trip down south, he came back the same old Cornell. At times she wondered why she ever let CoCo talk her into dealing with him. The truth was, she hadn't been with anyone since Henry left, and besides feeling sorry for Blast, she had also been feeling alone for two plus years.

"So," Sin began, "did he ask about me," she finished.

Thank God no. Could you imagine in front of Cornell?"

They both laughed at the thought.

"In front of me what," Cornell suddenly said.

They both nearly jumped out of their skin and turned to see Blast standing in the doorway.

"Huh," Sin replied, damn near trembling.

"Imagine what," he asked with his tone as serious as the look on his face.

"Nothing," CoCo answered.

"I don't know what the fuck you two bitches is up to, but I'll fuck this shit up and murder both ya'll asses!" Neither woman uttered a word as he stared back and forth between the both of them. "You hear me Sincerely?"

"Yes…," she answered just above a whisper.

"Chanel," he called but his sister didn't answer, so he yanked her by her hair.

"Ow," she yelled in pain. "Yes, I hear you. You bastard get off of me!"

He let her go and picked up the ash tray. "And what I tell you about smoking weed around her?"

CoCo sucked her teeth. "Sin I'm leaving," she replied picking up her bootleg Prada bag. "I'll talk to you in the morning."

"Lock the door behind your ugly ass," Blast yelled as CoCo walked out the room. He was pissed, because he knew what they were talking about, that bitch ass nigga Henry. He wished he could've murdered the nigga right there in the hospital. He hated him since they were kids, but truthfully he hated all of them and before this shit was over, all of them would pay for the years of turmoil, even Mark and Maurice. Henny would get it the worst, because he would torture that motherfucker. Blast promised himself he would do Henny dirty, for all the times they laughed at him. Even this little grimy bitch carrying his baby laughed, and now look at her. If it wasn't for him she'd be dirty, hungry, and homeless. He bet she wouldn't laugh now.

His cell phone rang and it was Drama. "Yo, where you at," Blast asked.

"A warehouse in Brooklyn by the docks," said Drama.

"What the fuck you doin' there?"

Dog, you wouldn't believe that all dem niggas here and they got Wild Appache!"

"Tior," Blast replied in shock.

"Yeah, man. Yo, the fools must think ah him do it!"

"Yo keep an eye on that nigga. I know he live somewhere upstate and I know he holding!"

Right away Sin knew he was talking about Henny, and through the mirror, Blast watched her face to see her reaction. "Yo that bitch ass nigga Henry dead. You hear me?"

When he said it, he saw the look of concern on her face and that triggered his rage. He hung up, fell back on the bed kicking off his shoes and unbuckling his belt. "Come here baby," he called her to him, in the sweetest tone.

She tried to smile through her nervousness. On all fours she crawled up the bed to him, and he quickly grabbed her by her neck.

"Aww," she groaned in pain.

"You miss that nigga," he asked through clenched teeth.

"Please... Cornell you're hurting me!"

"You miss him bitch?"

"Whooooo," she cried out.

"Henry," he screamed, while pulling his belt off with his other hand.

He wrapped the leather belt around her neck and she was too afraid to fight back. "You miss him bitch?"

"Nooo," she tried to scream.

"Yeah, I see. You think I'm stupid?"

"No... Cornell please, please," she pled.

"Tell me you hate 'em!"

She cried but said nothing.

SMACK! He slapped her busting her lip.

"I hate him." The tears ran down her cheeks, mixing with the blood from her busted lip.

He hit her again and she tried to scream. Then he quickly tightened the belt and squeezed her small neck, closing her throat passage and trapping her screams. She began to gasp. "I'll kill you bitch. Tell me you love him!"

She shook her head 'no', unable to speak.

He began to yank the belt back and forth, smiling as her head jerked from side to side.

"The bay..." Each time she tried to speak, he yanked the belt again. He found it hilarious, but finally she was able to get it out. "The baby..."

His mood changed, as if she ruined the joke. He pulled the belt from around her neck and once free, she fell flat on her stomach gasping for air. "Who you love," he asked, as his face displayed an evil grin.

"You," she managed through the tears. "You!"

"Get yo ass in the bed."

With the little strength she could manage, she crawled under the covers. '*Why*,' was all she could think .Why her? What did she do to deserve this? The worst thing was, she couldn't even run. She had no where to go, because CoCo and Blast were all she had.

It was his own insecurities that made him the monster he was, because deep down he knew he could never be Henny. He really loved Sincerely because she was the only one that never really shitted on him. Back in the day she would laugh when her boyfriend made jokes about him, but she was always apologetic. He laid there ignoring her sobs, or at least trying to. He lit his backwood trying to think of something else, but all he could see was Henny's face. Crazily, the thought made him smile. Then he thought about the Brown brothers because they had Tior. That could also work out in his favor, so he decided to go see the white boy in the morning. He poked out the backwood to save that for a nice morning wake up.

*****

Once Henny and Mark walked through the doors of the abandoned warehouse, Sha Asiatic pulled the pillow case off of Tior's head. "Oh shit," The Wild Indian yelled, seeing the six men standing around him. "What the fuck boy," he added as a question.

Mark handed Moe a brown paper bag containing fifteen grand. Moe added this to his money and passed it to Sha. "30 gee'z," Moe said.

Sha nodded.

"You can count it," Moe added.

"I know your money is good Black Man. So you good," Sha asked.

"Yeah good look," Moe answered.

"It's nothing! Send my love to Lace."

"For sure," Moe replied.

With that Sha and his team left the warehouse.

The so called Wild Appache was already begging for his life. "Yo, I swear I don't have no money or nothin'!"

"This ain't about no money Indian."

"So what's up man?"

"You had a problem with my cousin," said Moe.

"Who's your cousin," asked Wild Appache.

"Lace," Henny offered.

"Lace," Tior repeated, as if contemplating.

"Lace from Web?"

"Yeah that's it," said Moe.

"Yo, we deaded that. Ask him!"

"Lace is laid up in the hospital."

"What happened to him," Tior asked.

"You tell us," Moe asked. "I don't know shit. My word."

They went on like that for minutes, and when Tior still refused to tell them anything they began to beat a confession out of him. That only brought out the Appache. He must have realized he was going to die and decided to die with his pride.

"Who hit my cousin?"

"Fuck you," he replied between breaths. "Fuck you and your cousin," he spit blood on Moe.

They beat him bloody until they were tired, but got nothing out of him. "He ain't gonna talk," Mark finally said. Moe panted and nodded his agreement.

"Alright... Alright." Moe dug through the bag he had sitting on the old, dusty table and pulled out a jar of honey. "I guess the Wild Appache is gonna die here in this rat infested warehouse."

Tior could barely speak, but still he cursed the men that had him duct taped and on the bloodied floor. The blood soaked his clothes, as well as the duct tape. The blood weakened the glue, and if he had the strength, he might've been able to break free.

"What the fuck is the honey for," Henny asked, also winded from the beating they gave the Indian.

"You'll see," Moe replied.

Moe opened the honey and began to pour it all over the still cursing Indian. "Let's go," Moe said.

"Kill this nigga," Henny replied.

"Trust me he'll be dead before the sun comes up."

Before they slammed the door shut, the rats began to appear and were sniffing The Indian, as he lay out on the dust covered floor. The dirt beneath him quickly turned to mud, as his blood mixed with it. They could hear the man's low squeals of pain, as the rats began to nibble at his sweet and salty flesh. There was no doubt in the men's minds. It was now 2 a.m. and The Indian would be dead before dawn.

Henny had all kinds of thoughts, as he rode north on the New York State Throughway. Mostly thoughts of Carol, being around Lace, and seeing how easily life could be over danced in his mind. He began to think about how he had been cheating himself out of enjoying life. He always wanted a child but had been afraid, especially after Sincerely lost their baby. Now she moved on and was carrying his worst enemy's child. Henny thought he could never get over her, but apparently she had gotten over him. He had been denying Carol, because deep down he still wanted to be with Sincerely. It was now time for him to move on, and the first thing he'd do is tell Carol the truth.

It was 3:45 a.m. when he pulled up to their apartment in middle class suburbia, Nanuet, New York. Maybe Marisol had been right, that the streets didn't love anyone and drug dealers had a short life expectancy. Maybe he'd just ride out to Middletown, gather all his money, and devote his time to the salon and starting a family. Carol proved herself worthy of that. As he got out the car, at the end of the parking lot he saw the van parking. It was early in the morning, a little too early for one of these folks, but he just shook it off and headed into the house. He missed Carol, and was kind of upset about not calling her and telling her what happened. He'd been gone two days and left his phone. She had to have been going crazy with worry and he felt bad for his selfishness.

It was Tuesday morning. Carol had barely been able to sleep the past two nights because all she could hear was that mystery woman Ceily telling her she wasn't as important as she thought. Then this inconsiderate bastard didn't have the decency to call. She was so miserable that she didn't even bother going into the shop Monday, so she let Heather and Monica run things for the day. Carol couldn't stand to be around Monica, or her jokes and snickers. It was almost 4 am and she still couldn't sleep. She thought maybe if she smoked a joint she could finally get a few hours of sleep and be able to go to the shop in the morning. Carol sat at the kitchen table, and as she smoked the weed by candle light, she twirled his phone on the table. His little bitch hadn't called back, but she really didn't expect her to.

Henny walked through the door way. They startled each other, because the house was so dark and quiet. Henny thought she was in the bed, and she didn't hear him come in. "Why you sittin' here in the dark?"

She didn't answer his question. She just looked at him twirling the phone.

He looked at the phone. "You alright Carol?"

"Do you even care how I am," she quickly spit back.

"Look Carol, some shit happened that I needed to take care of…"

"And you couldn't take two minutes to call and let me know something Henry," she interrupted.

"You're right! I should've called. I was just a little busy."

"Ha! Busy? I bet you was busy. Here, call her," she replied pushing the phone towards him.

He looked at her confused. "What the fuck are you talkin' about?"

"Call your little bitch!"

"Are you smoking more than that weed?"

"Don't fucking play with me Henry. Call her, she's been calling you since you left!"

"Who Carol? Who," he yelled.

"You think I'm stupid?"

"No, but your acting stupid." When he said that, she sat back and folded her arms across her chest. "Listen I was wrong for not calling. I apologize for that. It was definitely selfish and inconsiderate…"

"Ha! You think?"

"But seriously Carol, we need to talk."

For some reason, when he said that, all she could think was that he was breaking up with her, and she refused to give him that opportunity. "Fuck that Henry! Call your fucking bitch Ceily," she yelled.

"Carol I don't know no fuckin' Ceily," he yelled back.

"She's called you over twenty fucking times. She even knows me, but you don't know her," she said, with her voice cracking. She was on the verge of tears.

"You know what? I'm gonna take a ride and let you calm down. When you ready to talk, just call me." He reached for his phone, but she quickly snatched it.

"What you gonna run to be with your lil girlfriend?"

"Carol please give me my phone."

"Fuck you and that bitch." Her anger superseded her intelligence. Before she had time to think about what she was about to do or before she could stop, it was too late because she released it. The phone smashed into the wall and landed on the kitchen floor in pieces. Henny looked at the phone then looked at her. She jumped to her feet. "Henry, I'm sorry," she pled. He just shook his head in disbelief. She knew the phone was his livelihood. For years it was the reason she was driving her Expedition and the reason she had her beauty salon.

"Nah Carol, don't be sorry. I AM," he said as he turned and walked out of the kitchen.

She chased him. "Henry wait!" She grabbed his arm but he just pulled away. His Mark Bocanon leather still sat of the love seat where he left it. "Please Henry, talk to me. I didn't mean to…"

He put his hand up and the motion caused her to flinch. He never hit her nor raised his hand at her before, so her fear angered him. "Just think about the dumb shit you just did. I'll be back later!"

"But Henry…"

He just ignored her as he headed out the door and hit the short button on his key ring.

"Henry please," she yelled.

"Carol," he spoke quietly and calm. "Don't wake up my neighbors!"

He jumped in the Lexus and pulled away. She stood there in the cold early morning air. The warm tears ran down her cheeks and quickly turned ice cold as she stood there til the Lexus was gone. What had she done? She acted like a fool. That's what she did. His best friend got shot and she didn't have the decency to ask if the man was alright. All she did was throw a school girl's tantrum. Carol sat on the sofa and cried uncontrollably. Why did she throw his phone out of all the things she could've done? He would never forgive her for that.

Suddenly, there was a knock on the door that nearly made her jump out of her skin. "Thank you God," she said in a whisper. "He came back." She wanted so much to tell him she loved him. She rushed to the door and flung it open. "Who are you?"

SMASH! Everything went black.

*****

The sound of Blast's cell phone ringing woke her up, but she laid there still. She didn't want him to know she was awake. "Dog, it's almost six in the morning," Blast answered.

"Yo, we got his bitch," Drama replied.

Blast knew just who Drama was talking about. He looked over to Sin and she was still sleep, so he slid out of the bed and into the hall.

"Yo, you still there?"

"Yeah," Blast replied just above a whisper.

"Where you at?"

"Just hit Bk," Drama answered.

"Brooklyn, for what?"

"Dog, she had a bad accident and we droppin' her off," Drama answered back.

Blast couldn't help but smile, "What about Henny?"

"Let him go. We saw a chance to hit the nigga crib, so we took it!"

"Tell me."

Before he answered, Drama sucked his teeth. "Nothing."

Blast didn't know if he should believe him or not. He hid over fifteen keys of coke from them, so why wouldn't they hide a good lick from him?

"Alright. I'm gonna check ya'll later." Blast hung up. He quickly pushed the door to the bedroom open, but Sin was still in the bed. He could've sworn he heard something behind the door, but maybe it was just paranoia. Still he couldn't erase the smile off his face. As he got back in the bed, Sin didn't move. He pulled the covers over his head and hoped that the rest of the morning he would sleep well, because by the afternoon the rest of his plan would be in full effect.

Sin laid there with her eyes tightly closed as she tried to fight back her tears. Blast let his boys murder Henry and it was all her fault because she gave him the plan to set Lace up with CoCo. She let out a soft, low sob. Blast didn't respond because he must've already been sleep. Thank God.

The ride to Brooklyn had been fast and there was almost no traffic. Drama and the D.D.B carried Carol's dead body into the same abandoned warehouse that the Brown brothers and Henny took The Wild Appache. Once they finally got the doors open, to their surprise Tior's body was gone. Maybe the Brown brother's came back, found The Indian dead, and took his body somewhere else. That was their sign to dump this bitch's body and go, and that's just what they did. There was no telling if anyone would ever find Carol's body this year.

*****

It was 10 a.m. on Tuesday morning and Lace was feeling shitty. He tried to smile through the pain so his mother wouldn't worry herself. His sister and Marisol had been arguing for almost an hour which was adding to the aggravation he felt, but for the past two minutes he had been trying to focus on the local news. A reporter was talking about a break in and abduction of a local Guyanese man, but Lace could barely hear over Nette and Marisol's bickering. "Will you two shut the fuck up," he screamed.

"Boy watch your mouth!"

"Sorry mom, but I want to hear the TV."

They all got quiet and focused on the news broadcast.

"Oh shit," Nette started, "that's Tior," she finished.

"His face looks familiar," Mrs. Anderson added.

"Yeah Mommy, I dated him for a few months!"

"Who didn't you date girl," Mrs. Anderson said with a smile.

Lace just laid there quietly. Although the police and neighbors knew nothing, he knew just what happened. His mother sighed as they showed the reporter interviewing The Indian's grandmother. Her head was bandaged and her face was swollen. Lace couldn't believe his cousins would do such a thing to an old woman. It was obvious whoever broke into Tior's house was ruthless.

"This just don't make sense," Mrs. Anderson started. "What is wrong with you kids? That's why I hate you out there doing what you doin'!"

"Ma, I ain't doin nothing."

"Boy don't you sit there and lie to me. People don't get shot doin nothin'."

Lace didn't even bother saying anything because his mother had a point, regular everyday people didn't get gunned down in the street unless it was by the police.

"Just imagine," Mrs. Anderson continued, "if somebody kicked in your door and hurt Marisol or Tish trying to get to you."

"Thank you Miss Anderson, I tell him this all the time."

Before Lace could respond, there was a knock on the door and then entered the two detectives, Hobbs and Mason.

"Well I hope ya'll came to tell us you've found who did this to my brother," Nette said standing up and walking to Lace's bedside.

"I'm sorry Mrs. Jackson," Hobbs said with a smile, "but we just came to ask Mr. Anderson a few more questions."

"Mrs. Jackson? Well, who are you two gentlemen," Mrs. Anderson asked.

"Mom these are the detectives assigned to my case," Lace answered.

Hobbs and Mason introduced themselves to Lace's mother and then asked for everyone to leave the room so they could question

Lace in private. Marisol and Mrs. Anderson were already late for work, and Nette needed to get home so she could watch Tish and let Elise get to school. They all departed leaving Lace alone with the cops, and as soon as his family left Hobbs got right to it. It was a much different method from the day before. "So Lace", he began as Lace looked at him strangely. "Yes, I said Lace. Isn't that what they call you on the streets?"

Lace shook his head.

"Don't fucking bullshit me kid! We know all about you and your cousin Maurice, and as a matter of fact he's probably in cuffs right now. So tell me what the fuck happened."

Lace stuck to his story, but the police refused to believe him. All he wanted was for them to leave, so he could call Mark, to see what the fuck the detectives were talking about. They must've known that would be the first thing he would do, so they sat around just harassing him about shit he didn't know. They even asked questions about Henny.

"I swear I don't know shit!"

"What the fuck are you into?"

"Nothing," Lace yelled as Hobbs grabbed his injured shoulder. Lace groaned in pain.

"Alright, tough guy! Your cousin is going down and since you want to dick with me your next. 225th and Bronxwood will be my breakfast, lunch, and dinner spot. Maybe even my midnight snack corner, so get used to seeing my face! Mason, lets go."

As soon as the detectives walked out, Lace snatched up the phone and dialed Moe's cell number, but there was no answer. Then he dialed Mark, and it was the same. Voice mail. Finally, he tried Henny but again all he got was a voice mail.

All he could think was that the news reporter lied and that his cousins, as well as Henny, were in custody. Maybe they had been caught leaving Tior's house. Anything was possible, but one thing was for sure and that was that Lace wanted out of that hospital before the dicktectives came back. As soon as the nurses took that piss bag out of him he was gone!

*****

Blast wasn't up yet and Sin was in the mirror crying as she looked at her busted lip. It wasn't swollen, but it was split pretty badly. As she came out of the bathroom she stared at him as he slept, and all types of thoughts flowed through her mind. She knew what his problem was. Even though they had been together for almost a year now, he was still jealous of Henny. She devoted herself to Blast and tried to give him all the love she had for another man, but he proved he didn't deserve it. The past few months her life had been miserable and now she was pregnant. It couldn't get any worse. She just needed a pull of his backwood because she knew it would ease her nerves just a little.

Sin picked up the half of backwood and lit it. She took two pulls and they went right to her head. She felt much better as she turned to put it back in the ashtray. At that very moment he grabbed her wrist.

"What the fuck is your problem?"

"Nothing, Cornell. I just wanted two pulls!"

"What you tryin' to kill my baby?"

She pulled her arm away. "No, it ain't gonna do nothing. All I took was two pulls, Cornell!"

"Oh, you's a little hard headed bitch…"

She sucked her teeth and got up to walk out the room, but Blast quickly jumped up. He was barefoot and in his boxers as he ran behind her.

"You don't hear me talking to you," he yelled as she made her way into the kitchen.

"Are you hungry," she asked trying to avoid an argument or a fight.

"Bitch," he started as he pulled her shoulder turning her around to face him, "you crazy?"

"Please, Cornell, I'm not in the mood."

Before she could say anything else he punched her in the eye. She fell on her back without a sound, except for the thud of her body hitting the floor. A flash of light came and went, and then she realized she was staring at the ceiling. Blast was yelling something, but she could hear nothing except a ringing sound in her ears. She struggled to get up and in an instant he was gone. With her hearing returning, she could hear him in the bedroom still cursing. She laid down on the sofa, closed her eyes, and quickly dozed off.

Blast washed his face, brushed his teeth, and quickly got fully dressed because he had things to take care of. As he walked out, she was lying on the sofa and he didn't bother saying a word. When he got downstairs he realized he left his gun upstairs, but then again he was going out to play the peace maker so it was probably for the best. First he headed up to Boston Road. It was early, but money didn't have a timecard and drug dealers didn't punch in or out. As he pulled up to the block, Homicide's crew recognized the Acura Integra right away and quickly got on guard. Blast parked and got out of his car.

"What the fuck you want," Baby Homicide called out lifting his sweater to show the nine on his waist.

"Yo, I come in peace. I just wanted to holla at your brother," Blast answered.

"What the fuck could you possibly have to holla at my brother about?"

"Business, strictly business," Blast answered making sure his hands were in everyone's view.

"What kind of business," Homicide asked as his voice now took on an interested tone.

"Well, I'm sure you heard about The Indian," Blast replied.

Homicide nodded. Everybody in the hood was talking about it.

"Well," Blast continued, "The Brown brothers and that little prick Henny from my buildings are moving on the hood."

Homicide knew the Brown brothers well. He found it strange that they came out and now were asking questions. "What you mean moving on the hood," Homicide asked.

Blast smiled nodding his head. He realized he had the young, hot headed Homicide's ears. He was beginning to think it was better that he spoke to the little brother. "Just what I said," Blast started. "Henny's back in town, so they trying to take over a couple blocks," he added.

"How you know this," Homicide asked. He knew the Brown brothers were above block hustling. They hooked up with this chick uptown, known as the Cocaine Princess Francis White, but Henny and Lace were different because they were street hustlers.

Blast needed to think fast. "You know Lace just got hit up over the weekend?"

Homicide nodded.

"Niggas tried to move on some Yardie boys uptown." Blast came up with an excellent lie.

Homicide knew Blast was Jamaican so there was no need to question his knowledge.

Blast continued, "Now I hear they're moving on Washington. That's why they snatched The Wild Indian, because with him gone, it's open seas on the white boy!" Blast could see the wheels turning. Maybe Homicide was thinking something totally different. He wanted Washington for himself and knew his brother would want it too.

"Yo, that's good lookin' Blast! We'll watch out for them niggas. Now what's the deal with you?"

"Well, I know your brother would want info and would even hit me for it." Blast didn't need anything but his enemies eliminated. Still Homicide smiled while digging in his pocket. Digging through his wad of green he counted out two hundred dollars and handed it to Blast. Although Blast felt like spitting in the man's face, he fought the urge and smiled. "Peace," he said stuffing the money in his pocket.

He jumped in his car and pulled off. Next he would hit Washington and sell some bullshit to the white boy. Yeah this shit was gonna work, and in a few days he'd have his drugs moving on Boston Road and Washington. He pulled up on 172nd and Third Ave, and as usual the white boy was surrounded by more women than men and they were all on point. "Yo Chad," Blast called out to Hard White. "Can I holla at you?"

*****

It started out like any other morning, except Moe woke up with Asia in his bed. He didn't have anything valuable in the house, so he let her sleep, and after a shower and getting dressed he headed out. It would only take him a half hour to forty minutes to do what he had to do, but he was already late, thanks to last night's adventure with his shorty's sister. Although Asia was dealing with his brother, Mark wouldn't care because these were hood rats.

Mark left the message that he left for Philly the night before and would be back that afternoon. Everything would be in the usual spot for Moe, but he begged Moe to handle the business early, before 9 am's morning rush hour traffic. At 7 or 8 a.m. the post office would be empty. Here it was 9:30 a.m. and Moe just picked up the package. It was two nights worth of work that had been sitting in the P.O. Box. At this time, the Post Office was crowded, and it was impossible to see if anyone was watching or seeing more than they needed to.

Moe held the parcel package in his hand and walked out. A woman held the door. He thanked her and began to head to his car when his personal phone rang. It was his house telephone and he knew Asia was awake. "I'm on my way back now," he said as soon as he answered.

"The police are here."

"What?"

"The police are here now."

Moe paused with the key in his hand. "What the fuck did you say?" He wasn't sure if he heard her correctly.

"The police, Moe. The police!"

"Where are they?"

"Here," she answered.

"In the house?

"Yes, they kicked in the door!"

"Don't say a word. The house is clean."

Just then a man's voice was on the line. "Maurice Brown," the voice said. Moe didn't say a word. "You don't have to talk, just turn around."

Moe turned to see three people holding guns pointed at him, including the woman who just held the door for him. He fucked up.

"Maurice Brown, drop the package and get the fuck on the ground." Moe did as he was told and the officer took his phone. "Hobbs, I got 'em, just stay there. I'll be there in a minute," Donald's hung up Moe's phone and placed it in a clear plastic bag. "This is evidence. I got you, you fuckin' bastard. I got you." The woman placed the cuffs on him and read him his rights.

Chapter 4

The nurse took the catheter out and that was it, because Lace couldn't take the hospital any longer. He had to get out of there. Everything was bothering him, including the police and the food. Mark, Moe, and Henny hadn't answered their phones. Nette would never help him escape, and he needed a ride really bad. He opened the drawer next to his bed. His sister left him a few cigarettes to get him through the day, and that's when he saw the paper with CoCo's cell number written on it. He smiled as he took it out along with a cigarette and lighter and tried to decide what he'd say. Lace hopped to the bathroom to smoke his cigarette. He couldn't tell her the truth because she'd do the same as his sister and tell him he was crazy. Lace decided he would just lie to her, because he had to get the hell out of there before detectives Hobbs and Mason came back. He dialed the number and after four rings, CoCo answered, "Hello?"

All Lace could think about was how sweet her voice sounded. "Chanel, its Lace."

She couldn't believe how his voice sent chills through her body. She literally had to force the smile off her face. "Oh, hey Lawson. How you feelin'?" It surprised her that she really cared about how he was.

"Considering the fact that I have five holes in my body, I'm good!"

"So were you thinkin' about me," CoCo asked sincerely interested.

Although he hadn't been, he found it to be an opportunity to get to why he called. "Of course, that's why I called!"

Again the smile was plastered on her face. "So what's up," she asked.

"Well," Lace paused for a moment, "I'm trying to get out of here now."

"So soon?"

"Yeah, I'm made of good material."

CoCo laughed at his little joke. "That was cute," she said.

"Not as cute as that laugh. I wish I could've seen the smile that came with it!"

"Oh? Where is all this coming from Lawson," she questioned.

"I'm grown up now. You know? I'm not scared to say what's on my mind now!"

"Oh is that right," she asked.

"Yeah," he replied.

"So what's on your mind right now?"

"Spending some time with you…"

"Um, I might have to come get you myself," she responded.

That's what he wanted to hear. "I wish you would, so I could get the hell outta here."

There was silence as CoCo thought what she should do. This would definitely put her brother's plans in motion. "Can you give me about an hour?"

"I'll give you whatever you want and need," he said in a low voice that made her shudder.

"I'm on my way," she said as she hung up. His words had her feeling him. She had to keep reminding herself that this was business. She found a pair of tight fitting jeans, put on a blouse that would show off her cocoa brown, flawless cleavage, and pulled on her calf high leather boots. It was pretty cool outside for late October, so she also put on her matching waist length leather. CoCo smiled at herself in the mirror. She looked good and she knew it. She had to run upstairs to Sin's apartment to get the keys to Blast's Plymouth Sundance. He never drove it anymore, since he'd brought his 2002 Acura Integra, and Sin didn't have a license, so it just sat in the parking lot.

CoCo knocked on the door. "Come in," Sin called.

CoCo walked in. "What's up girl," CoCo asked as Sin stayed with her back to her washing dishes.

"Ain't nothing," Sin answered. Her voice expressed signs of her frustration.

"What's wrong with you?"

"Nothing, Chanel!"

"Excuse me! I just came to get the keys to the Plymouth. Where are they," CoCo asked.

"Over there," Sin said, pointing to the china cabinet. "In the ashtray," Sin finished as she still didn't turn to face her friend.

"I'm going to pick up Lawson, so you know shit is about to be poppin'!"

Sin sucked her teeth. "Who cares," she shot in response.

"Whatever, Sin! Where are the keys?"

"In the fuckin' ashtray," she yelled.

"What the fuck is wrong with you?"

"You," Sin said finally turning around.

CoCo now saw her black, swollen eye.

"You Chanel... You're what's wrong with me. You and your fuckin' brother," she said with tears rolling down her cheeks.

"What'd he do?"

"What the fuck do you think he did Chanel?"

"I mean why…"

"Because he's a miserable, selfish, son of a bitch just like you," she yelled.

"Me? What the fuck do you mean Sin?"

"Its fuck any and everybody, as long as you get what you want. It doesn't matter who gets hurt! Just take the keys and get the fuck out," Sin yelled out of frustration.

"I don't know your problem, but you ain't never had no problems before. I'm sure you won't have a problem spending this money either." CoCo just needed something to say, because Sin's words hurt her.

"It's a shame Chanel. You'll sell your fucking soul for a dollar. Go ahead, set up one of the only people that ever cared about you for you."

CoCo just rolled her eyes and left.

Sin looked at her face in the mirror. "Fuck you, it's all your fault! You did this to me! I hate you! I fuckin' hate you and I'm glad he killed you! Fuck you Henry," she yelled in the mirror. She really didn't know if she meant what she said, but it was his fault she was in this situation. He left her, after all of his promises. He left her and never came back.

*****

When Henny left the night before, he hopped on the Palisades and headed up to Highland Falls. Lately he had feelings about getting out of the game, but if he did, what would he do? He picked up sixteen grand and locked up the crib, thinking that he'd never see Highland Falls again. It was a little after 11 a.m. when he got back to Nanuet, New York, and since Carol broke his phone that was the first thing he needed to take care of. It took him about a half hour to transfer the info from the broken phone to the new one. While in the Nanuet Mall he figured he'd stop by Carol's favorite spot, Golden Wok. She loved their BBQ chicken and vegetable rice. After getting her food, he walked passed Kay Jewelers and was tempted, but he fought the urge. He was ready for a child, but wasn't too sure about marriage.

He got to the house and was pissed that the door was unlocked, and the house was a mess. Henry had no idea what Carol had been looking for, but she didn't hide the fact that she was searching for something. He called the salon. Heather answered and reported that she hadn't seen Carol yet, but would definitely tell her to call home when she got there. Henry kicked off his shoes, turned on the television, and got comfortable. He refused to clean up the mess Carol made. He hadn't had a decent sleep in days and quickly drifted off into a deep slumber.

*****

It was almost 1 p.m. when CoCo walked into the hospital room. She was a little surprised to see him still in a hospital gown bare bottomed and staring out the window. "Ahem, I told you I'd be here in an hour." He jumped closing the back of his gown. "Why aren't you dressed," she asked.

"Nobody bought me any clothes!"

"Why didn't you tell me? I could've brought you something."

He just shook his head and hopped on his left leg back to the bed. "It's all good. I'm just ready to go," he replied.

"Like that?"

"Yeah, just go out there and get a wheelchair."

CoCo did as he said and found a wheelchair at the end of the corridor. In seconds she was pushing the wheelchair into his room.

He couldn't help thinking to himself how good she looked. "Can't you help a crippled ole man into his wheelchair," he said with a smile. The thought of him being naked underneath the thin gown made her a little hesitant, but she held her arms out. He purposely fell into her and she jumped when she felt his manhood pressed against her stomach. She just smiled as she helped him get comfortable in the chair.

"All set," she asked.

He nodded while saying, "Wait, grab my cigarettes out that drawer." '*Mmm, mmm, mmm,*' he thought, while watching that ass move in the jeans.

She turned to see the Kool-Aid smile on his face. "What's your problem," she asked.

"God Bless your moms!"

His statement touched her in a way she couldn't understand. Her mother had been dead now for a little over two years. Lace was one of the ones that showed up, that she least expected.

"Why… why you say that," she stuttered.

"For having you," he answered.

Her words were caught in her throat. Most guys that approached her always used the same tired, predictable lines, but the man she grew up with had her at a loss for words.

"Thank… thank you. You ready?"

He nodded.

She begged herself not to let this boy get in her head. "Where to," she questioned.

"The elevator," he said pointing.

"Don't you have to fill out some paperwork or something?"

"I did all that already, now get me out of here."

No one paid attention to them. This was a hospital, so there was nothing strange about a man in a hospital gown rolling through in a wheelchair. They made it outside with ease, and she pushed him to the raggedy old Plymouth Sundance. He looked at the car and then looked at her.

"What," she said to him.

"Now you know you look too good to be riding in that!"

She couldn't help but smile. "Lawson, you don't even have a car!"

"Just for that I'm gonna get something fly for you...," he started.

"For me?"

He nodded.

"What about your Spanish baby mama," she said surprising herself with a hint of jealousy in her voice.

"I'm starting to feel like my baby mama should've been Jamaican," he answered.

CoCo didn't know what to say, so she just opened the door and helped him in.

"Don't forget the wheelchair," he called out.

"What?"

"Put the wheelchair in the trunk!"

"You want me to steal this wheelchair," she questioned quite seriously.

He nodded.

"Are you sure you're supposed to be leaving," CoCo asked, now being skeptical.

He smiled at her. She shook her head as she folded the wheelchair and put it in the trunk.

"I need to stop by 239th and Carpenter first," Lace ordered.

"Now I'm a cab?"

"Shit, I'd ride with you all day if you let me."

"Lawson, what's up with you," CoCo asked having a bad sense about things.

"I told you I'm not scared to tell you how I feel now!"

"And how do you feel?"

"Like I've been robbed and cheated. Let me see your phone."

She passed it to him. "What you mean robbed and cheated," she asked, as he held up his hand for her to wait a minute while he made a call.

"Yo, Hitz its me... Yeah I'm good... Yeah... I'm on my way to your crib... I need something to wear... five minutes." He hung up and out the corner of his eye he saw it. "Stop the car," he yelled wincing in pain.

CoCo quickly pulled to the side and stopped the car. "What happened? Are you alright," she asked.

"Yeah come on," he said opening the door and hopping out a little too fast causing himself to bend over in pain.

"Slow down Lawson," CoCo said rushing to his side. He put his right arm around her shoulders for support. "Maybe you should go back to the hospital!"

"Hell no," he groaned. "Just help me," he added.

"What are you doing," she asked while Lace pointed to the car dealership. "Lawson you don't even have on pants," she said patting him on his bare ass and smiling.

"I just want to see something. As they entered the dealer's lot, all eyes were on them.

A young salesman approached them. "Can I help you," he asked staring at the half naked man and the young pretty woman he was using as a crutch.

"I… I saw the black… BMW going… going past," Lace stuttered as he spoke through the pain.

The dealer led him to the car he saw. It was a 1999 525 BMW, with an eleven thousand dollar price sticker in the window. "Thirty thousand miles." The dealer began to mention several different things, but Lace ignored him.

"Chanel, get in the driver seat," Lace told her.

She just looked at him in confusion.

"Go head," he added and she did as he said. As she sat in the driver seat she began to smile, Lace nodded, liking the way she looked in the black man's wish. "What time you close?"

"Ah, 6 p.m…"

"I'm gonna send my man by to pay for it. I'll pick it up tomorrow."

The salesman smiled believing the young man was lying, just trying to impress his girlfriend, and CoCo kind of felt the same way. Just in case the young man was serious, he gave Lace his business card not wanting to miss the 'could be' commission.

CoCo and Lace got back in her brother's hoopty. "Can I ask you a question Lawson?"

"Only if you'll stop calling me Lawson," he replied with a smile.

"Well you keep calling me Chanel!"

"Excuse me, CoCo! Go ahead and ask your question."

"What did you mean when you said you've been robbed and cheated?"

He smiled as he pointed to his man Hitz's house and she pulled over and parked. "Let me see your phone again." She handed it to him and he smiled at her, and then dialed the number. He told his man he was out front, and then gave her back the phone. She stared at him and he turned at the right time to see her watching him. "What's wrong with you," he asked.

"I want you to answer the question!"

He smiled at her again and stared into her pretty, brown eyes. She couldn't take his stare and had to look away. "CoCo?"

"Yes," she answered but didn't look at him.

Hitz was already coming out with the shopping bag in hand. "CoCo look at me…"

She slowly turned to face him.

"For years I knew we could've been happy together, at least I know I would've done whatever it took to make you happy. I just didn't know how to approach a woman like you."

She sat there at a loss for words. Why was he saying these things? Why now? Why was he making her simple task so hard? She didn't deserve this attention, especially from someone as sweet as Lace. The look in his eyes told her that his words were sincere. It felt as if her heart would burst through her chest.

Lace grabbed her hand and she looked at it. It was as if she could feel his energy passing through every inch of her. She tried to pull away. Well, at least she wanted to pull away, but couldn't find the strength.

"Say it?"

"Say what," she asked.

"Say what's on your mind!"

There was so much she wanted to say but couldn't. It wasn't out of fear or worry of rejection, but because this was business. She pointed to his passenger side window. "Your friend…"

Hitz stood there. "Do you mind if he gets in," Lace asked. It was still hard for her to find words. He mentally fucked her up, because she didn't expect any of what had occurred. Could her feelings be getting the better of her? Was she allowing emotions to supersede her intelligence?

She just nodded her consent.

Lace reached behind, opened the door, and Hitz jumped in the back. "Dawg, I'm glad you good my nigga! Damn shortie you bad," Hitz said, which caused CoCo to smile. "Here son," Hitz said passing the shopping bag to Lace. Lace dug through it and pulled out the Rocawear sweatsuit. "So what's your name ma," Hitz asked.

CoCo looked at Lace who was pulling up the sweatpants.

"Excuse me ma for asking!"

"Chills Hitz! This my new wifey!"

CoCo looked at him, eyes wide open. "Is that so," she replied.

Lace just ignored her and continued talking to Hitz. He gave Hitz the shopping bag still containing the money and the man's business card at the car dealership.

"It's about time you got a whip dawg!"

"I know…"

"So what's up Lace? We gonna move on 221st Street?"

Since the big man on 221 Street got knocked over a month ago and the block had been for the taking, a few small street hustlers came through but none seriously tried to lock it down. Hitz and Rich were trying to get Lace to take it for weeks, but Lace was leery about the heat and attention it could bring. Now he was beginning to understand the saying, 'scared money didn't make money.' His boy and his family were living off the drug game while he was surviving, and it was time for him to love.

"We'll talk about that later, just make sure you take care of my whip!"

"I got you," Hitz said stepping out of the car and closing the door. "It was nice meeting Mrs. Boss' wife," Hitz said to CoCo as he walked off.

CoCo just looked at Lace as she pulled off. "I guess your going home to your wife now," she replied with an attitude. However, he couldn't understand why she had one.

They were at his house in minutes. CoCo pulled up right in front of the small two family house and parked. "Is it all right if I park in front?"

Lace smiled at the question. "You don't have to be upset Chanel!"

"Upset... Upset about what?"

"When can I see you again," he now asked.

"Lawson what's this game you playin'?"

He shook his head before answering. "It's no game. I really want to see you!"

Now CoCo shook her head. "I don't know Lace. Its... Its just..." Again she was at a loss for words. He took his right hand and placed it gently under her chin, slowly pulling her to him. She wanted to stop him, but she couldn't. It had been so long since she'd felt genuine affection, but was this even real? It couldn't be, but she had alternative motives and maybe he did too. Maybe he knew Blast's plan and was just playing along. Oh God... He was kissing her. What should she do? Her heart was pounding in her chest and now his tongue was in her mouth. At first she fought with him, but now her eyes were closed and she could feel her own heat increasing. Something was wrong. It wasn't right. Now she wanted more, but he was pulling away. He broke the kiss, but why? She exhaled in frustration.

"So does that mean I can see you later?"

She couldn't speak, so she just nodded as he got out.

"I got your number. Just hold on to the wheelchair. I'll probably call you tomorrow. Stay sweet!" He hobbled away, struggling up the small flight of stairs, which were the same stairs her brother tried to murder him on.

She just sat there in the car, even as he disappeared behind the doors followed by some old woman. CoCo didn't know what to think, but Lace had her wishing it was a different time, because now she wanted nothing to do with Blast's plans. She wanted what Lace offered.

*****

Moe had been at One Police Plaza over eight hours. He was given a phone call after hours in the freezing room while he was chained to a desk. The P.O. Box wasn't in his name, so maybe he'd be able to beat this possession. That seemed to be the only thing they had on him. Now he was faced with a real dilemma, should he call his brother or should he call his lawyer. The truth was, he needed to warn Mark, so he dialed his brother's personal phone and after four rings he finally answered. Moe knew what took him so long. Mark was very cautious about phones and didn't recognize the number.

"Hello, this is Mark…"

"Its your brother."

Mark knew something was wrong if Moe called him on this line, but Mark's business phone battery had been dead all morning. He just exited the Holland Tunnel on his way back from Philly.

"What's wrong," Mark asked.

"C cipher poison."

Mark knew just what the code meant. C, cipher representing O, poison for the letter P, The Cops.

"You got knocked," Mark said.

"Yeah," Moe replied.

"Shit, Moe. For what?"

"I don't know yet."

"Where are you?"

"One Police Plaza!"

Click! Mark quickly hung up. One Police Plaza wasn't just local task force or detectives, that was the feds. He quickly rolled down his window and tossed both his phones, because he couldn't risk taking any chances. If they had his brother, there was no telling if they were coming for him.

Moe knew the deal. He was on his own. There was no way Mark was getting close to him especially with the feds involved, but he did know a lawyer would be there in a few hours. He and Mark always made that promise, that if anyone of them got pinched, the lawyer was the first thing the other would take care of. All court fees, but no face to face or phone contact. Moe knew his brother was planning his escape from New York as soon as he hung up. He sat back. Now, it would just be a waiting game.

As soon as Mark exited the Bruckner, he flew to his stash apartment in Co-Op City. No clothes, no gunz, no drugs, just six hundred thousand dollars and the keys to his '88 Chevy Cavalier. Very inconspicuous. The next stop was the office of Joshua

Berkowitz, one of the best criminal lawyers in the city. He dropped the lawyer fifty grand and hopped on the interstate. Goodbye New York. The sad part was he couldn't stop to say goodbye to anyone, including his cousin Lace. He'd contact them in a few months, but he'd definitely stay in contact with Berkowitz. He wasted no time and within an hour Berkowitz was sitting in front of Moe getting the entire story.

*****

If the pain wasn't enough, now Tisha was crying as he and Marisol yelled at each other. "No antibiotics? No pain medication? Are you stupid?"

"Listen Madi, I had to get the fuck out of there," he yelled back.

"What asshole leaves the hospital with holes in his body? I mean, dammit Lawson look at the blood under your arm," she said as she pointed at the blood staining his white t-shirt.

"I'm sick of this shit! I'm not gonna argue about this, I'm a grown ass man!"

"You're a fucking idiot! I'm calling your mother!"

"You know what Madi call whoever you want," Lace shouted.

"Then you run out and spend ten thousand dollars on a car! Why?"

"Cause I fucking wanted to. It's my money!"

"So what happened to not wanting the attention?" she yelled.

He didn't answer.

"So what happens to Tisha and me when your ass is sitting in jail?" Still he ignored her. "Dammit Lawson," she yelled. "What the fuck am I gonna do when you go to jail?"

"Honestly Marisol, Tisha's straight. But YOU, I don't give a fuck what you do!"

Slap! She smacked him.

'*What did she expect him to do,*' he wondered. Did she want him to hit her? Did she expect him to grab her and hold her? It didn't matter, because at that moment he just hated her. He couldn't even stand to look at her face. He struggled to stand up, wincing in pain. She flinched, but he just laughed. "Don't worry. I ain't mad at you," he started while still smiling. "I'm mad with myself because for years everyone told me you weren't shit, even the friends you think you turned your back on, the ones that laugh at you because you actually think you're different!" He paused letting out a low, painful chuckle. "Nobody likes you, not even your own mother!"

"What?"

"You heard me, Marisol. You selfish, little, miserable bitch. I saved you! I took you from the South Bronx, your pissy ass mattress, roach infested hole in the wall apartment! I took you out of Levi's and ten dollar dress for less outfits! I put you through school and I showed you there was more to life than getting pregnant and being an heiress to welfare, and what the fuck have you ever done for me besides my daughter? All you ever gave me was a fucking headache!" He picked up his phone and dialed a number. As it rang he continued, "Like I said, my daughter is straight but fuck you! Yeah, can I get a cab to 728 East 224th Street? Yeah... thank you." He hung up.

"Where you goin'," she asked.

"That's all you can say huh? Don't worry, I'll still pay your rent and I'll be by tomorrow to pick up my daughter."

★ ★ ★ ★

He didn't even bother packing a bag or anything as he slowly made his way down the stairs. It felt good, because for years he wanted to give her the reality check that she needed. The relationship between them fizzled years ago, but he tried to make it work for Tisha. If he wasn't happy, there was no way he could make his daughter happy. It was time to let go of the love that wasn't there.

His cab arrived. Lace slowly crawled in and went to his mother's house. They were all glad to see him walk through the door, but a little disappointed that he didn't have Tisha with him. They could all pitch in to raise his daughter without her.

Henny looked at his watch. It was 11:30 p.m. and Carol still hadn't come home. Although it was late he called her mother. He explained that they had an argument, he left, and she hadn't been home for the day. She also hadn't shown up at the salon. Her mother told him not to worry that she was probably out trying to frustrate him and that she was probably staying at one of her girlfriend's houses. Henny couldn't stay there by himself, because all kinds of thoughts ran through his mind. He pushed the 50 cal. under his seat, and with the engine idling, he contemplated not knowing where to go. He put the Lexus in drive and literally let it drive itself.

Less than an hour later, he was parked in a place he had been avoiding for years, the parking lot of 1239-1240 Webster Avenue. At first, his nerves wouldn't allow him to get out of the car. It wasn't fear, it was memories. He left so much behind and that's what was keeping him away from his place of birth. He left the desert eagle under the seat as he got out, and a smile erupted on his face as he walked into the old courtyard. It was hard to believe how small it was, because as a child they had so much space to play stickball and two hand touch. So much changed, and not just the doors on the tenement, but everything. It didn't seem real. His entire life changed because of this courtyard. He had dreams of playing third base for the Yankees. Then STAR came into his life and changed his entire world.

God took his parents and life seemed hopeless, but then God gave him Star and he gave him the world in the form of cooked up cocaine. It seemed like only yesterday he was running to the store to get Star and his team Philly Blunts and Chico stick candies. When he saw the power Star demanded, he began to mock everything he did. He had literally become the man. Police never found the man or men that murdered Henny's savior, but the love and respect Star gave his little protégée, a seventeen year old kid named Henry Charles, was amazing. The older cats quickly began to call the young hustler Henny or Hen Roc.

Henny never changed anything about the way Star controlled the block. It was now Henny who sent shorties to the store for dutches and Chico sticks. A Chico stick, now that was something else he hadn't had in years. The twenty-four hour store's lights were bright. He thought maybe he should go get the burner, because a lot of these young thugs tried to make a name for themselves by lurking the streets at night trying to find a victim. Then again, this had been his hood for years. He was sure if they didn't know him, they'd at least heard of him. He pushed up off the same bench he had sat on for years looking out for police while his workers pitched.

He just made it out of the courtyard when he heard his name. Henny turned to see a woman walking towards him.

"Henry is that you?"

There was no doubt in his mind it was her, but what was she doing outside this late. It was 1 a.m. "Sin?" Her smile seemed to light up the darkened courtyard as she ran to him. He held out his arms to embrace her. As her stomach made it before the rest of her, it brought him back to the reality of what he had already known. Still he held her tightly in his arms. It was an embrace that let her know he missed her as much as she'd missed him. She realized they were standing in the open where anyone could see them and she broke the embrace.

"Look at you," she said. "I can't believe this, it's like I'm seeing a ghost," she said as she held his hands at arm's distance with sunglasses covering her eyes.

"Look at you," he now replied, pulling one of his hands free to rub her belly.

"I know I'm so fat!"

"Nah, you look good with the belly, but what's with the shades," he asked.

"Let's go over here," she said looking around, still holding one of his hands with her brown bag stuffed under her arm. She led him to the small playground, and as they sat down she pulled off her shades exposing her blood shot eye, which was still a little puffy.

"What happened," he asked.

She shook her head. "So how have you been Henny," she said emphasizing Henny. "What brings you to the ghetto?"

"I just needed to see the hood and I'm sure you heard what happened to Lace."

She nodded putting her head down.

With one hand still free, he lifted her chin. "So tell me," he started again rubbing her belly, "what's goin' on with you?"

★ ★ ★ ★ 106

"Well as you can see, I'm four months pregnant!"

"And your baby daddy?"

She sat back and exhaled a deep breath. "Doesn't this bring back memories? Me and you in this playground," she said changing the subject.

"Yeah, I was just sitting in the courtyard thinking about you," he said.

"Yeah right!"

"I was," he said.

"You, Star, my moms, your moms, and even Mrs. Winston…"

"I think that was the last time I saw you."

He nodded. "Yeah it was," he said.

"So much has changed since you left," she said. "Bet I know one thing that hasn't," she added as she dug into her brown bag. "Do you still love these," she asked pulling out the candy.

A huge smile came across his face. "A Chico stick. I was just thinking about these," he said.

"I was craving these things so bad," she said as they both opened one.

"So did your baby daddy do that to your eye," he asked.

The smile quickly left. "Does it matter Henry?"

"Of course, you deserve so much more than this!"

"Cut the bullshit Henry!"

"It's not bullshit, it's the truth…"

"If it's the truth Henry, why the fuck did you leave me?"

He couldn't answer.

"And if I deserve so much more, why is it that you're living in white suburbia while I'm living in the poverty stricken South Bronx?"

"Sincerely, I didn't want to leave you…"

"But you did, so let's change the topic while we can still be friends."

Friends. It sounded alien to him because they were supposed to be so much more than friends.

"So who's your baby father?"

She smiled. "You probably won't be my friend if I tell you!"

"I don't think I could ever stop lov— being your friend," he said as he caught himself.

She heard him. "Cornell," she answered barely above a whisper, but Henny heard her as if she had yelled it.

"Blast, how?"

"Duh, you know the birds and the bees? We had sex!"

"I know that Sin, but I mean you hated him."

She wanted to say she still did, but instead "things change" came out of her mouth. "He's not the same kid you used to bully," she added. He lifted her chin again and stared at her eye, but she pulled away. "Do you remember when you beat him up over there on the swings, 'cause I brought him an icy," she said.

They both laughed. "I should've known back then he was after my girl!"

She heard what he said, but chose to ignore it. "I just always felt sorry for him, I guess," she started. "That's how this happened," she added.

"And this," he said again, holding her head up and looking at her eyes.

She stood up. "Well some relationships go through their ups and downs and if it's worth it, you stay and try to work it out!"

"So I guess it's worth it…"

"I'm sorry Henry. I'm not a track star," she replied and he knew the point she was making with her statement.

★ ★ ★ ★

"Sometimes Sin, the only option is to leave."

"You mean run."

"No Sin, I mean leave!"

"Well news flash Henny... some of us can't just pick up and leave everything behind."

"I didn't leave everything behind," he answered.

She smiled. "No you didn't, you just left me!"

He shook his head. "I never wanted to leave you Sin, I swear."

"You know that's hard to believe Henry because for months I sat around lying to myself and telling CoCo you'd come back... because... that's what you promised me." She was on the verge of tears.

"You were always special to me."

"If I was so special, why didn't you come back to get me?" She paused, waiting for him to answer, and when he didn't, a single tear rolled down her cheek. "I know why Henry, because I wasn't as important to you as I thought I was." She remembered saying that same thing to Carol days ago, when she tried to warn him not to come to the Bronx. When she said it to Carol, it had been what she was thinking about herself. She turned and began to walk away.

"Sincerely," he called.

She stopped and faced him.

"You know it's not too late,'" he said.

"For what," she asked.

"For me to take you away from here."

She smiled as she rubbed her belly nodding. "It is," she answered.

"Why? We could leave now." He couldn't believe he said it.

"Things change like you said Henry, and now I'd rather be with someone for the wrong reasons than to be alone for the right ones." She turned to walk away again because she didn't want to cry in front of him. She wanted so bad to leave with him, but then she wouldn't be any different than CoCo.

"Wait, Sin! Wait!"

She turned and he was right there, pen in hand. "Please," he said ripping a piece of her paper bag. "This is my number. If you need anything, please call me."

She looked at the number and balled it up. "It's alright," she said tossing it on the ground as she turned and walked away. The truth was, she had the number.

"Sin," he called out, "you know I'll always love you!"

She stopped and nodded her head, she answered, "I know. That's why I have a black eye because he knows that too."

As she disappeared into the darkness, Henny went to his car and drove home. The house was just as he had left it, miserable, and now he was being haunted by the ghosts of love, lies, and loyalty. The next morning he and Carol's mother drove over to the Clarkstown police station to file a missing persons report. None of her friends had seen or heard from her. After a small investigation, neighbors mentioned hearing a small commotion and a green Dodge Caravan speeding off.

*****

3 weeks later...

Clarkstown Police still hadn't turned up anything on the missing persons report and police had begun to look at Henny.

They watched him closely and he knew it, so he focused his time on the salon. All the women there gave police the same statements that Carol and Henry loved each other and he would never hurt her. Henry turned to Monica and the other girls for support, and he was feeling it. He knew someone did something to her to get to him, but who was the question. Monica told him about the nights he'd been in the Bronx, how Carol told her a certain number continuously called his phone. Both Monica and Henny went to Verizon in the Nanuet Mall to check his phone records. (718) 321-1234. That number appeared over twenty-one times in one day, but now the line was disconnected.

Henny remembered the night of their fight. Carol mentioned a woman named Ceily, but he knew no female with such a name.

In Carol's absence Heather and Monica ran the shop. Heather knew Monica's motives. She was using Carol's disappearance as an opportunity to get closer to Henny, and for that reason Heather began to wonder if Monica herself had something to do with Carol being gone. She could see the pain in Henny's eyes, because they told the truth. He loved Carol and paid money to thugs in the hood and PI's to find his girl, but there were no suspects, only a green Caravan.

*****

For the past two weeks, Lace and CoCo had been inseparable and most times Lace was riding shotgun in his 525 BMW. Marisol begged for him to come home, but he had already moved into his own studio apartment. Everything was going good, except Moe being locked up and Mark was nowhere to be found. He heard several tales about it being bad luck to visit a man in jail, but he needed to see his cousin. Some kind of move had to be made, because his block had been dry for two days now. He needed to see Moe, and of course his road dawg CoCo went with him.

Visiting someone in jail was like being in jail. They searched everything and even made CoCo take off her bra, because it had a wire rim in it. By the time they made it to the visiting room, they felt as if they had been physically violated. As Moe walked out, he looked terrible. He was bone thin and it looked like he hadn't eaten in days. His once three hundred and sixty waves, was now a tight, nappy afro, and his facial hair was rough and thick.

"Ain't this a hell of a couple," he said giving CoCo and Lace a weak smile.

"How you doin," Lace asked giving him a hug over the table. CoCo did the same while kissing his cheek.

"I'm fucked," were his words.

"How?"

"This cat I was fuckin' with in Brooklyn. Kid caught a body few years back and it caught up to him, so he gave them me!"

"What do they have on you?"

"Everything! My lawyer says they got video, audio, phone taps, and pictures. So much my plea is one hundred and twenty months."

Lace began to do the math. "Damn that's ten years," he replied.

Moe just nodded his head.

"So where the hell is Mark," Lace asked.

"Gone. He paid my lawyer and bounced!"

"Why would he just leave you?"

"Lace, they offering me ten years as a plea bargain. Imagine what they offered the boss!"

The boss was all Lace could think of. For years he had thought Moe was the man, not Mark, but now it all made sense. Mark was never dirty. Whenever a family member needed help, Moe would call Mark. Moe was always the flashy one, while Mark would tell Lace to lay low and move in silence, but Lace was so ignorant wanting to be like Moe and thinking he was the brain of the operation. Moe continued to tell Lace everything, but before long the visit was over.

They seized over a hundred grand and a brick and a half when they arrested Moe. It was obvious he needed help now and wouldn't be any help to Lace. Lace left Moe two hundred dollars for commissary but was still stuck with a problem, he had no drugs.

"Shit," he yelled, pounding his fist into the dashboard.

"What's wrong," CoCo asked.

"Nothing!"

"Are you sure Lace?"

"Yeah it's nothing you could help with."

She saw the opportunity. "You never know, try me."

Lace looked at her with a blank expression

"I'm serious Lace. Maybe I can help."

"Only way you can help me is if you can get me five ounces of coke at wholesale prices!"

She smiled.

"I'm glad you find shit amusing."

"Well Lace, what if I told you I could get you enough coke to last you a few months and it wouldn't cost you a dime up front?"

"I'm listening."

CoCo went on to tell Lace about her brother coming up on a couple of keys and having nothing to do with them. Of course Lace had his doubts about even talking to Blast about any type of business arrangements, but he was desperate. He was still knee deep, and besides stick up kids and drug dealers didn't mix.

"Your brother?"

"Yes Lace."

"I don't know CoCo. I really don't trust your brother!"

"I swear Lawson, he's different," she replied.

Lace just shook his head and sucked his teeth, while riding shotgun in his BMW.

"Lace I mean it. Sincerely is pregnant. He knows he can't live like he's been living and he's trying to find an exit out of the bullshit. Just talk to him and if you don't like what he's saying so be it, but just give him a chance."

He knew somehow he would regret it.

"Call em." With a smile, CoCo pulled out her cell phone and dialed her brother. "Cornell, where are you," she paused as he answered on the other end. "Lawson wants to talk to you. We'll be there in a half an hour, so don't leave... alright... I know, see you in a minute." She hung up. "I'm glad you're giving him a chance."

Although she knew her brother's original intentions, she found herself in a tight spot. The past few weeks spending time with Lace felt like for the first time in her life, that she was in a real relationship. Although he spared no expense wining and dining her, it wasn't about the money because she honestly enjoyed herself. The thoughts made her smile as she headed home on the Westside Highway. Lace had done things with her in a few days that she had only saw in movies, including walks in the park and dinners in Mid-town. He actually held her hand and opened doors for her. In days, she had caught feelings and he never once tried to have sex or take her to a motel. Lace didn't even try to fondle her like the other guys she dealt with, because he was a gentleman. Now, all she had to do was convince her brother that it was best to use him as his worker.

If Blast did this properly, he could actually take care of himself, Sin, and their daughter off of Lace's hard work. CoCo knew she would definitely be taken care of.

"What you smiling about," Lace asked.

"I was just thinking," she answered not realizing she had been grinning from ear to ear.

"Thinking about what?"

"Us!"

Now Lace smiled. "It's about time."

"Why you say that," she asked expecting him to mention sex because she had become accustomed to being just a fuck toy to hustlers. It was hard for her to recognize sincere feelings.

"Because," Lace started, "the only reason I'm doing this is for you," he added.

She sighed and was somewhat relieved that he didn't say what she expected. "I know Lace."

"I hope you don't make me regret this!"

She hoped she didn't either.

*****

6:30 p.m. On the other side of the Metro North train tracks, the Yukon Denali just pulled up across the street from the Washington Houses. Hard White saw it. This was the third time it pulled up that day. "Faggets back already," Hard said to his little man Most. When Tior disappeared, Hard expected dudes to push up on him. He was far from stupid, unlike his business partner The Wild

Appache. Several times he told Tior to move away from the hood, because too many eyes watched. Now he paid the price for his arrogance and ignorance, and Hard now had to pay out of his pocket.

"You want me to tell them anything," Most asked.

"Yeah tell them bitch ass niggas come back around 11:30 and I'll definitely have it."

Most nodded as he looked at Hard disappointedly. Most and a few other loyal soldiers were ready to take the brothers to war, but Hard knew it would make shit too hot. He had to move carefully and plan his strategy properly. In two weeks, he paid Homicide and Genocide over ten grand and was told to have five more today. Although his team was loyal, he knew he'd have to set an example because sooner or later somebody would get brave if he allowed the murder brothers to pressure him.

As Most approached the Denali, Geno rolled the driver side window down. "Where's my money?"

"Yo, Hard said he'll have it by 11:30."

Homicide laughed. "I can't believe ya'll calling this pussy ass white boy Hard."

Most rolled his eyes. He wanted to clap Homicide right then and there.

"You tell that spiced ham lookin' motherfucker I be here at 11:30, and if he don't have my money that's his ass." As Genocide finished, Homicide cocked back the forty-five for special effects as the truck pulled off.

As Most began to walk back, Hard pulled out his cell phone and hit three on his speed dial.

"What's up baby," the voice said from the other end.

"Keisha, what's up mami?"

"Whatever you want."

"I need you tonight."

"By myself?"

"Nah a couple of friends."

"So it's a party," Keisha asked.

"Of course baby girl, bottles poppin'!"

"What time," she asked.

"I wanna be out of here before 11:30."

"That's what's up!"

"Peace baby…"

"You know it daddy." Keisha hung up first.

Most stood there heated. "What's up," Hard asked.

"Niggas talking shit man!"

"Fuck that, you told 'em 11:30?"

"Yeah, they talking bout have they money or it's your ass man. You gotta give it to the niggas Hard, word!"

"Don't stress it Most. Niggas like that don't last long because greed is a man's downfall!" "Whatever," Most answered.

Hard knew little Most didn't want to hear it. He was young and still hungry for props and not much of a thinker, which also made him dangerous. Hard knew he was one of the cats he'd have to show sooner or later he wasn't to be played with. "How many cats was in the truck," Hard asked.

"Five. It don't matter Hard, we could handle them niggas!"

"Chill Most. Don't worry when they come tonight we won't even be here. I got some ladies coming through, some bad bitches."

"Word!" The young hustler's mind was quickly taken off the extortionist, and that's what Hard was hoping. So quickly women could take a man's mind off of any problem. No matter how big, pussy always clouded judgment.

"Yeah they'll be here before 11:20 and I got something nice picked out for you…"

"That's what's up Hard."

They quickly went back to business, but Hard still had his mind on the brothers. Pussy couldn't take his mind off of that problem.

*****

Blast almost grabbed his gun when Lace came walking through the door, but quickly shook it off. This was business, and Lace hadn't even noticed.

"Oh shit," Lace started. "There's my girl," he said holding his arms open for Sin to hug him. Although he was moving a lot better, he winced in pain when she hugged him.

"Lace what's up baby," she said realizing she had been a little too affectionate. She looked back at Blast, who put on a fake smile.

"Lace what's up? Good to see you up and about!"

"Yeah, well bitch ass niggas can't keep a good man down," Lace replied.

Blast had to literally bite his tongue not to react to the statement. "That's good, that's good."

"Damn Sin what happened to your eye," Lace asked as it still showed signs of Blast.

She swallowed a knot in her throat, "Clumsy that's all!"

"I don't remember you being clumsy."

"Well," Blast interrupted. "She is. She's also a little stupid at times," he added. Lace didn't like what Blast said about his old friend. He looked at her and she quietly put her head down. "Sin why don't you go upstairs and make something to eat," Blast said. She nodded and turned around.

Lace called out to her, "Sin, congratulations!"

"For what," she asked.

He pointed to her belly. She looked at Blast and just nodded her head because she felt like she had betrayed him also.

Blast sat on the sofa with his sister next to him, and Lace sat across from them. "So, lets talk business," Blast said.

"Talk to me!"

"Well," Blast began and told Lace a lie about how his man got knocked uptown in the Bronx and left him with fifteen bricks. Blast also mentioned that he knew nothing about the drug game, but was willing to go in as partners with Lace and would do whatever he had to do. He had a daughter coming in a few months and wanted to be able to put some money away for her. Lace understood the man's worries. He had a daughter, but there was no way he'd allow the man to be his partner.

"Fifteen keys? That's a lot of shit Blast!"

"Can you move it?"

Lace sighed, "Yeah, but it would take months."

Would you be able to hit me off with something weekly?"

Lace nodded as he did the math in his head. If he allowed his team to move on 221st, as well as 223rd, he might be able to see around ten to fifteen grand a week, but there was no way he'd split the profit fifty/fifty with Blast. After moments of calculations he answered Blast. "Check it, I got workers to pay, so what I could do is maybe give you twenty a brick, and it would probably be five grand a week."

Now, Blast did his own math. Twenty grand a key? That was three hundred thousand at twenty grand a month. "That's not bad," Blast said a little nonchalantly looking at his sister.

"You could live good off five grand a week Cornell and you could put up a nice piece of change for your baby," she offered.

"And truthfully Blast, I might be able to give you more than five grand a week. I'm just giving you an estimate!"

"It's a deal." Blast wasted no time, "You want it now?"

Something was telling Lace to say no and just walk out of there now. His mind told him to leave both of them alone. Blast is the devil, which makes CoCo the sister of Satan, and you can't trust them. He looked at CoCo. There was something in her eyes and he couldn't tell what it was. Good or evil? Anxious or concern? Disapproval or eagerness?

Regardless of what it was, Lace and CoCo left that apartment with fifteen kilos of cocaine in a dufflebag. It was the beginning of something and Lace didn't quite know what, but he began to think about that look in CoCo's eyes, as well as Sincerely's. What the fuck had he done?

*****

11:15 p.m. The platinum colored Lexus pulled up. "Damn," Most said out loud. "Where the fuck is the bitches," he asked.

Hard just shook his head because he told Keisha he wanted to be out of there before 11:30, and now here were the brothers. The window came down and Geno was in the passenger seat of the Lex. "Most go upstairs and call this number. Just say Hard is ready!"

"Who is this," Most asked.

"Just hurry up, you got five minutes!"

Most ran into the building. Hard held up his ten fingers, indicating ten minutes. Homicide nodded gesturing a gun aimed at the man and pulling the trigger. Now, Hard held up his hands, palms out gesturing his surrender.

"Bitch ass nigga," Homicide said out loud. "Yo, Hah light that weed," he said to his man in the back seat. Hah quickly lit up the blunt.

"Damn what's that," Geno said, noticing the thick sexy thing walking towards them.

"Damn shortie right," Hah said from the back seat. "Holla at that," he added.

The girl was about to walk in the Arab store.

"Yo, shorty," Geno said before she walked in the door. The girl stopped and pointed to herself.

Homicide laughed.

"Yeah, you! Come here," Geno said as his brother laughed.

"Pretty as hell but obviously she ain't that bright," Homicide said as the three of them laughed.

She walked up to the passenger side window. "Yes," she said as if they were bothering her.

"What's your name," Geno asked.

"Ke-Ke," she answered.

"What's yours," she asked.

"Genocide."

"Um," she smiled. "Why you a killer?"

"All I kill is pussy baby," Genocide said causing his brother to laugh out loud.

"Why you laughing? Is he lying?"

"Nah Mommy!"

"So what's your name," she asked.

"I'm Baby Homicide and this is my man Hasan."

"I guess you the only one in the car that don't kill pussy, huh?"

"Nah baby girl, I paralyze it." Again the men in the car began to laugh.

"I see," she started, "Ya'll got jokes," she added.

"Nah ma, it's definitely not a game," Geno said.

"So what ya'll doin tonight," she asked.

"Whatever you wanna do," Hah said from the backseat.

"You cute. My girl Slelia would love you!"

"Word you got friends," Homicide asked.

"Of course," she answered.

"They all look as good as you," Hah asked.

"No doubt, you know birds of a feather, flock together," she answered.

"So where they at," Homicide asked.

"At the crib around the corner waiting for me. I was just goin' to the store to get some dutches so we could get smoked out."

"Oh word? Ya'll blow trees," Geno asked.

"We blow more than trees," she said licking her lips.

"That's what's up," Homicide added.

"Let me hit that blunt and I'll call em, they'll meet us out here."

Hah quickly handed her the blunt. She took two small pulls and choked. The men laughed at her. "That's that Bronson Mommy, be careful!"

"That shit is good," she said passing the blunt to Geno.

"So what's up, call your friends," Homicide said.

"Can I use your phone?"

 122

Geno passed her the phone. She dialed the number as Geno stuck his two fingers in her belt loops, pulling her closer. She smiled and blew him a kiss. "Lee, Lee... I am at the store... I know... chill listen, I met three cuties... yeah... they in a silver Lex."

"Platinum," Homicide yelled, as Ke-Ke just smiled.

"Tell Hell Relle she'll like the driver."

"Hell Relle," Homicide repeated and Ke-Ke nodded her head to him.

"Yeah...," she said. "They look like they got money." Hah pulled out a knot and Ke-Ke smiled. "Yeah girl the one for you got paper... Oh god, they look like they could pop bottles all night."

Homicide sung the latest T.I. song. "You could pop bottles all night, Hell Relle you could have whatever you like!"

Again Ke-Ke smiled at him. "Yeah, come right now." She closed Geno's phone, but didn't hand it to him. "They'll be here in two minutes."

"So what we doin' tonight," Geno asked.

"I ain't had this pussy murdered in months," she said with a smile, still holding his phone.

He pulled her close trying to grab her ass, but she pulled away. "What's up with this Hell Relle," Homicide asked.

"Here they come now," Ke-Ke said pointing to the black Tahoe pulling up in front of the courtyard, obscuring their view of Hard and his boys. They didn't care at the moment, as two thick ass shorties hopped out the truck.

"Shit," Hah said from the back seat.

"Which one is Hell Relle," Homicide asked.

"Black shorts," she said. Black shorts was the baddest of the three, even Geno forgot about Ke-Ke in front of him. "Excuse me," KeKe said.

"Chill, chill," Geno said as he watched the thighs in the black pum pum shorts approach. Relle stopped at the driver's window. Hah slid across the back seat.

Ke-Ke began to introduce. "Relle, Lee Lee... This is Genocide, Homicide, and Hasan."

"What's up fella'z," Lee Lee said as she stood in front of Hah.

"You are fine," Relle said to Homicide.

"So what we doin' tonight ladies," Geno asked.

"What time is it," Relle asked.

Homicide looked down at his fifteen grand Movado and answered, "11:28."

"Just in time," Ke-Ke replied.

The three men turned to face her and she smiled. "In time for what," Geno asked.

She gestured for the two to look at her girls, and as they turned, Homicide and Hah were facing two guns. Ke-Ke had her hand behind Geno's neck. It happened in seconds.

"Oh shit," Homicide yelled. It was too late Ke-Ke's gun was pointed to the middle of Geno's forehead.

Over nineteen shots riddled the Lexus, to the point that there was no doubt the job was done. They quickly crossed the street jumping into the Tahoe, with Hard and Most already in the truck. With Hell Relle behind the wheel, they pulled off.

"That's better," Hard asked the wide eyed Most. He was so shocked, all he could do was nod his head. "Hell Relle, I like that," Hard said.

"I pop bottles all night daddy!"

Hard smiled. "Seriously Keshia," Hard said.

The driver looked at him through the rear view mirror. "Yes daddy?"

"This my little man Most. I told him I'd have something nice for him, so what's good?"

"You mine tonight Most," the black shorts replied.

Most didn't know if he should be excited or scared to death. Hard sat back thinking to himself how pussy took a man's mind off all matters at hand. He relied on that tonight; and once again it proved to be the most dangerous weapon God ever created.

Chapter 5

Lace set up shop and Rich put together a small crew on 225th, while Lace and Hitz played 221st and Bronxwood. This had been the first time Lace ever handled more than five ounces in his possession. Twenty grand a key gave him room to test the competition. The dimes on 225th were the biggest they'd ever been, while the nickels on 221st were the size of the other hustler's dimes. The flow was unbelievable, the fiends were lining up, and the speed they came made Lace nervous, but Hitz controlled the tempo with ease. It was just as Hitz said, 221st was proving to be a gold mine.

Usually by 8:30 p.m., Lace would be leaving to meet Marisol at the train station, but now it was all about his paper chase. He and Hitz came out about 4:30 that afternoon and by 12:20 a.m. he made three trips back to his mom's house. Twenty-five hundred packs were moving with ease, but Rich was still on his first pack at 3 a.m., so they called it a night. After picking him up, they rode over to Hitz's crib to do the math of the night's work.

"Yo, shit did alright," Rich said.

"What you came off," Hitz asked.

With a small smile, Rich dug through his pockets and began counting out his night's intake. "Two thousand and seventy-five after shorts," he answered with pride.

Both Hitz and Lace laughed.

"What the fuck is so funny," Rich asked.

Lace nodded. Rich was four hundred and twenty-five short, not bad at all. Now Lace and Hitz began to count what they made, and after about fifteen minutes, they'd counted out eight thousand ninety-seven dollars.

"Get the fuck outta here," Rich replied in amazement.

In ten hours, 221st made damn near nine thousand, just four blocks away. That meant an average of a grand an hour. Lace split seven hundred dollars and fourteen cents a piece, which was eight grand for the stash and ten grand in one night. Not only would this be the new block, but Lace was already thinking of a way to organize it, because he had a plan.

He was feeling CoCo more than he thought he would, but still he didn't trust her like he wanted to. He had a small crib not far from Bronxwood, but didn't feel safe stashing there yet. So after dropping Rich off at his mother's house, Lace took the Deagan to his mother's house at River Park Towers. He tried to be as quiet as he could, but it didn't matter, because when he walked in, his mother was sitting at the table sipping a cup of tea.

"So now my house is your safe house," Mrs. Anderson asked. She was far from stupid, as she knew what her only son was involved in.

"Nah ma. Not really. Well, just for a few days!"

"Look at you boy. You can't even give me a straight answer. I guess lying up in that hospital wasn't enough for you?"

"Why you say that," Lace asked.

"Because you're just digging deeper into the devil's business. Do you think I don't know how many times you been in and out of this house tonight?"

Lace just laughed as he pulled out a rubberband knot. "Here take this," he said, handing her a thousand dollars.

"You know I'm a take it, but ain't nothing funny boy. This is your life and ain't nothing good in them streets."

"Ma, I'm safe!"

"Boy you ain't safe," she yelled. "If you were safe, you wouldn't be walkin 'round here limping," she added.

Elise came walking into the kitchen. "Good morning mommy," she said stretching as she kissed her on the cheek.

"Good mornin' baby."

Elise went to the stove and poured herself a cup of tea. "What you doin' here so early," she asked her big brother.

"Here, put this up for me," he said giving the seven grand to his sister.

"Look at you, getting my only good child involved with this mess!"

"Mommy chill," Elise said with a smile.

"Cold nothin'! Next thing you know she'll be bringing drug dealers in this house at all times of the night."

"I'll never need no man. I got my big brother to take care of me," she said sitting on her brother's lap, causing him to wince in a little pain.

"I never liked that Marisol girl, but she's my granddaughter's mother, and you were never in the streets this time of night when you were at home with her," said Mrs. Anderson while looking at her son.

His mother had a point that he couldn't argue with, more so because it was almost seven in the morning. He had to visit his cousin Moe later on, and he and CoCo were suppose to go out to lunch, so he decided to kiss his two ladies and leave so he could get a couple of hours sleep before getting his day started.

One month later....

The feds handled their cases much different than the city or state court systems. In criminal court, cases were drawn out for months, even years. In two months Maurice was being sentenced, and everyone showed up except for Mark of course. It had been a long time since anyone heard from him. Maurice tried to be strong amongst the tears, as he was sentenced to one hundred months in jail. CoCo held Lace's hand tightly, because she found herself worried that it could one day be him. She wondered if she was in love. The sex had been much better than she expected, and their relationship had been unreal to the point that she'd forgotten how it all came about. Now, she wondered how it would feel to lose him.

In a month's time Lace, Rich, and Hitz organized 221st Street very well. They had an apartment in the corner building and paid Poppy at the corner bodega. Lace's aura and personality made people love him. The tenants in the building never complained about his activities, he bought the kids ice cream, flirted with the older, single women, and gave the men the utmost respect. This block was pulling in anywhere from five to seven grand a day. Lace gave Blast over thirty grand, and Rich and Hitz full control of the block, so all he did was drop off the product and pick up money. Lace had one rule, all business was to be handled in the building and nothing was to be sold outside.

CoCo on the other hand, tried her best to keep her brother under control, but the cash that was coming in didn't help. Blast ran out and brought his team D.D.B. links because now he was a king pin. He forgot his murderous plans of revenge and was just living the drug dealer's dream life. Of course he pampered a now six month pregnant Sin, but her only thoughts were of escaping.

*****

It had been almost two months since the disappearance of Carol. Henny asked Heather to take charge of the salon, which made Monica pissed. To Henny, Heather was more trustworthy which helped, as the shop pulled in about four or five grand a week, that paid the bills. Henny didn't mind, as he still had around ninety grand in the office safe. Since he'd been the only suspect in Carol's case, he decided to lay low, only leaving the house to check on the shop. About three or four nights a week, Monica would stop by to cook and clean for him. Several times he had to reject her offers to stay the night, because he had too much love and respect for Carol.

It was a little after 2 p.m. when Carol's mother called him. Realtors showing dock properties in the Cock areas of Green Point, Brooklyn found a woman's body. They believed it to be Carol and wanted her to come ID her daughter. Henny drove her to the city morgue, and although the body was mauled by the rats, there was no doubt in either's mind that it was Carol. The NYPD sent DNA samples to the federal lab to try and identify a second blood sample in hopes of finding a suspect. Henny knew the other sample was The Wild Indian's, but couldn't figure out what happened to the man's body, or if Maurice and Mark had something to do with Carol's death.

A week later, services were held in Nyack, New York for her and more than one hundred people attended; including her co-workers, clients, family, and friends. Henny couldn't help but think that Carol's mother blamed him. However, she gave him encouraging words, like he had to be strong and Carol loved him just as much as he loved her. They sat hand in hand as the eulogy began, Mrs. Francis in tears and Henny's rage not allowing tears to form. Just then, a hand landed on his shoulder and he looked up to see Lace, Nette, and CoCo. As he stood, they all hugged him and introduced themselves to Mrs. Francis as Henny's family. Nette kept Henny up to date on Moe's case, and the fact that Lace and Blast were now business partners.

"Let's go outside and talk," Lace said.

Nette and CoCo sat with Mrs. Francis, hugging her as if they'd known her forever, and she appreciated the affection. Although Henny hated Blast, Lace's business moves had nothing to do with his emotions. Lace led Henny to his 525 I.

"Nice ride," Henny said.

"You know, tryin' to keep up with ya'll now. Get in!" Henny jumped in the passenger seat. Lace reached under his seat and pulled out the fresh bottle of Hennessy. He then cracked it open and poured some out of his window, in respect to the dead. After he took a gulp he passed it to Henny. "Ah," he began with the liquor burning. "So how you making it," Lace asked.

"I'm, not," Henny answered.

"Talk to me."

Finally a tear ran down Henny's cheek. "Who the fuck would do this to me?" Now it was more than just a tear.

"You think it was meant to get at you?"

Henny looked at him with a 'don't be an asshole' look.

"Brooklyn Lace, this is a girl that's never been to the city until she met me. How would her body end up in Brooklyn?" Lace now understood. "It's not a coincidence, Lace. It was the same warehouse we took The Wild Indian."

Lace never knew what happened the night Tior was kidnapped, but it all made sense. Henny downed more than half of the bottle, then passed it back to Lace.

"You think maybe the white boy had something to do with this?"

Henny never thought about Hard White, but the thought stopped his tears. The emotion was now vengeance. "That fuckin' pale faced son of a bitch! I'm a kill em!"

"You just chill. I got some boys that'll handle it," Lace said.

Just then, there was a tap on the window and CoCo stood outside.

"You feel safe talkin' in front of her," Lace asked.

"I think the question is, do you?" Henny replied.

Lace nodded, as he hit the button to open the automatic lock.

CoCo crawled into the backseat. "How you feeling, Henry," she asked.

Henny gave her a weak smile. "I'm trying Chanel, I'm trying."

"My girl wanted to come, but she thought it wouldn't be appropriate."

Henny laughed. "No disrespect Chanel, but fuck her!"

"Why would you say that," CoCo asked.

"Ha, she's pregnant by your brother!"

"That's not fair Henry, you left her! So many nights I told her fuck you, and you know I love you, but I told her she had to let you go and she refused."

"Don't seem like it Chanel," Henny shot back.

"Well I was there those nights she cried. She spent months and then years lying to herself and defending you, swearing you were coming back."

Henny sucked his teeth as he looked out the window staring down the hill towards the Hudson River.

"You don't have the right to be angry at her Henry, and you don't have the right to be angry with my brother, at least not for that."

The door opened and it was Nette. "Services are over," she started. "Is everything alright," she asked.

"Yeah," Henny answered as he opened the door. "Everythings good," he added stepping out.

"Shotgun," Nette called jumping out the car, as she ran around to get to the passenger side. She was now face to face with Henny. She hugged him, and then kissed him on the lips. "Call me," she said.

He nodded.

"I'll come up and spend the weekend with you," she added.

He smiled, as she got in the car.

"Thanks for comin'," he said to Lace. Lace extended his hand, giving his man a pound.

"Henry," CoCo called from the backseat.

Henny stuck his head in.

"Please don't be mad at her, because she loves you," CoCo said.

They all knew who CoCo was referring to.

"I know," he replied and then focused back on Lace. "You heard what happened on 3rd Ave," Henny asked.

"Yeah, Hamo and Genocide," Lace answered.

"They gave us the heads up on Tior, so it might've been the white boy that set this up. Dawg, it's on you. Don't let shortie have died in vain."

Lace nodded. No one paid attention to the look of distress on CoCo's face as Henny walked away. CoCo was in love with Lace and she couldn't deny those feelings, but the white boy had been there for her in many times of need. As much as she hated to, she'd have to let him know to watch himself; she owed him that much.

They were on the Tappan Zee Bridge when Lace picked up his cell and dialed The God's number. The God from the four building would do it, as long as the numbers were right, although it would take a chunk out of his stash. Henny was his man, and he would go broke or die to hold his man down. After three rings The God answered. "Sha its Lace!"

"Peace Black Man," Sha answered.

"I need a favor…"

"It's all about the mathematics Black Man."

"Yo, my man Henny…" Lace didn't even get to finish his sentence.

"The God Hen Roc?"

"Yeah, Sha Cat."

"Favors on me," Sha said, again interrupting Lace.

"Just give me the science."

"The white boy."

"Hard?"

"Yeah!"

"Taken care of Black Man. Peace." Sha hung up.

Two Days Later…

Sha took his time, because this was a move he needed to make on his own. Although 3rd Avenue was on fire since the triple homicide, it was business as usual for the white boy and his team. Due to the heat, Hard was forced to switch the daily operations. After two nights of watching Washington's 3rd Avenue side, Sha saw that Hard switched his flow to the Park Avenue side of the projects, which would make Sha's hit more complicated, because now he would have to go deep into the courtyards. Today he'd just talk, unless it came down to disrespect.

It was a school day, so there weren't any children around. One less worry. Ski mask was out of the question, so The God allowed his dreadlocks to hang freely and cover most of his face. This allowed him to get closer to the white boy. Years ago, Star solidified Henny's name in the neighborhood. The gangsters were told to protect Henny, the same way they would protect Star himself. The God himself rode after the death of Star, which began the beef between the four buildings and the thirteens. It was a beef that would carry on years after Sha Asiatic was dead and gone. Ashes to ashes and dust to dust.

Desert eagle tucked safely in his waist, Sha had made his way across the courtyards from the 169th side of the projects. He knew the white boy's look outs would spot him, so he carried himself in a nonchalant manner, as if his presence was normal. He would be upon the group by the time he was recognized. As he entered the playground of the courtyard, no more than a hundred feet away from the white boy's crew, three men, most likely young teenage boys, and five women began to form a barricade around the man. As he reached the small group and was in the young Caucasian man's circumference, Sha began to rethink his plan. Maybe he miscalculated the outcomes of this hit. As he studied the perimeters and angles of his equations, it was almost mathematically impossible for him to get out. Still, there was no turning back, because he was here.

Instantly, Hard White recognized him. "Sha," Hard spoke. "Peace God."

Sha laughed. "Peace is not a word to play," Sha replied.

Hard swallowed a knot in his throat. Some men had names they gave themselves and reputations were given by those closest. Sha The God Asiatic's face only meant one thing, but Hard had been warned and was prepared for the visit. Although the man lacked the heart to commit certain acts, he made up for a lack of physical ability, with mental capacity and was a master of the art of manipulation. Those around him were ready to die and had already given their souls to Shayton, which he considered himself.

"Excuse my choice of words God. What could I do for you?"

"We need to talk," Sha responded.

"About what," Hard's little man Most asked.

"This don't concern you shorty," Sha replied. The shorty offended little Most. "What nigga," Most started.

Nigga was the wrong word for Most to use toward The God and Hard knew it. He quickly put his hand on Most's shoulder to quiet him and he took the hint. "I ain't sure I have shit to say to you," Hard answered.

The anger caused Sha to smile. "Oh word," he said as he began nodding his head. "What makes you think you have a choice," Sha asked. Now it was Hard's turn to smile. He looked at his small army to answer Sha's question. "You think they'd stop me if I wanted to do more than talk," Sha responded.

Keisha, the same one that wore the black shorts the night the brothers and their man were gunned down, pulled out her 32 and pointed it at Sha. Never flinching, Sha smiled pulling the 50 caliber from his waist and cocking it back. In the same motion, the other four women pulled weapons. Sha expected it, as he figured the women were around for that purpose. If the police pulled up, the women holding the guns and drugs would front like money hungry chicken heads, and in all actuality they were the ones that needed to be watched, while the men stood out there clean as the Board of Health.

"Now, once again white boy," Sha said with emphasis on the white boy. "Either," he continued, "we can talk or right here in broad daylight shit could get real ugly!"

Hard knew The God's style and since he had approached the way he did, he figured all he wanted to do was talk. "Be easy," Hard said and his team of assassinettes, and all but Keisha put away their guns away. "Relle baby, be easy," Hard said again.

"I am easy Daddy," Keshia answered. Keisha was known as Hell Relle, because of the work she put in with her thirty two. Hell was for the viciousness and Relle for the revolver.

"Trust 'em Ms. Relle, he's good," Sha added.

"I know he is," she replied.

"Let's walk. Relle, Le-Le, come on." The two men began to walk, while Relle and LeLe were not far behind them.

Sha began his street interrogation. "So what happened to my man Lace," Sha asked.

Hard's face expressed his confusion. He expected The God to ask about the Murder Brothers. "Lace? You mean Lawson from Webb?"

"Exactly…"

"God, only reason I know about that is through a mutual friend," he answered.

"So you don't know nothing about him getting hit up?"

"God, all I know is The Wild Indian disappeared," he looked back at his female body guards and lowered his voice so only The God could hear him. "And with The Indian gone, I know everybody is gonna try to push up on the skinny white boy."

Although Hard's statement shocked Sha, he could tell the words he spoke were sincere. He also knew for sure the white boy had killed the Murder Brothers and Hasan the God. Most likely, it was the pretty ladies behind them that had put the work in.

Hard continued to speak, "With the Indian gone I got a lot of enemies, and Lace isn't one. I do my numbers over here, so whatever Lace and his boys do has nothin' to do with me. They could take over whatever they want because my clients are loyal. I'll just move my product else where."

Sha was now confused. Had Lace been trying to take over and gassed him to be a henchman? "Where you get that," Sha asked, concerned about his own business affairs. He took a number of clients from Henny and Lace once they moved out, but now it was a possibility that Henny and Lace wanted their block back.

Although Blast hadn't been reliable or a trustworthy source in the past, he warned Hard that the Murder Brothers were coming and he dealt with that problem. A few days ago, he received a call from CoCo that The God was coming, and here he was. Hard knew better than to give up a source he might need again. "Let's just say, I got the info from a mutual associate!"

Sha couldn't knock the white boy's reply, but now he had his own thoughts. After talking to the white boy a while longer, he broke out the way he came. Something was going on that didn't make sense, but women were always the best sources of information. So many of them accidentally gave out too much info, and since everyone knew CoCo and Lace were now together, Sha knew right where to go for what he needed to know.

*****

A Month Later…

Although her belly was getting bigger, she seemed to be losing weight rather than gaining. Even her face seemed skinny and her eyes kept a dark, sunken look. She knew it was the stress getting to her that she made an irreversible mistake. She was carrying the man she loved enemy's baby, and even worse, her best friend was now in love, with the best friend of the man whose baby she should have been carrying. As much as she tried, she couldn't be angry with CoCo's happiness. Whenever she was around, which wasn't often anymore, it was all Lace this and Lace that. It reminded Sin of how she used to be with Henny. Now, more nights than often, she sat around the old projects by herself dying for someone to talk to.

With Blast's new found fortune, he was never around. He had money, so he was always out partying with D.D.B. CoCo was always out with Lace, so Sin would spend her nights in front of the sixty-two inch television that Blast brought her. Sin was depressed with thoughts of calling Henny, but never acted on the idea. She was pregnant and miserable, had no appetite, and no friends. All she had was just stress and she was wearing her emotion all too well. It all began the night she saw Henny. Again for the eighth or ninth time that night, she dialed his number but hung up before it even had a chance to ring. He had his own problems, because he lost the woman he loved. He chose to replace her, so why bother him with her problems. Instead, she sat on the sofa starving herself and praying for an accidental death of the life she carried in her stomach.

*****

Marisol finally came to reality that it was over with her and Lace. He did as he said he would and continued to pay all her bills, and spent all the time he could with their daughter. Still, Marisol couldn't lie. She missed him so much, and was tired of being lonely and horny. Many nights she begged him to stay for a while, or she would call him and beg him just to come over and fuck her, only to be laughed at. His exact words were, she disgusted him. Still, she never changed the locks or asked for his keys, hoping that one night he'd just come over and surprise her, with a stiff dick and a strong tongue.

As she exited the 225th Street train station, she began to wish he'd be waiting for her like he used to, not even with his new BMW. She just longed for his company. Marisol missed the walks home, and nagging him about any and everything she could possibly think of. She had been such a bitch, only because she knew she had him because of their daughter. Now she wished she could take away all the aggravation she caused him. It was true, that you never miss the water til the well runs dry.

She was lost in a wide awake daydream, when she heard her name, "Marisol." She turned to see an old friend, truly just an old friend named Daniel. He nodded. "Oh my God! I haven't seen you in years!"

"I know, you're still beautiful as hell I see."

The man's compliment caused her to blush openly. Although Daniel was quite a few years older, during her late teens, he had been one of the older hustling cats her friends were trying to get with, because he had money and was willing to spend it. He had been dealing with one of her friends Amanda, and hanging with Amanda and going to see Daniel was how she met Lace.

Still blushing she replied, "Thank you, and of course you still look good."

"Yeah right. I'm an old man now! Shit you've gotta be at least twenty-five now."

She nodded.

"I know you married," he added.

"Married? No." She shook her head a little disappointed in her own answer.

"Nah, I always knew cats in New York was stupid, mainly me. I know I chose the wrong one." She knew he meant her over Amanda but left it alone, truly just enjoying his compliments. "So where you coming from," he asked.

"Oh I just got off of work."

He nodded his approval of her doing her thing. "It's kind of late and this is a rough neighborhood. Your man ain't here to pick you up?"

She shook her head. She took a deep breath and let it out before answering. "No man." Now Daniel shook his head in disappointment. "I do have a baby father though."

"Word? You gotta seed?"

"Yes, a four year old little girl…"

"I know she's beautiful just like her mom."

Again Marisol began to blush. "I got pictures," she said digging through her bag. She found her wallet and quickly flipped past the photos of Lace to find a more recent photo of herself and Tisha.

"I knew it! Beautiful. So where's your baby daddy?"

Marisol just shrugged her shoulders. Daniel sucked his teeth. "No, don't get it wrong he handles his business. We're just not together," she defended him.

"Well if he ain't with you he's gotta be an asshole, no disrespect!"

Again Marisol exhaled, "None taken."

"Listen it's late. Can I give you a ride?"

Marisol looked around.

"Look, just a friend giving you a ride. I'm not asking you to dinner or anything."

Marisol smiled. "Shit that would be nice, I haven't been out in months!"

"So it's settled. I take you home tonight and this weekend we go out to eat, see a movie, and maybe do a little dancing. That's if you can find a babysitter."

She smiled. "Okay, I live up the street. You can take me home, but I don't know about the date thing."

"Fair enough. I'm right here," Sha held open the door of his Denali, which right away impressed her. Then again, he was an older man who knew from experience how to treat a lady, and although she was a little lonely, even vulnerable, she now knew from experience not to be a nagging little selfish bitch.

Two Months Later...

Sin was eight months pregnant and Blast, thanks to Lace, was on top of the world living the fast life with fast cars. To make a statement, he brought five 1986 325I drop top BMW's, each one white with the Jamaican flag in the window. None of the team asked where the money was coming from, but they all enjoyed it. In four and a half months, Lace brought Blast over one hundred grand, which was way more than Blast expected to see. Blast had no problem spending the money on any and everything he wanted, literally forgetting about his original plans. The drug game had the stick up game beat by far. He felt like a king pin and this was a life he could get used to. One thing he didn't like was how close his sister was getting with Lace, but as long as the money kept coming he didn't care.

Blast had always been clowned as a child. They laughed at his clothes and his hair, because he couldn't get hair cuts but once a month. So now that he was a grown man and could afford the finer things in life he loved to floss. He no longer parked his car in the back parking lot. He liked to park right in front of his building, so everyone could see his BMW, with his country's flag representing in the windows.

This day he had been window shopping in Mid-town all morning, looking for one specific item. Once he found it, he headed back to the Bronx and couldn't wait to show his sister. She had to see it first. He pulled up in front of 1240 Webster Avenue with the sun shining bright in the mid afternoon sky. As he got out of his whip, he smiled at the sun's reflection off his chrome rims. He locked the doors and headed to the building. That was when he saw the old man; at least he thought it was an old man. His skin looked almost rotted, as if he'd been burned badly. As Blast approached the courtyard, the sight of the man made him feel nauseous.

His ears gnarled, a piece of his right nostril was missing, and a part of his bottom lip hung, as if a gust of wind would cause it to flap. The man had an old rag on and would continuously dab at the raggedy piece of flesh to wipe away the freely leaking saliva. Blast found himself praying the man wouldn't look directly at him, but just then, the man stopped in front of him. Slurping spit before he spoke, the man said, "Beg…" Slurp. "Beg you a dollar…," the man said, slurping again as he finished. That's when Blast saw the man's eyes, which instantly caused his stomach to turn. As yellowish goo seeped from the corner of the eroded iris, he noticed that the pupil was torn in a jagged gash.

Blast reached in his pocket, pulling out a five dollar bill. Although he could barely look at the man, Blast felt a small inkling of compassion for him. He raised his hand for the bill with Blast holding only the end of it, not wanting his hand to get anywhere near the man's scabby, moist looking flesh. The man nodded, and slurped before and after he spoke. "Thank you." His voice was barely above a whisper. Blast nodded and quickly continued to his building, looking back at the old man watching him. Blast murdered men, tortured women, and duct taped and pistol whipped children, yet the look of this man gave him the chills.

As Blast disappeared, the old man just watched. He became accustomed to the half looks and glares people gave him, as the sight of his own face was hideous to himself. He felt the thick saliva running down his chin and wiped it away, as a young woman passed him, jumping as she turned to see his face. "Ooh, excuse me,' she spoke while quickly looking away and hastening her steps once she caught sight of the man. He smiled as she entered the building and she glanced over her shoulder at him. He winked at her and she almost fell, trying to escape his eyes.

CoCo looked back again, just to make sure the gross looking thing wasn't following her. She could taste the bile in her mouth, as the sight of the man almost caused her to vomit. The elevator stopped on her floor and was on its way back down. She and Lace had an appointment at six. She needed to get dressed, but first she had to tell Sin the news. The elevator couldn't rise fast enough because her excitement built more and more as every floor passed. Finally, the doors opened on the 9th floor, she almost ran out.

Sin's door was unlocked, so she walked in. As usual, Sin was parked on the sofa, remote in one hand and telephone in the other. Although she would never say it to Sin, she couldn't help but think how bad her best friend was looking. "Hey girl," CoCo said in a bright cheerful voice. Sin just looked at her and nodded, then focused back on the television which was muted. "I got some good news girl. Lace and I are going to look at an apartment. Well, actually an apartment in a private house."

"Good," Sin said. Maybe CoCo would now stop coming by.

"Good? That's it? I thought you'd be happy for me!"

"What you want me to say Chanel? Oh that great! Lucky you finally getting out of the projects."

Sin hadn't called her Chanel in over six years and it hurt CoCo to see her girl in the condition she was in, but what could she do. For the first time in her life, CoCo was happy. Sin had always been the one in a meaningful relationship, with sincere feelings involved. CoCo loved Sin, but the way she was behaving wasn't fair because she was always happy for Sin, and now CoCo felt Sin should be happy for her. "You can't tell my brother. Lace doesn't want anyone to know where we're living!" Sin just sucked her teeth. "Sin please don't do this to me," CoCo said kneeling down in front of her best friend and grabbing her hand with both of her own.

Sin gave a smile. CoCo knew her long enough to know it wasn't meant, but Sin's next words let her know for sure. "I'm starting to understand life Chanel…"

"What you mean?"

Now Sin's smile was sincere. "Ms. Nice bitch finishes last. So now it's my turn not to give a fuck about anything or anyone. Maybe my luck will change."

CoCo didn't know what to say. Sin quickly pulled her hand away, as if she was infected and CoCo could feel herself tearing up. Why was Sin doing her like this? She needed her girl to be with her. She needed her friend.

Just then the door opened. Blast walked in and seeing his sister on her knees said, "Everything alright?"

CoCo took a deep breath, trying to clear away signs of her emotional state. "Yeah, what's up Cornell?"

Blast smiled and as he approached CoCo stood up. Still Sin's facial expression remained the same. He leaned down and kissed Sin's cheek. She rolled her eyes, as his touch repulsed her, like the sight of the mutant she saw days ago standing outside of her building. She felt rigid and Blast could feel her coldness to his affection.

"What's wrong with you," Blast asked in concern, while staring at her. Sin rolled her eyes again, this time making sure he could see it. Her actions shocked him and caused him to go into his defensive mood, but Sin honestly didn't care, because hopefully he would flip and beat the baby out of her.

"I don't know what the fuck your problem is," he started, but before he could finish, Sin loudly sucked her teeth.

CoCo could see the rage building in her brother as his muscles tensed. She quickly moved to her friend's side. "It's just her pregnancy, you know, giving her mood swings that's all. Right Sin?"

"Whatever," Sin replied.

CoCo couldn't believe Sin. "I know what she needs," Coco started. "Lets all go out tonight to dinner or maybe a movie. Sin your hair looks like shit," CoCo said with a smile. "After I do what I have to do, I'll come back and do your hair. We'll find you a nice outfit and go have some fun. How does that sound," she finished.

Sin just changed the channel, still with no sound. She just held up the telephone, holding it in her hand. CoCo asked Blast to walk her out. She didn't tell him it was because she was scared of the creature she had seen coming into the building. Still, Blast didn't mind, because he had something he wanted to show her anyway.

*****

Lace was feeling good because he just paid the first month's rent and security on a two bedroom apartment on Mundy Lane in North Bronx. He gave her seven grand to furnish the place. The next week would be the first, and in two days he had another surprise for CoCo. He'd be picking up their 1998 Range Rover, and he couldn't help but feel himself. After dropping CoCo off on Webster to get ready for the double date, he really wasn't too enthusiastic about heading back uptown. He wanted to see his daughter and he also wanted to give Marisol her rent money.

It was a little after 8 p.m. He was supposed to meet CoCo, Sin, and Blast at BBQs at 10. He still couldn't believe Blast managed to get one of the baddest females in Webster Projects, and not only did he get it but he had her pregnant too. Although Henny hadn't said a word, Lace knew his boy was hurt. As he pulled out the keys to Marisol's apartment, he thought about calling Henny, but he didn't. He'd make sure to give him a call in the morning. Lace made it up the stairs. He hadn't seen his baby girl in two days and couldn't wait to hold her. He put his key in the door and opened it.

The apartment was quiet, but he could hear Madi in the kitchen singing. He crept through the kitchen door. "What the fuck," were his first words.

Marisol jumped and turned around to see her daughter's father. She quickly began covering herself, as if he'd never seen her in a negligee. "What are you doin' here," Marisol asked, "and how did you get in."

Lace held up his keys. "Where is my daughter and why the fuck are you wearing Victoria Secrets?"

"Tisha is downstairs with Ms. Maddy."

"Go put on some clothes and go get her."

"No…"

"What the fuck you mean no? Go get my daughter!"

"Can you come back tomorrow?"

"What? Make me a sandwich too and then go get my daughter. What the hell is wrong with you," Lace questioned, as he turned to go to the back of the apartment.

Marisol dropped the plate she held and ran to block his way. "Can you just come back tomorrow, damnit Lawson?"

"Get out my way Marisol!"

"No, Lawson. Please, I have company."

"Company? Move," he said, pushing her out of his way.

She quickly ran behind him, but was unable to stop him. He made his way through the empty living room. He was at the bedroom door.

"Daniel," Marisol called out before Lace could push the door open.

He looked back at her. "Daniel? Who the fuck is Daniel?" Lace opened the door and was staring down the mammoth barrel of the desert eagle point five o. "God," was all he managed to say.

Sha had been taught everything he needed to know about Lace and his cousins. Moe was serving ten years and was now in a federal pen in Virginia. No one had seen or heard a word from Mark, Henny was somewhere falling to pieces over some broad that had been murdered, and Lace was doing his numbers right down the block from where they now stood. Sha was now enjoying Lace's butter pecan rican and decided to have fun for a while. Marisol had a lot of freak in her and Sha had been seeing all of it for the past month or so.

"This is your daughter's father," Sha said, as if it had all taken him by surprise. He slowing placed the safety on the gun.

Marisol just nodded and finally Lace's heart beat returned to normal. It was damn near impossible for him to say a word to The God, that wasn't disrespectful. Lace knew the man was a heartless murderer, and that made him more nervous. This man was in the home his daughter lived in. "I didn't know," Sha replied.

"I... I just stopped to drop off the rent money." After speaking the words, Lace realized how much of a coward he must've sounded like.

"Rent is taken care of," Sha said. "Daycare too," he added.

Lace wanted to flip but couldn't. He just nodded and turned to leave with Marisol behind him.

"Lawson, I'm sorry. I wanted to tell you!"

"Yeah, you damn right you're sorry!"

"I can..."

"Marisol please save it. Just pack my daughter's things because I'm taking her this weekend."

"Oh, so I'll just pack three or four outfits."

"No, pack all her shit. I'm taking her for good!"

"But Lawson…"

"No buts, I want my daughter." Lace turned around to see Sha standing in the living room doorway in his boxers, D.E. in hand, with a smile on his face. "I'll be by to get her Friday."

With tears in her eyes, she nodded.

Lace turned to leave. "Yo, Lace," Sha called.

Lace turned to face The God. "You ain't gonna need those keys no more."

Lace nodded, throwing them on the floor and running down the stairs, because he had to get out of there.

Marisol turned to face Sha. "I didn't know you two knew each other," she said.

"Don't worry, he'll be alright. Just bring my sandwich."

She nodded and headed for the kitchen.

Once Sha found out what he needed to know about Lace, he began watching him and his business on 221st Street. Lace had a little gold mine going on, and now The God had his own plans for a hostile take over and not just the business. He went and laid down on the king sized bed with a huge smile on his face. Marisol was his and soon enough 221st would be also.

*****

It was after 11:30 p.m. as they sat in the restaurant with hardly a word being spoken. Lace's mind had been preoccupied with what he found out just a few hours earlier. CoCo was love struck and

Blast was thinking about what he would buy next. Sin just wanted to be anywhere but with the three people she was with. Sitting at the table with Sin and Blast just didn't seem right to Lace because he felt like she had betrayed his man.

"So Sin, how many months are you?"

She didn't answer.

"She's about eight and a half," CoCo replied.

"Fuck is your problem," Blast asked looking at Sin, but she still didn't answer. "You don't hear me talking to you," Blast said almost in a yell.

"Cornell, please," CoCo began. "Show her what you have for her," she added.

Blast reached in his pocket, pulling out the small jewelry box, and for some reason seeing the box pissed Lace off. Sincerely was Henny's girl and always would be. Lace knew Blast was about to propose and all he could do was pray for Sin to say no. "Sincerely, I know I've been an ass. I just always knew I could never be the man you needed, because I was so caught up into reputation. I let it fuck up my judgment and I let people control my behavior." Blast stopped, but CoCo urged him to continue. "Lace, no disrespect when I say this alright?"

Lace nodded to Blast.

"I just always knew I could never be Henry."

That wasn't what CoCo or Lace expected to hear, and at that point Blast saying the name made Sin feel sick to her stomach.

Blast continued. "I love you Sin. No woman has ever been by my side through all my faults and my fucked up ways like you, and you deserve so much more than the way I've treated you. I promise you I'll be a better man." He pushed the small box to her and she just looked at it.

"Go ahead," CoCo said. "It's beautiful Sin. Open it."

Sin looked at the box and then at Coco. Suddenly she stood up and walked towards the ladies room.

"Give me a minute, let me see if she's alright," CoCo said, getting up and running behind her friend.

Although he hadn't said a word, Lace had mixed emotions about what had just occurred. He was glad Sin hadn't accepted the ring, but he also saw something in Blast he had never saw before. He knew how much it must've killed Blast to admit that he hated not being able to compare to Henny. Most men could never admit that, which now made him think of Sha at his home.

"What's wrong," CoCo asked through the closed stall door, because she could hear Sin crying.

"I hate him," Sin called out.

"He's trying Sin. Please give him a chance."

"No, Chanel. I mean Henry…"

"What?"

"Why'd he leave me Chanel?"

As much as it hurt her heart to do it, CoCo had to be honest. "Sincerely, Henry loves you," she started, not meaning to put her words in a present tense, but it was too late to correct. "He had to go."

"Why," Sin screamed through the tears. "Baby, we were too young to realize it then, but think Sin. Where's Rob, Kenny, and Alf," CoCo asked.

"In jail."

"Sosa and Kevin?"

"In jail," Sin answered again.

"He had to leave or he'd be right there in jail with them, and don't act like he didn't ask you to go with him cause he did."

Sin was quiet now. Hearing it from CoCo made it make more sense why he did have to leave. Not even a week after he disappeared, the feds tore Webster Projects apart, arresting everyone. "You think he still loves me?"

"I know he loved you," CoCo answered, this time using the past tense. "I also know my brother loves you," CoCo added.

Sin just sucked her teeth.

"Open this door Sin." The latch slid and the door swung open.

"CoCo," Sin now spoke, wiping the tears from her eyes.

"What up girl?"

"I don't want it," Sin answered.

CoCo, afraid she meant the baby, rubbed Sin's belly. "Why Sin?"

Again Sin sucked her teeth. "Of course I want my baby!"

"So what are you talking about?"

"The ring," Sin answered.

"Listen Sin…"

"No," Sin interrupted her, "I love you CoCo, you're my sister. Always have been, and if you love me, you'll help me!"

"With what?"

"I can't let, no, I won't let your brother destroy my baby. I'm leaving!"

"What are you talking about Sin?"

"I gotta get out of here. If you love me, you'll let me. You're happy now Chanel and you deserve it, but me and my baby deserve to be happy too!"

"Sin, where would you go?"

Finally her smile was back and CoCo could tell it was sincere. "I'll be alright. If what you've told me just now is true, everything will be good. I promise you!"

★ ★ ★ ★ 153

"Whatever you need me to do girl, I got you," CoCo answered.

Sin stood up, throwing her arms around her best friend. "I love you!"

"I love you too, girl!"

"We're going out here and we gonna enjoy the night, but I'm gone in the morning."

Chapter 6

A week passed. CoCo and Lace moved into their North Bronx apartment. Lace made it clear that no one was to know where they lived, especially Blast. CoCo didn't complain, because she understood why. She was just glad that Sin hadn't left as she said she would. CoCo knew that regardless of her brother's behavior, he loved Sin. He just didn't know how to express his feelings. Sin's baby was due in the next two weeks and although she hadn't worn the ring once, Blast was being the perfect gentleman. Lace had given him over two hundred grand and somehow Blast managed to save only ten of it. As Blast and Drama sat in Blast BMW kicking it, Drama was determined to know what was going on and where Blast was getting the money.

"I need money man," Drama yelled.

"Jus' cool Drama!"

"Don't tell me ti cool mon! You runnin' round buyin' cars and tings while man starvin'!"

"Didn't I get you a vehicle?"

"Fuck dat Blast! I want in."

"In on what?"

"Boy you tink we no see ya sista ridin' inna she big Range Rover wit dat boy dere? What's up?"

Drama wasn't a fool, so Blast was forced to tell him almost the whole story. Since they'd shot up Lace and he didn't die, he put

⭐ ⭐ ⭐ ⭐ 155

CoCo on to Lace, and since then CoCo had been digging the man's pockets and blessing Blast.

"So the pussy boy holdin' like dat?"

"Muss be," Blast answered.

"Where him juggle," Drama asked.

"Uptown round 221st."

"So we ahgo hit him bumbaclod workers den."

Blast couldn't say no, because if he did it would bring suspicion, so he had to agree. All he knew, was he couldn't be down.

He gave all the info D.D.B would need. Drama, Take, and Cappo sat on the corner of 221st and Bronxwood, directly across the avenue from where they were told Lace and his crew hustled. The three men were strapped and ready to attack for whenever Drama gave the word. As of the moment, they just waited patiently watching the young hustlers who were harassing the crack heads. Nothing about the way they hustled seemed organized. Although these were Drama's thoughts he kept it to himself, but Take saw the same thing.

"Look at these fuckin' fools boy," Take said.

"Dem look like asses boy. Deez men here g'tting' money mon," Take added.

"Dat's what Blast sayin'," Drama replied.

"To me look like the boy Blast done sen man on some fuckery," Cappo added.

"We'll see when the sun go down," was all Drama could say, but in his mind it was time to start watching Blast. The man was into something and although he broke bread with his brethrens, he was holding out and Drama knew.

*****

Sha drove Marisol to work, but before he did, he dropped off the packs to Noodles and Mix. The day before, he'd sent a fiend to cop from 221st. Although he didn't have the product to deal with the sizes, he brought the same color bags. His dimes were slightly smaller but they could probably compete. Noodles and True were young and hungry, so Sha had no problem convincing them that they needed to get this money. All they had to do was catch all the heads before they made it to the building. If anything happened, Sha was willing to bet Lace wouldn't be ready for the war he would bring. If it came to that, Sha would take the entire strip from Lace. With Moe and Mark out of the picture, Lace wasn't strong and although Sha had love for the Legend Star, he was gone also. This wasn't Webster, so fuck Hen Rock and Lace.

*****

When his phone rang and Henny looked at his caller ID, he couldn't help but think he recognized the number (718) 321-1234, but couldn't think where he knew it from. When he answered, her voice lifted his down and depressed spirits. She was crying, as she begged for him to pick her up from the White Plains, New York Metro North train station. He rushed down to get her, and she had nothing with her. Not a bag, not a pocket book, nothing. He couldn't help but blame himself for what she'd been through. It was alright, because she didn't need anything. He had her and she deserved whatever she wanted. He would do whatever he had to make sure she had everything she wanted and needed.

His first stop was the salon, because he needed to get to his safe in the back office. He had over a hundred grand in the safe, and when he walked in, right away Monica began to show her ass.

"Hey baby," she called out looking at Heather and the other stylists, with a devious smile.

"What's up Monica?"

"Nothing. I was hoping you'd stop by. I was trying to get up with you," she said with her hands on her hips.

"For what," he asked disgusted. Since the death of her friend, all she tried to do was take Carol's spot.

"I just wanted to talk to you!"

"Oh yeah?"

"Yes Henry," she said trying to sound as if they were that personally involved. "Do you have time for me now," she added.

"No not really. Heather I need to see you right now."

"Me," Heather replied in a surprised tone.

Her innocence caused him to smile. "Yes, you Heather."

She looked around as if she was nervous, and the others looked just as nervous as she. Henry walked to the office door and opened it. He turned around to see that Heather hadn't moved. He laughed and this made them more nervous because he hadn't smiled since Carol went missing.

"Heather," he called as she practically ran to the office. Henny closed the door and sat down behind Carol's desk. Heather just stood there. "Heather, please sit down." She quickly sat in the pink leather chair Carol had picked out. Carol designed the entire shop, but Henny named it the Girl's Spot. "Heather," Henny started as he opened the safe. Heather turned her head, giving him the privacy she felt he wanted.

"Carol loved you," he stated.

"I know Henry. She loved you too and we all know you loved her."

Again Henny smiled. "Heather I don't know what's going on around here, but please relax," he said as he pulled out the stacks of money. Heather's eyes were wide open. "I'm sure you know what I use to do!"

Heather just nodded her head.

"Well, I can't help but believe what happened to Carol was meant for me, and I can't lie before it happened, I was really thinking of quitting and starting a family."

Heather wiped her eye.

Henny smiled as he continued. "Now Heather, I have a chance to make things right, a fresh start. It hurts me that Carol's not here to hear these words, but it was her that made me want to be a better man, so I'm leaving."

Heather put her head down.

"What's wrong," he asked.

"This is what we were all worried about, you're closing the shop."

"Nah," Henny started. "Heather look at me."

Heather looked up.

"I'm not closing the shop. Are you crazy? I would never shut down Carol's dream. That's why I chose you." He handed her the deed, fifteen grand, the combo to the safe, his cell phone number, and made her promise two things. One, if she needed anything she would call him. Two, she could never give his number to anyone. With tears in her eyes, she hugged him and they walked out. Everyone jumped and acted like they were busy.

"Can I have ya'll attention," Henny called out with his arm still around Heather's shoulder.

She still wiped away her tears. They all stopped what they were doing, and even the customers seemed to be bracing themselves for the bad news.

"Ladies, I thank every one of you for your hard work and dedication. You all helped build this beautiful place. To the clients, I thank all of you for your loyalty, but with Carol gone, this place is not for me anymore. Too many ghosts haunt me right now that I have to walk away." The "Ahs" began. "Relax, the Girls Spot will still be open but under new management." Now "Whats" came. "And Monica, you better not give Heather any problems, because if you do, I will personally come out here to fire you!"

Now the women cheered and hugged Heather, all except Monica. She looked disappointed as Henny walked up to her. "You're a beautiful woman and one day when you get your priorities straight, you'll make some man happy, but you gotta love you first."

While they all continued to congratulate Heather, Henny slid out the door. Monica just stood there watching him with a dumbfounded look on her face. Henny jumped into the driver seat of his Lexus. She finally calmed down and actually had a smile on her face.

"I see you feelin' a little better."

"Yeah," she answered nodding. "Your Girls Spot, huh? Nice name," she replied.

"Yeah, it was a name I got from my best friend," Henny said.

"Your best friend? What happened to him?"

"It wasn't a guy it was a beautiful woman, and what happened was I was an asshole afraid of the future."

"What about the future made you afraid," she asked.

160

Henny smiled as he put the Lex in gear and pulled off. "I guess," he started, "those ghosts."

Now she smiled, because she had her own ghost that she feared. It was like that old story '*A Christmas Carol*' with the ghosts of the past, present, and future, but that was a white man's tale. Where they came from, those ghosts had different names. They called them love, lies and loyalty.

It was after 9 p.m. and the white 325 I BMW had been parked there for hours just watching. Now it was time to move. The three men stepped out of the car strapped and ready for war. One walked up the street, and his job was to come from behind the victims, as two approached head on. No masks were necessary, because the victims didn't know them. As they made their way across the avenue with guns covered by black hoodies, the victims didn't even pay attention to the armed men creeping up. Now it was too late. Drama pulled out the big Browning nine.

"Oh shit," the first victim screamed.

"Run it boy," Drama said as the other turned to run, but he turned only to be face to face with the sawed off shotgun.

"Get on the fuckin' floor," Take said.

They had no choice, as they quickly fell to the ground. Cappo pulled off both men's shoes and found two small knots of money. Now the pants and then the shirts. People watched the event occurring, some laughing and others quickly trying to get away from the scene. As the two drug dealers lay on the concrete in their underwear, although the three gun men were pissed, they had what they came for and quickly ran off on 222nd street. The green Caravan was parked and they pulled off all cursing. "Twelve hundred bloodclot dollars dread," Take cussed. Drama didn't answer. All he could think about was having a sit down with Blast.

The man was definitely holding out, but on what was the question. A grand wasn't worth the risk the men just took. He'd go see Blast in the morning.

*****

The married life was growing boring. He sat in the bedroom while she was cooking dinner. Every night was the same routine, rice and beans with chicken, rice and beans with steak, rice and beans with lamb chops, rice and beans with oxtails, rice and beans. This bitch was rice and beaning him to death. He was one rice and bean meal away from shooting this chick and just then, "Baby dinner is ready." He was almost afraid to ask what she had made.

He got up and walked out of the bedroom, "What you make," he asked.

"Fried chicken," she answered.

All he could do was nod.

"And rice and beans," she added.

That was it. He turned around and was out. The sex was good and the head was even better, but he couldn't take it anymore. He couldn't kill her and get away with it, so he'd have to kill that nosey ass bitch down stairs too. As he grabbed his phone it rang.

"Who is this," he yelled.

"God we just got robbed!"

"What?"

"Yeah three Jamaican cats ran up on us!"

"Where you at?"

"On the block!"

"Don't move, I'll be there in two minutes." He hung up, stuffing his 357 in his waist band. He walked back into the living room, right past her to the door.

"Where you goin' baby," she asked.

"I'll be back," was all he said as he stomped down the stairs intentionally to bother the old woman downstairs. He also slammed the door. It took him less than three minutes to get to the block and as he arrived the truck jerked and he slammed it in park. He hopped out seeing his two pitchers sitting on the stoop half naked.

"What the fuck?"

"God, they caught us slippin'!"

"You fuckin' right they caught you slippin'! What the fuck did they get Noodles," Sha now yelled.

Noodles mumbled something.

"What the fuck did you say," Sha said grabbing him by the back of his neck and pulling him to his feet. "What the fuck did you say," Sha asked again.

"They got everything," Noodles said unable to even look The God in his eyes.

"Everything," Sha replied. His voice was calm and cool as he nodded his head. He was still holding Noodles by the neck. Smash! He gun butted the man and Noodles screamed in pain. "Noodles shut the fuck up! Mix get up."

Mix jumped to his feet.

"Come on," Sha said pulling Noodles as he walked around the corner. It was time to give Lace his ultimatum.

Kane saw the three men coming. "Yo Hitz," Kane called out. "Peep this shit!"

They began to laugh as the three men came closer. They were amazed that two of the men were in their undies. "Who the fuck is that," Rich asked.

Now Sha knocked on the door, and Kane opened it still laughing.

"Shit funny," Sha asked as his face was serious with anger.

"Hell yeah shit funny," Rich answered.

"Oh word, this shit is a joke," Sha now asked.

"Word, shit funny son," Kane added.

As fast as an old west gun slinger, Sha grabbed the 357 off his waist and had it shoved in the middle of Kane's forehead, and the laughing quickly stopped. "Shit ain't funny now huh?" Kane shook his head no. "Nigga, I'll blow your head off ya neck! Where the fuck is Lace?"

"He... He ain't around," Hitz answered stuttering.

Everyone stood there still in silence, including Noodles and True. That caused The God to laugh seeing the fear in everyone in the hallway. Sha tossed his phone to Hitz, "Call him now."

*****

Lace rode shotgun in the Range Rover, as he and CoCo just left New Roc City in New Rochelle, New York. They took Tish to the movies and then to Chuckie Cheese, and now she was in the back seat in her car seat knocked out. CoCo enjoyed herself more than the baby did. As she drove home, she continued to adjust the rearview mirror to check on Baby Tee, as she called Tisha. She couldn't think but how lucky Blast and Sincerely were. Any day now they'd have a baby, and now CoCo wanted a child. Thinking about babies, she wanted to check up on Sin to see how she was doing. CoCo reached in her original Louis Vuitton bag. Thanks to Lace there were no more knockoffs for her. She fumbled around the bag, until she found her phone.

"Shit," she said.

"What's wrong mommy," Lace asked.

"My battery is dead. Can I use your phone?"

Lace handed it to her. First she dialed the house phone at Sin's but got no answer. Thinking maybe she was downstairs with Blast she tried that phone, but still no answer. She then tried Sin's cell but only got the voice mail. "That's strange," she didn't mean to say it out loud.

"What," Lace asked.

"Sin is not answering."

"You think maybe she's having the baby?"

"I hope not," CoCo answered excitedly.

"Why not?"

"I want to be there Lawson. Let me try Blast," she said. Before she could dial the number, the phone rang. She sucked her teeth and passed it to him. Lace didn't recognize the number, but answered anyway.

"Hello?"

"Yo Lace, it's Hitz man. You gotta get over here quick!"

"Why what's up?"

"Somebody wants to talk to you man, word."

"Who is it," asked Lace.

"Dawg, some big nigga and he gotta gun!"

"He robbin' you," Lace asked.

"Nah, he just said he wants to talk to you!"

"Put him on the phone."

There was a brief silence then, "Peace Black Man."

Right away Lace knew who it was. His heart began to pound in his chest, "Sha Asiatic?"

"You know it. I suggest you come holla at me now!"

Click! The line went dead.

CoCo could see something was troubling him. "Lace you okay?"

He didn't answer, because he honestly didn't hear her because his mind was elsewhere. What could The God possibly want? Hitz said he had a gun, so it was obvious he didn't come in peace. Lace was on his own, no Mark and no Moe. Shit, he didn't even have a gun. He hated guns.

"Lace... Lace," she called him about five times.

"Yeah," he finally answered.

"You alright? Who was on the phone?"

He took a deep breath, "Look I'm gonna take you home. I have some shit to take care of."

What could he really do with no gun because he had no shooters. His thoughts had him so far away that he hadn't noticed they parked in front of the house. CoCo stood there with Tisha sleep in her arms. "Lawson?"

"Huh?" He popped up.

"What's wrong baby? What happened?"

He shook his head. "I gotta handle a situation and just don't know how to really go about it."

"Do you want me to come?"

Lace didn't know what to expect. The God was all about violence, and he would really hate to get gunned down in front of CoCo. "Nah, I'll be back soon."

She stood there, as he stared out the windshield. He hadn't even put the car in drive yet and he just sat there quietly deep in thought.

"Lawson, Lawson," she whispered not wanting to wake his daughter. "Baby?"

Now he looked at her. "Chanel, you know I love you right?"

She used that wretched word so many times in the past but only in a manipulative lie. It never meant anything to her, and now she was confused because she couldn't understand how she felt. It scared her to hear it, while she fought to hold her composure. "I... I love you too Lawson," she said, but more frightening was the fact that she meant it. Now her fear focused on something different as he pulled off. Would she see him again? That was the thing about that four letter complicated word because at any moment love could be ripped away from you, and her mother proved that.

Lace tried to take his time because he had no gun, no back up, and no idea what The God wanted, but before he knew it, he was parking the car. Hesitantly, he stepped out of the car and headed towards the building. Kane opened the door. Lace walked in with a shocked expression on his face when he saw the two men sitting on the cold, tile steps in their boxers. At any other time, Lace would've found this incident hilarious, but under The God's circumstances this was anything but funny. "What the fuck is this," Lace asked. Due to witnesses, and people going in and out of the building, right after speaking to Lace, Sha put away the gun.

"The guest of honor," Sha said standing up. "Where the fuck is my money," Sha added.

"What money," Lace said dumbfounded.

"My two assholes here," he started as he gestured to the two half naked men, "were playing the block. Who robbed them," Sha now asked.

Lace smiled while shaking his head. "So you had your boys posted up on my block, they got robbed, and now you're blaming me? That's… that's amazing!"

"Yo, don't bullshit me Lace," Sha now grabbed the gun off his waist.

"God put the gun away before one of these tenants call the police. It don't make sense to go to jail for some dumb shit! Let's talk," Lace offered gesturing to the front door.

Sha put the gun back on his waist. "You two dummies sit right the fuck here. Lace lets go."

Both men stepped outside and walked to the corner. "God, I ain't no stick up kid. I'm a hustler and I know you get money too. What's goin' on man? Why you terrorizing my life? First you fuckin' my baby moms and now you tryin' to move on my block."

Lace stopped talking and pulled out a pack of Newports. After pulling out a cigarette, he offered the pack to The God who also took one. Lace lit his and then lit The God's, and after taking a few pulls he began again. "We could get money God, but damn I left the hood so cats could eat and now you come uptown to harass me. I could use you on the team and not as an enemy man. Moe and Mark are your peoples! I watched ya'll ball together, but now both my cousins are gone. I ain't got nobody! I need real niggas with me. I already got niggas tryin' to kill me, and all I want to do is feed my daughter." Lace never thought it would be easy to convince The God to get down with the team, but he did. In five months he had close to a hundred grand and in a few weeks he'd have Blast completely paid off. Shit couldn't be any better. Now he had muscle on the team and couldn't be stopped.

He walked into the dark apartment, first checking on Tisha who was asleep. Her Nemo night light gave him enough light to see her pretty little sleeping face. He kissed her cheek, and then headed to his bedroom. The TV was still on, but CoCo was knocked out. As usual she was sleep in his four hundred dollar, Randle Cunningham throwback jersey.

He could tell she tried to wait up for him, but lost the battle. She looked so good, even in the dark room only lit by the light of the television, and her flawless, chocolate complexion seemed to glow. He took off his clothes and quietly climbed in the bed. He started at her ankles and slowly licked up to the inside of her leg, and the tingle caused her to wake up.

"Oh Lawson, is everything alright?"

"It is now," he whispered, as he blew between her thighs where he just licked, causing her to shake.

"I tried to... Ohhh," her words caught in her throat as he began to lick her spot.

This was something new. Lawson never went between her legs before. With her eyes tightly closed, she held on to his head as he feasted. She spasmed, as the orgasm flowed freely out of her. Letting go of him, she pushed her hands up, grabbing for the pillow because she was going to scream.

"Please, Please Lace! Tisha... Tisha's in the... other... other room!" He stopped with a smile. "Oh God Lawson! What was that?"

"Wifey treatment," he answered as he began to climb on top of her. She knew his routine so she reached for the night stand to retrieve a condom for him. "No," he said grabbing her hand.

"Lawson are you sure?"

"I want you to have my baby!"

With a smile and biting her bottom lip, she guided him inside her. She was so wet and throbbing, that she took him in, all of him.

*****

Lace was sleep. He came in and made love to her for over an hour, so she knew he was tired. She decided to wake Tisha and let him sleep. She and Tisha enjoyed homemade french toast and turkey bacon. "Are you my new mommy?" Tisha asked.

"Nooo," CoCo answered giggling. "Why would you ask me that?" Tisha was so cute, that all CoCo could think of, was how beautiful their daughter would be, and the night before was the first time in months they'd been together that Lace hadn't used protection.

"Well," Tisha started as she struggled with her bacon, because her front teeth missing. "My mommy said that Uncle Daniel was my new daddy."

CoCo knew exactly who Daniel was, The God from the four buildings, and it upset her that Marisol's grimy ass would tell this little girl, that Lace loved and would die to take care of, something like that.

"Tee-Tee," CoCo began. Tisha loved the nickname CoCo gave her, so Tisha gave her a big, beautiful toothless smile. "You only have one daddy that loves you so much and only one mommy, so don't let anyone tell you anything different. Okay?"

"Yesss, CoCo," Tisha said before she took another bite of her bacon. "So if you and daddy have a baby, will he be my brudder?"

CoCo couldn't help but to laugh. "Do you want me and your daddy to have a baby?"

"Yesss but only if it's a brudder!"

CoCo reached over and kissed the girl on her cheek. Then she heard her cell phone beeping in the living room. It had been completely dead the night before, so as soon as she came in, she plugged it in the charger. She picked it up, and then went back to the kitchen table with Tisha. She missed seven calls in all and smiled when she saw two calls were from Lynette. Since they'd been together, all of a sudden Nette had become her second best friend. Next she saw the other five missed calls was her brother, so she quickly dialed his cell, as she remembered not being able to reach Blast or Sin the night before. Now she worried she missed the birth of her niece.

"Chanel, where the fuck are you," Blast answered his phone.

"Home, why?"

"Where," Blast yelled.

She couldn't tell him, so she tried to avoid giving him an answer. "Cornell, what's wrong? Is everything alright?"

"Is Sin with you?"

"No, why?"

"I'm gonna kill this bitch," he yelled.

"Cornell, relax. What's up?"

"Chanel," he said her name a lot calmer now. "I ain't seen her in two days."

"What you mean?"

"Damnit," he yelled again, "I ain't seen her! Where are you?"

"Cornell stay at the house I'll be there in a half hour. Relax, I'm on my way." She hung up.

"Everything okay?"

She turned to see Lace standing there.

"Daddy," Tisha yelled pouting.

"Daddy's hungry baby," Lace answered.

"Here Tee-Tee. I have more for you," CoCo said as Lace put Tisha down.

"So, what's wrong," Lace asked seeing the stress on CoCo's face.

"Sin is gone," she answered.

"What you mean gone?"

"Cornell said he hasn't seen her in two days!"

"Maybe she wizened up and left his ass."

"Lawson," she uttered shaking her head, but that's what actually worried her. Sin had her plans, but promised she would let CoCo know her every move. "I have to go see him. He sounds… I don't know. Let me just go see."

As CoCo began to get dressed Lace thought about Henny and about Carol disappearing. He hoped no one got Sin trying to get at Blast. CoCo was ready to go. "CoCo do not let Blast know about here!"

"I'm not…"

"Chanel…," Lace said unconvinced.

"Damnit Lawson, I'm not." CoCo hopped in her Range Rover and headed for the other side of town.

*****

When the door knocked, Blast jumped up to answer it. He prayed it was Sincerely, but knew it was just his sister. He opened the door to see it was neither. "What the fuck you doin' here," Blast asked.

"Can I come in," Drama asked.

Blast just turned his back and walked back to his sofa. Drama closed the door and followed. Sitting across from Blast he just stared at his one time best friend.

"What the fuck you want," Blast asked.

"What the fuck is your problem," Drama replied.

Blast wasn't the type to share his personal business, and to answer so that Drama wouldn't continue to dig, he knew to change his mood. "What's goin' on," he now asked.

"That's what I'm tryin' to find out," Drama replied.

"What the fuck that mean?"

"Exactly what it sounds like!"

"Drama, I ain't in the mood for no bullshit…"

"So why the fuck you send us on some bullshit Jux?"

"What the fuck are you talkin' about," Blast yelled.

"Thirteen hundred dollars," Drama yelled back just as loud.

"Where the fuck you getting' the bread Blast?"

"Who the fuck are you to question me motherfucker," Blast said getting noticeably irritated.

"Who team you on Blast?"

"What the fuck? Didn't I buy you niggas cars and jewels?"

"Fuck that bullshit Blast. Niggas wanna eat," Drama said.

"So I look like your fuckin' father? I been feeding all ya'll niggas for years!"

"Oh word, Blast? That's what it is!"

"Yeah that's what the fuck it is. I built Do Dem Boys and I fed niggas, but now it's time for boys to grow up and be men," Blast finished.

Nodding his head with an evil grin Drama stood up. "That's good to hear, so from now on everything you eat, I'm eatin too," he said.

Blast smiled as he stood up. "So that's a threat?"

"Blast you know me. I don't make threats. I make bodies!"

"You threatenin' me," Blast said taking a step towards Drama who quickly pulled out the nine.

"Yeah, I'm threatenin' you! Your body'll drop in here!"

"Motherfucker," Blast yelled pulling the forty five from his waist. Both men held guns on each other. "Then both of us gonna dead in here. You ready to die?"

CoCo walked into the living room and screamed. "Cornell, Nathaniel…? What's wrong with ya'll? Put the guns down!"

Blast said, "Chanel leave!"

"No… Drama… Please, both of ya'll put the guns down," Chanel pleaded.

"Chanel, your brother is a fuckin' snake"!

"Please ya'll, please," she begged.

Drama nodded as he lowered his gun. "You know what Blast? Every fuckin' dog has him fuckin' day, and yours is coming!"

"When it come I'll be ready, and as of now Do Dem Boys dead nigga. All of ya'll dead to me!"

Drama just slid out the door. CoCo pleaded for an explanation, but all Blast could do was literally cry about Sin being gone. There was no way CoCo could tell him about Sin's plans to leave, so she just tried her best to comfort him. She never saw her brother like this.

*****

"Who is this?"

"Henny, it's Lace!"

"What's up dog?"

"Yo, I don't want to stress you out anymore, but yo Sin is missing!"

"What," Henny yelled.

"Yeah. Blast called this morning telling CoCo he hadn't seen her in a few days."

"What the fuck did he do to her," Henny asked.

"I don't know dog. I'm hoping she just left!"

"And went where, Lace?"

"I don't know," Lace responded just above a whisper.

"If this nigga did something to her, I'll kill him, Lace! Word to my dead mother!"

"Just be easy Hen. I'll let you know what's going on. I just… Well, when I heard she was missin', I couldn't help but think about Carol."

Henny was silent as his thoughts ran wild. As soon as Lace mentioned Carol, he thought about the day at the hospital when Blast and Chanel unexpectedly showed up.

He couldn't just jump to that conclusion, but it did make a lot of sense. He only had one enemy in life and that was Blast, but it still was far fetched, because no one knew where he lived and there were no signs of forced entry. Carol would never let just anyone in the house. Plus, the fact that they had found her body in Brooklyn, in the same warehouse they took The Wild Appache, wasn't right. Better yet, something was definitely wrong.

"Henny you there," Lace asked.

"Yeah. Yeah, just thinkin'. Listen, I got a job interview in a little while. Call me if you find out anything." Henny hung up.

Lace began to regret calling Henny, but he had to because he knew how Henny felt about Sincerely and he would've flipped if Lace hadn't told him. Then it dawned on him that it was his right hand man, the man that had hustled almost half his life. He was the same man that introduced Lace to the game and just said he had a job interview. Lace just shook the thought off. He had a busy day and Nette begged him to get her a Jeep. They were going to check a few out today, so he got himself and Tisha dressed and headed out.

*****

It was after 3 p.m. as Hard White and his team sat posted up on the 3rd Avenue side of Washington Projects. Months passed since the triple homicide and things cooled down, so they moved back to the parking lot side. Hard hadn't heard anything from The God or any other of the slum cats who were trying to dig in his pockets, so he was back to running his business smoothly.

His only problem had been this raggedy ole man that seemed to come by every other day. The man never said anything to anyone; he would just sit in the courtyard and stare in Hard White's direction. The man even spooked Keisha, and this girl was afraid of nothing. He wasn't the police or anything, and that was easy to see. He just sat there for an hour or so with his filthy rag, dabbing at what must've been his lips at one time. Most offered the answer that maybe the man was a survivor of a fire, but Hard suggested the man was burned by acid. Still, no one had the balls to approach him. The man had been gone about an hour or so and everyone was a little at ease with his departure.

It was Keisha that spotted the white BMW first. When she pointed it out, the girls were quickly on guard. The white Beamers were now considered the Do Dem Boys' trademark in the hood and meant trouble.

Just when White thought his days were once again at peace, here came some drama, and as he looked, that's just who hopped out the Beamer, Drama. With his hands in plain view, Drama approached Hard White and his small entourage. Keisha was the first to speak, reaching in her Louis Vuitton hand bag. "What the fuck you want," she asked.

"I need to speak to you big man," Drama replied looking at Hard White and putting emphasis on the big man.

"Why doesn't that surprise me," White answered. He, Keisha, Le-Le, and Drama walked off, leaving Most in charge of the other young pitchers.

Drama knew what he was doing was a snake move, but he rode with the snake Blast so long that it became his nature. He told the entire story to the white boy of Blast trying to murder Lace and how they followed the Brown Brothers to Brooklyn where they tortured The Wild Appache. Although White couldn't understand why Drama was telling him these things, one thing came to mind. Tior had been his right hand man, the man that took him from a white trash, project kid to a well respected street pharmacist. As Drama spoke, White only thought about revenge for his partner and just as quickly an epiphany came to him.

Drama gave him the info on Lace's uptown block, and he tried to exaggerate about its profits, telling how they robbed the men a few days ago, for ten grand right on the block. By the end of his story, Keisha was ten times more pissed about what happened to Tior than White was. For everything The Wild Appache did for

Hard, he did ten times more for Keisha. He took her off the streets when she was a young weed monster that was sleeping with any and every thirsty hustler that would give her money for sneakers and weed. Tior also took time out and taught her the game. He showed her how to eat without destroying herself. Instead of making her his mule, he gave her a gun and put his trust in her that she would protect him and Hard with her life, and she happily accepted the job. Furthermore, he took the time to teach her more in a year, than any man she dealt with in her seventeen years on earth. Now at twenty-five years old, she was a heartless, ruthless killer and someone would die for what they did to her mentor.

"So, what you tellin' me all this for," White asked.

"Because I wanna eat," Drama answered.

"Eat," Keisha yelled. "You should eat a fuckin' bullet motherfucker!"

"Listen Girl," Drama started.

"Girl? I'm a fuckin' woman!"

"Well listen woman… I ain't do shit to The Indian!"

"So where the Brown brothers at," Keisha now asked.

Drama shrugged his shoulders.

"I know," White answered. "Moe Money in the feds for the next decade."

"What about Marcus," she asked.

"He bounced. Scared the feds would grab him."

"So what's good," Drama asked.

"Yo, give me your number and when the time is right I'll give you a call. I might need you for an uptown move."

Drama gave White his cell number and walked off. He could see Keisha was pissed.

"I want Lace dead Hard! That's my word," Keisha hissed.

"In due time baby girl, in due time. I give you my word.

*****

He hadn't seen the Bronx in months and really didn't want anyone to know he was home. His shortie on the Concourse kept him up to date with everything, while he was O.T. Now he was walking up the stairs to her apartment, and he knew she would flip when he walked through the door. It felt good to be home, and as much as he wanted to go see his family, especially his cousin Lace, Mark just wanted to stay under the radar. He was pissed when Ebony told him Lace partnered up with Blast and now he was running with The God. That wasn't bad because The God was definitely peoples, but how could Marisol be dealing with him. That he didn't understand.

When Mark walked through the door, Ebony attacked him. She wanted sex so bad, but he had business to tend to. While he was down south, he still had to hustle. He needed to cover what his brother lost, because the supplier didn't give a damn about Maurice getting locked up. It was his own carelessness and she wanted her money. He stopped to pay off the Queen of the Castle, Castle Hill's own Francis White, the Diamond Princess, as it said on her CLS license plate. Mark had Ebony call the one person he knew would keep her mouth closed about him being in town, his little cousin Elise, Lace's little sister.

She met him by Pelham Parkway and all Mark could do was smile when she pulled up in her 2001 Ford Expedition. Seventeen years old and pushing a big truck. Lace loved his sisters. Elise was in the Expo and Nette was in a Tahoe. Mark definitely didn't want Nette to know he was around, but before sundown everyone would know. Ebony rode shotgun while Mark was in the back of Elise's Expo. She was taking him to Lace and CoCo's crib. Mark didn't even want CoCo to know he was there because he didn't care how much Lace trusted or loved her, she wasn't family. Mark didn't understand that relationship anyway. Elise went to the door, CoCo answered, and she went inside. Seconds later, Lace came out with her.

"Lise, I'm tired," Lace argued. "I need some sleep," he added.

"Just come on boy," Elise said grabbing his arm and pulling him to the Expo.

Lace couldn't see through the dark tints in the back, but he could see the female in the front seat. "Where you takin' me," he asked.

"Just get in," Elise said jumping in her driver's seat.

Lace grabbed the handle and opened the door. "Oh shit," he screamed seeing his cousin.

"Chill son," Mark said calmly. "Just get in," Mark added.

Lace jumped in and Elise pulled off. "So how you been," Lace asked.

"I'm good, but it's you I'm worried about. I'm hearing a lot of shit. What's up with you and CoCo?"

Lace told everything from Moe's trial, to Blast having the work, to The God and Marisol, and now being on the team.

"The God, Lace? Why?"

"Ya'll was gone and I needed back up!"

"Back up, what about Henny?"

Lace sucked his teeth. "I don't know about Hen man. That nigga gotta job and shit. I think he called it quits since Carol!"

"Lace, The God is good peoples but…," Mark was shaking his head as he spoke. "I don't think he can be trusted. I just want you to watch what you doin' man and make sure the cats you runnin' with know what loyalty is. Most of the shit these cats say are lies and all they show is fake love!"

It all made sense to Lace, but his team was tight. He was making more money than he ever had in his life and everyone was straight thanks to him. When everyone used to run to Moe and Mark, they now ran to Lace. His moms, his sisters, and his girl all had the latest whips, and his next move was to get his moms out of River Park Towers. She'd been out of Webster Projects for five or six years now, but Lace wanted her in her own house. Now he was sitting on close to a hundred grand and had five bricks and a half left. In the next few months or so, it would be time for him and Blast to make a move. It was good to see Mark, but Mark couldn't understand how much Lace changed in the five months he was gone.

They rode for a while and kicked it, but then took Lace home. If Lace needed to contact Mark he would have to contact Ebony, and Mark made it clear never to call Ebony from his cell no matter what time it was or where he was. He was directed to use a public payphone. Still the same ole paranoid Mark, and once again in two days he was a ghost of the Bx.

Chapter 7

Regardless of what Mark thought or said during his visit a month ago, Sha had been a valuable asset for Lace. Sha had contacts up and down the east coast and in a short time he knocked off close to four bricks. The movement had Lace ready to hit the road because here was money in NYC, but too much competition and haters. Lace and Sha kicked it about hitting the road with the last brick and a half and the plan sounded good to Lace, but for some reason he felt that he needed to talk to CoCo before agreeing to bounce.

When he walked in the house Coco was on the phone, and Lace could tell she was trying to comfort her brother. That's all CoCo did lately, which was understandable, because his daughter would be almost two months old now and he had no idea if she was alive, straight, or even where she was. The only thing that seemed to ease Blast's pain was spending money, and as a matter of fact he just brought a pearl white GS Lexus. Still he was miserable, but Lace couldn't concern himself with that because a brick and a half and it would be time to re-up. Lace didn't want to be rude so he just gave her a look.

She put up her hand asking for a minute, as she continued talking to her brother. "Cornell trust me, she'll be back soon. Baby,

you can't worry yourself because she probably just needed some time. I know she loves you!"

"No the fuck she doesn't. She loves that bitch ass nigga. I should've killed him when I had the chance!"

Blast was yelling on the other end and Coco looked up to see if Lace heard what he just said, but he didn't. Silently CoCo thanked God that he wasn't paying attention. "Don't say things like that! Just relax and go take a ride or something. I'll stop by tomorrow."

"Oh, what you gotta go now?"

"Yeah," she answered as Blast sucked his teeth.

"So that other bitch ass nigga there, huh?"

"Cornell, please!"

"Fuck that nigga. I swear this bitch don't come back I'm gon' flip Chanel!"

"She'll be back, I promise. I'll call you later." She hung up before he could say anything else. Looking at Lace, she sat back on the leather sofa and let out a deep breath.

"Still no word from Sin?"

Sadly she just shook her head.

Lace sat down next to her. "So how is he doin'," he asked.

"Not good. I wish she'd call me or something!"

"Sin is a soldier. Wherever she is, she's safe."

"I know that. I just feel sorry for Cornell…"

"Well CoCo, you know they say you never miss your water til the well runs dry. He had a good girl, but didn't know how to treat her."

CoCo knew it was true. Her brother treated her best friend like shit, and now she disappeared with their baby and without a word. "So what's on your mind baby," CoCo asked throwing her freshly pedicured feet in his lap.

★ ★ ★ ★ 183

He massaged her feet as he told her about the trip Sha wanted to take. She knew The God well, but never dealt with him, although friends of hers had. He'd been a part of the drama that separated Webster Projects from Butler Houses. Many people thought the entire projects were considered Webster, but those that lived there knew differently. CoCo, Henny, Lace, and Sin were from Webster, although Henny hustled right across the street.

"I don't know Lawson. I mean, you're the boss why can't they just go?"

"I ain't no boss. I'm just a hustler tryin' to live," he replied.

"Well I don't want you to go. Let him take that risk. Isn't it his idea?"

"I just think I should go to make sure everything goes right…"

"Everything been goin' right Lawson. Why can't they handle it? I don't want you to go, because if something happened to you I don't know what I'd do!"

Lace wasn't a sucker for love, but he didn't focus on the mistakes made in the past with his other relationships. So maybe he'd listen, besides a woman's intuitions were real things that he knew all too well. He just sent Hitz down south with The God. He called Sha and Hitz to set it up and they'd be leaving in two days with a brick and a quarter, which left Lace and Rich with a quarter to hold 221st for at least a week. After the calls were made, Lace decided he was in for the night, so CoCo cooked a nice dinner for two. Tisha was with Elise, which was who she was always with. So after dinner, they made love once again unprotected, which they were doing more and more often.

Sha, Hitz, and True were in Ga. for two weeks and were now sitting on over forty grand for Lace already. Hitz was having the time of his life, as this was his first time out of New York, besides a few trips to Jersey with Lace. It amazed him how much love the dirty south boys showed them, and in two weeks, he'd been with six different females who were all bad. The day started off right and by 11:30 am they made close to two grand at the crib they were staying in. It belonged to a fiend named Charlotte, so most days they hit the blocks with the drugs stashed in the trunk of the rented Dodge Caliber. Everyday the block was like a party, with an abundance beer, women, and dice.

For days Sha had been breaking the southern boys' bank playing Cee-lo, and this day The God couldn't wait. He had seven grand of his own bread to toss around at the dice game. The three men all had at least five grand a piece with three quarters of a key left, so today was all about kicking it. True linked up with some broad with a Buffy the Body figure and was gone by 12 pm, so Sha and Hitz loaded up the rental car with the drugs and money, and headed out to the country boy's dope block. By 1:30 pm, the game was on and popping, for the first time in two weeks The God opened the game with the bank in his possession. There were five Gee'z in it, which was the minimum. Hitz saw the bank grow to as much as fifteen grand, but the holder would walk away with no more than ten or twelve.

The God started off hot and within a half hour the bank was at eleven, and he was still bowling strong. By this time the crowd of players went from seven to three, Sha, Cool and Porkchop. For thirty minutes Sha controlled the bank and talked shit as he shook the cubes in his hand. "Yeah Black Man, don't worry after this one here I plan on getting rid of Cool. So, it will just be me and you swine chop!" Every time Sha called the man swine chop, it got a laugh from the onlookers. They knew it was a joke made by the black man from New York that believed himself to be God.

"Whatever New York boy," Porkchop started. "Your luck is bound to run out sooner or later! Give me five of that," Porkchop finished.

"And you too Cool," The God asked still shaking the dice.

"I'll take two," Cool replied.

"Oh, Cool takin two grand. Your pockets must be coolin off," The God laughed and the crowd, including Porkchop, laughed with him. "Seven grand! Alright get em girls," The God yelled releasing the dice.

They hit the wall spinning off four... five... The dice read five and Cool quickly snatched them up. "Square ain't good enough in these parts New Yalk," he said in his southern drool, as he shook the dice and released a three... five... six. "Ooh wee boy that bank 'bout to be mine, here we go," he yelled out releasing the dice again two... three... three.

"Well, my man swine chops... I guess it's just me and you," Sha said bending down snatching up Cools two grand. "I'll take that! It's on you my man swine!"

Porkchop grabbed the dice and began to shake them in his hand. With Cool's two grand on the next round, Sha would have thirteen grand in his bank, and once swine fell to the square, that would be
eighteen.

"Take you time swine," The God chuckled.

"Whatever New Yalk! Jump ladies," Pork Chop yelled, as he let go of the dice one...three...two.

"Ah the big man aced out," The God teased, as he scooped up Pork Chop's pile.

"I swear this fool gotta rabbit foot up his ass," One of the other southern hustlers offered from the side line.

"Nah," The God began smiling as he counted the money. "Ain't nothing in my ass, but you country motherfucker's money is in my pockets! Don't look so sad Cool," The God said as he dug in his other pocket. "Lets ball for real," he said placing stacks neatly in front of him. "I got twenty grand in the bank." This move even shocked Hitz, as he leaned against the Dodge Caliber sipping a forty of St. Ides. "That's right, Twenty grand. Ain't nobody bowling," The God said as if he were disappointed nobody called a bet.

"You know what New Yalk," Pork Chop said walking towards his candy painted Caddy.

Sha was mad he left his strap under the seat of the dodge because for some reason he thought Pork Chop was getting a gun. The God gave Hitz the look, but the dumb mother fucker didn't take the hint. Just then Pork chop popped out his passenger seat, holding stacks of money.

"Yeah Nigga," Pork Chop said tossing his stacks next to The God's. "I'll take that bet. I stop the bank!"

The God honestly didn't expect anyone to take the bet or much less stop the bank. "Alright swine chops, these rocks is hot in my hand." He began to shake em up. "Come on baby, swine chops 'bout to give me a down payment on my new CLK. Get 'em girls." The God let them go six...four...one. "Ooh, it's close baby! Four, five, six...," he called releasing them again. Three, four, five. "Shit boy, it's comin'. Get up girls!" Six, five, six. "Fever," The God yelled with a smile.

"New Yalk, I think you got 'em hot for me!"

"Whatever man, I need rims too," The God said.

Again The God's words made the crowd laugh, and without hesitation Pork chop tossed the dice. All that could beat The God's point was triples, four, five, six, or head crack, which was a six. Pork Chop's first throw was a two five one.

"Next stop 123rd ," The God called out.

Pork Chop ignored him and rolled again. Four, one, three. "Come on baby," Pork Chop whispered to the dice, as he shook them in his hand.

"You might want to say a little prayer to your mystery God," Sha now said.

"Come on," Pork Chop said releasing them one by one.

'*One. No six, no six,*' the God said silently, as the last die spun finally landing on one. Triple ones.

"That's what I'm talkin' about," Pork Chop said snatching up the pile. "You see New Yalk, swine is devine. You wanna run that back," Pork Chop asked.

"What's in the bank," The God asked.

"Yo twenty grand," Chop answered.

"Yo, Hitz give me five!"

"What!" Hitz answered.

The God was going crazy. "Give me the five," The God yelled.

"Ahh looks like New Yalk ain't got no more paper. Better go hit Charlotte for a while!" Now the bystanders and hustlers laughed at Pork chop's jokes.

"Hitz these niggas can't hit again. Please… man trust me I got this." Hitz dug in his pocket and gave up his piece of change that he stacked in the two weeks.

"I got five of that," The God answered.

"Well I guess slow grind's better than no grind," Pork Chop replied again and the crowd roared with laughter.

Now, The God was silent. It was time to gamble for real with none of the bullshit. There was no talking, just bowling. Pork Chop shook the dice and it was his turn to mock. "Let's go girls it's time to send The God home. Get 'em," Pork Chop said as he let the dice roll out of his hand. The sound echoed as they hit the wall and seemed to stop simultaneously. Five, Six, Four. "Ceelo motherfuckers," Pork Chop yelled, giving his boys pounds as he scooped up Sha's money. "I hope you can give Hitz an IOU," Pork Chop laughed.

The God was pissed and Hitz was crushed. "Give me the keys," Sha said to Hitz through clenched teeth.

"Dog let it go, we'll get that back," Hitz said.

"Fuck that Hitz, these niggas ain't breakin me. Give me the keys!"

Lace told Hitz that The God was in charge, so if he fucked up it was on him not Hitz. Hitz gave Sha the keys. The God popped the trunk and was digging through the JanSport bookbag. He pulled out twenty-five grand of the drug money which was supposed to go to Lace. Sha threw the rubberbanded stacks on the ground. "Bank stopped," Sha called out and the crowd was quiet. There was now fifty thousand dollars lying on the ground.

"You New Yalk boys just don't know when to quit huh? Alright, you want the CLK? Well I'm ole skool, I want the CTS Caddy baby," Pork Chop shook the dice. With no words from anyone he released them. One,.. three... five...two... four... six...six... one... three... then finally one... one... two. "Shit," he called out rolling a deuce, which was known as Doo-Doo on the streets.

With a smile, The God picked up the dice. On his worst day he could beat a deuce, so he shook the dice and let them fly. "Come on girls!" Four... five... three... five... four... one... It was coming and he could feel it. Five... six... three. "One more," he said as he twirled the die that read three. It was one away from what he needed. "Let's go girls," he said as he picked them up and began to shake them again. "Dance for daddy girls!" He tossed them. One... two... one.

"Push," Pork Chop said. That only meant Chop had to roll again and all bets were still the same.

Everyone stood around quietly, while Pork Chop tossed the dice again. Three... three... two. Deuce again.

"Fuck this," The God said snatching the dice. He shook them hard and tossed them Five... four... three. Again. Four... five... three. "That six is comin'," he called out. Five... five... one. The oohs and ahh's echoed through the crowd and even Pork Chop's boys felt sorry for Sha. He aced to the deuce.

"Yo good game New Yalk," Pork Chop said extending his hand to The God.

The God accepted it." Yeah man, I'll be back tomorrow!"

"Yeah man, I'll be here. Henny on me!"

Hitz jumped in the passenger seat as The God got in the driver's seat. Hitz said nothing, as he just stared out the window.

The God knew he fucked up and it didn't have to be said. He started the car but just sat there. "You alright," Hitz asked.

"Nah Black Man, I'm pretty fucked up right now," The God answered.

"We'll get it back!"

"You damn right I'm a get it back," Sha replied reaching under the seat and pulling out the chrome Desert Eagle.

"What the fuck you about to do?"

"I'm gonna get my money back," he answered cocking the hand cannon and placing a shell in the chamber. He opened the door and stepped out. Hitz quickly slid over to the driver seat.

"Looks like New Yalk gotta couple more snaps to lose."

"Fuck ya'll niggas," Sha said raising the gun.

"Oh shit," Pork Chop yelled with the gun pointed only at him. The others ducked, with some running for cover.

"New Yalk, mane it ain't that serious dawg! Come on Mane!"

"Yo it ain't no robbery! All I want is what I lost!"

"Dawg, I thought it was all love mane!"

"Just give me what I lost and I'm out. No love lost…"

"C'mon mane…"

"Fuck it, get on the floor! I ain't got time to be talking 'bout bullshit."

Pork chop laid on the ground and The God began to empty everyone's pockets. He did it hastily, as he heard yells of 'call the police', and with all he could fit in his pockets Sha stuffed the 50 cal in his waist and raced back to the car. He didn't have to say a word. Hitz pulled off and headed back to Charlotte's.

*****

This working 7 to 5 was a lot tougher than Henny expected it to be, but it was time for a change. He traded in the Lexus and got a 2005 Town and Country Caravan because he was trying to change his entire lifestyle. Although he had over a hundred grand stashed in his crib, he was living a totally different lifestyle. It was payday, and after forty hours of work that week, it broke his heart to see the bullshit four hundred and eighty dollar pay check. He couldn't understand how regular folks did it. This little bit of money definitely wasn't worth the hard work and sweat, but after all he'd seen and been through; he was willing to give it a try. He owed it to his moms, pops, and grandmother, because they worked so hard and literally worked themselves to death to provide for him.

So many ghosts were haunting him in his dreams, and even while he was wide awake, he constantly had thoughts of Star and how different life may have been, had he not been murdered. Then there was Sincerely. Yeah he left her, but it was for all the right reasons; reasons she may never understand. She moved on to have the child with his enemy and he wasn't sure he could ever forgive her for that. It seemed as if his entire life had been an illusion filled with love, lies, and loyalty. These were the ghosts he would never be able to escape, and no exorcism or séance could rid his mind of them, because they would be with him forever. Henny pulled up in the driveway of his Orange County, New York home. It was in another quiet suburban neighborhood.

It was almost unbelievable how much money he made, just blocks away with crack cocaine. Even now, trying to be a productive member of society, he was haunted on a regular basis by zombies that roamed these streets. He could be in a supermarket and they would recognize him. They would attack him while being dirty, stinking, and reeking of the aromas of urine and other foul, questionable odors that filled him with fear. What had he done? What had he become a part of? Henny wanted to run, but she told him we can't run from who we are, or what we've done. There's no serenity in running because our past would always be with us as a ghost lurking in even the deepest, darkest corners of our minds. Some ghosts will never go away no matter how far we run and no matter where we try to hide.

Now, as he walked in the door, he could smell a different aroma. This was the smell of dinner after a hard day's work. He could also hear the sounds of a crying ghost, that was also there to haunt him for the rest of his life, but he chose this one. Henny would give his life to see that this one wouldn't become a demon.

*****

It took a few minutes for Charlotte to open the door and let True in. "What took yo ass so long," True asked. She didn't bother to answer and just stared out the door into the dark night. When satisfied there was nothing lurking out there, she closed the door. "You high or something?" Still, she didn't answer, so True made his way into the back room where he and the small crew stayed. He walked in the room and was shocked to see Sha and Hitz sitting there, with only the television giving them light. "I ain't think ya'll was here," True said. "Where is the car," he asked.

Hitz looked at Sha and then back at True.

True sucked his teeth. "Don't tell me ya'll crashed the vee!"

"Nah, it's up the street," Sha answered.

"Up the street? Why," True now asked.

"It's just up the street," The God barked as Hitz just shook his head.

They parked the car a few blocks up, in case Pork chop and his boys came looking for them. The God thought maybe they'd think they left and headed back to New York, if they didn't see the car. His plan was to quietly knock off the last seven hundred and fifty grams and get the hell out of Georgia.

"Get down," Hitz yelled as he dropped to the floor and pulled True down with him.

"What the fuck is wrong with you," True yelled.

Hitz pointed to the red beam on the wall. Sha and True both saw it now shining through the window. The God quickly grabbed the fifty cal.

He was ready. He jumped up and fired shots on the window. Charlotte screamed from the back room, as shots erupted shattering the windows. Fire returned from outside, that ripped up the interior walls and then bright lights flashed inside. Right away, The God knew this wasn't the country boys coming back for their money. Just then, there was a loud boom in the direction of the front of the house followed by thunderous foot steps. "GAPD! Everybody down!" The God's first thought was to empty his clip, but it didn't make sense, because they had the house surrounded. There was no way they'd make it out alive, so the three men surrendered, without any further incidents.

*****

Lace couldn't believe what he was hearing. Rich and Noodles had been robbed inside the 221st building, and Noodles claimed it was the same men that robbed him and Hitz a few months ago on Bronxwood. "Who let them in," Lace yelled and both men looked at the other. "So how much did they get," Lace now asked.

"Three," Rich mumbled.

"What," Lace yelled again. "I didn't hear what the fuck you said!"

"Three," Rich now answered, a little louder.

"Three grand," Lace repeated.

Noodles nodded.

"So ya'll ain't see nothin' huh," Lace said clearly agitated.

"I saw a white Beamer," Noodles answered.

"A white Beamer?"

"Yeah Lace, a two door joint!"

Lace was deep in thought. The only clues he had were a Jamaican accent and a white, two door BMW.

It had to be Do Dem Boys. That son of a bitch Blast! How could he have been so stupid to trust that snake? He gave the man over two hundred and fifty thousand over the past seven months and it wasn't good enough now, because he robbed him. "I don't believe you two mother...," Lace started shaking his head. "So how much drugs you got left?"

Noodles shook his head now.

"They got the drugs too?"

"Yeah..."

"How the fuck," Lace started, but then stopped abruptly. He just turned and walked out of the building.

Both Rich and Noodles followed him outside. "Yo, Lace man," Rich started.

"Yo, don't even say a word. Neither one of ya'll. Just, just get the fuck away from me," he said sitting on the hood of his 525. He wanted to kill Blast. Lace pulled out his cell phone and called the house.

"Hey baby," CoCo answered on the third ring, after she checked the caller ID.

"Your brother robbed me!"

"What?"

"You heard what the fuck I said. Your brother robbed Rich and Noodles!"

CoCo was speechless. What could she really say?

Then Rich stood up and said, "Lace, it wasn't Blast!" He'd met Blast a few times in passing.

"How you know? The white Beamer is his trademark," Lace answered Rich.

"Baby, Cornell doesn't have that Beamer no more. He is not even dealing with them no more!"

"How you know?"

"Damnit Lawson. I've spoken to him everyday and about a month ago I was at the house. He and Drama had guns pulled out on each other. It was something about Cornell not telling them about a robbery, and that day they said D.D.B. was over."

Lace couldn't help but believe her, because he didn't think she would lie to him, but if Blast wasn't behind it, that meant Drama moved on his block on his own.

Beep. Beep. "Hold on baby, someone is on the other line." She clicked over not knowing the area code displayed on the caller ID.

"Hello," she answered only to hear a computer automated operator.

"You have a collect call from: Hitz, an inmate being detained in Georgia Detention Center. Do you accept the charges? Press one to accept the charges."

CoCo pressed one, because she knew Lace would want her to.

"Yo Lace…"

"This is CoCo."

"Oh, CoCo thank you. Where is Lace?"

"He's on the other line. What happened?"

"Dammit CoCo, we got knocked! The God robbed the block and these coward motherfuckers went to the police!"

"Everybody," she asked.

"Yeah."

"What did you get caught with," CoCo asked.

"Everything."

CoCo knew it was over. Down south with all those drugs and knowing The God, they had to have guns. They were fucked. "Did you get a bail," she asked.

Hitz sucked his teeth, "Yeah two hundred and fifty thousand."

She didn't mean to discourage him, but she exhaled. Lace had close to enough, but there was no way he'd spend it to get Hitz out.

"Yo, please CoCo... tell 'em come get me!"

"I'll tell 'em. Just hold your head and call back tomorrow. I'll make sure he's here!"

"Yo, thanks CoCo. Please man, tell him to come get me!"

"I will, call tomorrow." She hung up with him and clicked back over to Lace. "I'm sorry baby that was Hitz."

"Why the fuck he call the house," Lace said angrily.

"They all got locked up with guns and the drugs."

"What," Lace said in shock.

"Yes, Daniel went out there robbing niggas and police raided the house."

"Get the fuck outta here! With everything?"

"Yes, baby."

"I don't believe this shit! Does he have a bail?"

CoCo was silent. She knew Lace was loyal to his boys and would spend his money, no it was their money. She couldn't afford that and besides it was true stupidity that got them locked up.

"Chanel, does he have a bail?"

She was shaking her head, as if he could see her through the phone as she told the lie. "No."

Lace sucked his teeth. "Damn, listen I'm on my way home. Call your brother and tell him we're coming to see him tomorrow."

"For what, Lace?"

"Business ma, that's all!"

"Alright, but we're not going to Webster. I'll have him meet us somewhere else."

"Whatever." Lace hung up. He was pissed that these assholes got robbed for three grand of money and a little less than seven grand in drugs. Those assholes got knocked with a brick and a half. It was time to re-up. Even if he and Blast could put together and get five or six bricks, that would be good. It would hurt his stash a little because he had been relying on the seventy grand coming from GA, and these stupid fucks were in jail with no bail. Meanwhile, CoCo had her own business to handle. After calling Blast and setting up a meeting at the Spanish buffet La Caridad over on Pelham Parkway, she called the phone company to have a collect block placed on the phone.

The next afternoon they headed to Pelham Parkway. CoCo refused to tell him why she didn't want to go to her old apartment. She honestly feared the old burned up man that harassed her every time she went home. Everyone in Webster talked about him, kids pointed at him, women ran from him, and even the men tried to avoid him. He was hideous, and for hours he would just stand in front of the building, as if waiting for someone. No one had any idea who he was or where he came from. Even the thought of his scabby, raggedy skin gave Coco the chills. She and Lace sat in a back booth enjoying their lunch, and of course, Blast showed up almost a half an hour late. He looked horrible, worse than Sin looked before her disappearance. It was now Blast showing signs of depression and stress.

Lace began to tell Blast about the robbery, which he already knew about. These days CoCo and Lace were the only friends he had, so he had to be honest about the stick up. He told about the first stick up, how he cut D.D.B off, and because of it, Lace was impressed about the man's loyalty. Next, he told Blast about The God and Hitz getting knocked in GA.

"The God?"

"Yeah Sha Asiatic," Lace answered.

"How the fuck you get involved with The God?"

Lace didn't find it necessary to tell Blast that it was The God's men who he originally robbed, so he just explained his reasons. "I just figured he'd be good to have on the team," Lace answered.

"Do you know how Sha blew up?"

Both CoCo and Lace shook their heads no.

"The God and his team from the four building murdered your boy…"

Lace sat in confusion, because he had no idea who Blast was talking about. He looked at CoCo and she just shrugged.

"Who you talkin about," CoCo asked.

Before answering, Blast smiled. "The Legend!"

Right away, Lace knew who Blast was talking about. "How you know that," Lace asked.

"Lawson, can't shit go down in Web and I don't know about it. It was just back then I hated you and Henny so much I didn't care, but now for you to tell me you fuckin' with The God, I gotta tell you."

Lace sat back. This was the same man who promised to always watch out for Henny and Lace; and the same man that laid up with his baby moms.

Still, CoCo sat there lost. "Who did Daniel kill," she asked.

Both men answered at the same time, "Star!"

Now CoCo sat back, because they all loved Star. Lace couldn't help but think it all had been an alternative motive. Had Sha

★ ★ ★ ★ 199

fucking with Marisol and the entire situation all been a set up? If so, for what? Maybe it was Sha that tried to murder him.

"So what you need to holla at me about," Blast said, breaking Lace out of his thoughts.

"Lawson, Lawson," CoCo called.

"Oh, yeah it's time to re-up," Lace said as Blast just sat there dumbfounded. "That means get some more COKE!"

"Oh okay, do you," Blast answered.

"So what you got to put in," Lace now asked.

"Put in," Blast repeated as he questioned.

"Yeah, the drugs don't buy themselves!"

"Lace I ain't know nothing about re-ups…"

"It's alright, I'll put up thirty or forty and you do the same."

"Thirty or forty grand," Blast asked.

"Yeah," Lace answered.

"I ain't got that!"

"What," CoCo interrupted. "What the hell did you do with all the money we gave you," she asked.

"I spent it," Blast answered.

Lace shook his head, because he knew he gave this man over two hundred grand. "So what you got," Lace asked.

"About fifteen grand…"

"Damnit, Cornell," CoCo shouted. "How could you spend all that money?"

"What the fuck Chanel," Blast yelled, causing everyone in the buffet to turn and look towards the back booth. "Nobody told me nothing," he finished.

"CoCo come on. I gotta make some moves!" Lace got up and went to the cashier to pay for lunch. CoCo got up disappointed, because she knew Lace wanted this partnership to work badly.

After all the years they'd never gotten along, Lace grew to like Blast in the past few months.

As she stood, Blast grabbed her wrist. "You make sure I'm taken care of! You hear me," Blast said through clenched teeth.

"Yes," CoCo answered just above a whisper.

"CoCo lets go," Lace called walking towards the door.

Still Blast held her arm. "You make sure he takes care of me!"

"Alright, Cornell," she answered, pulling away from him and following Lace out to her Range Rover.

*****

Hitz and The God were both locked on the same tier. Hitz told Sha he spoke to CoCo and was supposed to call back the next afternoon. They tried seven times and couldn't get through, and The God was getting pissed. "Yo this bitch ass nigga put a block on the phone son!"

"Nah, God. Lace wouldn't do that."

"Yo, that's my word Black Man. Your boy don't get me outta here, and that's my word, you and him outta here! So you better pray to your mystery God that man answers the call."

In the short time they'd been down, Hitz knew Sha to be a man of his word, so if Lace didn't answer soon, Hitz knew he would have more to worry about than his new court date. Sha separated himself from Hitz and quickly solidified his position on the tier. By his second day, he beat down three of the cats claiming they ran the tier.

The God had the southerners setting him out with food, cigarettes, and weed. Although Lace wasn't answering, Marisol was. He had a little twenty grand stashed in her house. She cried the entire conversation, which pissed The God off because he needed her to stay focused. His bail was two hundred and fifty thousand cash, and seventy-five thousand bond. The way drugs moved in jail, he knew if Lace didn't get him out, he could hustle the money up. It was up to Marisol to be his mule, and his plan would start immediately. She was to go check his peoples to get a half pound of weed and an ounce of crack.

He couldn't believe how loyal Marisol proved to be, as he convinced her in two days to quit her job, pick up the drugs, and move to GA until he hustled up the money to get himself out. Fuck Hitz and True, and once he got out, fuck Marisol too. Her baby father was a dead man walking. With his next plan in effect, less than seventy-two hours after the raid, it was time to apply the pressure to the jailhouse hustlers. He approached the young cat sitting in front of the day room TV. He knew from skid bids on Rikers Island that the cat that sits in front of the TV controlling what everyone watched was usually the man under the man, so this cat would know the runnings of the jail's underworld.

On his fourth day in the jail, he used a lighter to melt down an old tooth brush he found in his cell. It wouldn't cut, but it would poke a man deep, and with his hard plastic ice pick in pocket, he approached the middle man. "Peace God," Sha said pulling up a plastic chair next to the young man. Dudes usually paid no attention once they heard his New York accent, and Sha paid their rudeness no mind. He knew outside of NYC their swagger was hated. Not only did NYC cats come into these small towns and get money, but they also ended up getting their women too. They had reason to hate so he just sat back. "So what's on TV today," Sha asked the cat, who just looked at him and rolled his eyes. This caused Sha to smile to himself. This young punk thought he was tough, and in a few moments The God would find out how tough the young punk was.

Sha laid back to peep his surroundings. The others seemed surprised to see Sha sitting in the front row, as it was obvious those seats were reserved. "What the fuck is this bullshit we watchin'? Ya'll wanna watch this," The God asked looking around to the others sitting in the room. None answered and a few of the old timers got up to leave the room. It was safe for The God to assume this cat was known to pop off for the television.

"Yo, dawg, these foolz gon' watch whateva I put on!"

"Oh word? So this your TV, Black Man," the God now asked.

"Yeah," the cat answered focusing back on the TV.

"Fuck this punk motherfucker," The God said standing up and walking toward the television. The cat stood up without turning his back. The God watched the kid's reflection in the window.

As The God turned the channel, the kid rushed, and just as he was about to swing, The God turned just in time to snatch the cat by his neck and slam him to the ground. "Gutta," one of the others yelled running back into the cell area. The cat struggled underneath Sha but had no wins because The God overpowered him by a mile. He just man handled the poor kid. Seconds later, three men entered the day room, one of which had to be Gutta. More than likely he was the man The God was looking for. "Aye boss, I suggest you let that man up!"

"Yo, no disrespect Black Man, but ya man here attacked me over this idiot box," Sha said to the man that had to be Gutta.

"Fuck that," one of the goons standing beside him said approaching.

"Ease," The God said quickly snatching his toothbrush ice pick from his pocket and shoving it into the side of the young cat's neck. He broke the skin just a little, causing a trickle of blood to run down the cat's neck.

"Easy Mook. Yo, Black Man," Gutta started. "I'm sure we can talk about this!"

"I hope we can, 'cause I'd hate to kill a man over this tell-lie-vision!"

"Well, let 'em up, and you and I can talk," Gutta replied.

"You the man in charge," The God asked.

Gutta nodded as he answered. "The HNIC," he said.

Sha let the cat up slowly and with the kid finally on his feet, Gutta rushed to his side. With Sha at six foot two and two hundred and sixty pounds, Gutta could see The God was a strong man just looking at him.

The God put his plastic ice pick in his pocket and extended his hand to Gutta, introducing himself. "Sha Asiatic, Bronx, New York."

Gutta accepted the pound and did the same. "Gutta Man. Columbus, Georgia." While his crew stayed in the day room, Gutta and The God went back to Gutta's cell and kicked it. Gutta had been in the detention center over a year fighting weapons charges. He controlled this part of the jail known as the D Ward, while his cousin and co-defendant controlled B Ward. They kicked it about an hour, in which The God broke down his plan. It would also allow Gutta to make some money to help pay his lawyer fees. No man could argue with the money making plans The God offered. So it was set, The God had the country boys on his team. Now, the rest was on Marisol.

*****

For two days, Lace tried to use his resources to find a connect that would charge him under twenty-five grand for a brick, but it wasn't working. Late 2008, everyone wanted twenty-seven and better. He knew if he contacted Ebony from the Concourse, he could get in touch with Mark, but that had to be a last resort. So he called the one man he knew he could always count on, because fucking Blast really put him in a fucked up predicament. Lace dialed the cell phone number. It rang four times, which was the usual, and finally someone answered.

"Hello?" It was a female voice, which caught Lace off guard.

"Who's this," Lace asked.

"You called this phone. Who is this," the female quickly answered.

"It's Lace. Who is this?"

"Lace? Oh… oh hold on."

After a few seconds of silence, Henny was on the phone. "Lace, what's good?"

"Hen Rock, what's the deal baby?"

"Ain't nothing man, just got in from work," Henny responded.

"Work? You really doin' the 9 to 5 for real," Lace laughed in disbelief.

"Yeah man, ain't nothing in the streets for me no more. So what you up to?"

"Just chillin' man. Oh yeah, who was that who answered your phone?"

"Nobody," Henny quickly answered.

"Henny, I've known you my entire life and you'd never let a chick answer your horn!"

"Yeah… Well, since I quit the game I still get a lot of cats calling me for work. So, I let her answer, because cats figure they got the wrong number, or I changed numbers and don't call no more."

"So you really done?"

"Yeah," Henny replied.

"Hen you introduced me to the game," Lace gloated.

"I know… I apologize because you could've been so much more…"

"What you talkin' about?"

"Lace you was nice in baseball. You could've been like Griffey Jr., A. Rod, or something. I ruined your life, and I pray your moms or even Marisol could forgive me."

Lace could not believe what he was hearing. "What you goin' to church now or something? Who the hell is this chick got you changin' your life?"

"Nah, no church or nothing. I'm just gettin' too old. Time to grow up."

"I gotta meet this girl," Lace said laughing.

Henny even had to laugh. "Tell you the truth, shorty is just a chick I met a few years ago before Carol. It's not her that got me wanting to change; it's what happened to you and Carol. You know? Shit could've been different. Suppose you would've died. Latisha wouldn't have her dad! Shit, suppose whatever happened to Carol would've happened to Nette or Elise. Suppose they would've killed me. I don't have no children or nothing. Think about Star. His little man is sixteen and doin' a state bid already. Life is too short Lawson, and it could all be over in seconds!" Henny's words were kind of haunting. There were too many could'ves and would'ves, and Lace couldn't deal with that thinking, not right now.

He was doing too well and everything was right. Even after all the money he lost in the past few days, he was still holding six digits and it was the man on the other line preaching, that showed him the way. Nah, it was too late to walk away now.

"Lace?"

"Yeah, man? I was just calling to holler at you. You know, just been busy."

"So, yo I'm a holla at you soon, and I want to meet the new wifey. You heard?"

"Yeah for sure, but yo Lace, don't think it's too late to walk away man!"

"Yeah, I hear you. Peace!" Lace hung up and quickly dialed Ebony's number before Henny's words could get to him. "Hello Ebony?"

"Yes, who is this?"

"It's Lace…"

"What up boy? I've been waiting for your call!"

"Oh word?"

"Yeah M.B. told me you'd be calling. I got something for you."

Lace knew M.B. was Mark Brown and he also knew his worries were over. Or were they?

Chapter 8

A Week Later...

Marisol, Nette, Lace, and Elise stood in Lace's mother's kitchen. Well, everyone sat except Marisol and Lace.

"What the fuck, are you stupid?"

"Lawson, watch your mouth!"

"I'm sorry mom, but I don't believe this dummy," Lace added.

"You can call me whatever names you want Lawson, but why am I dumb? You riding around living the life and I'm supposed to just sit around like an ass?"

"No, but why would you chase some nigga down south that's in jail," Nette asked.

"Because I love him and he loves me!"

"Please, Marisol. You don't even know this dude!"

"What about Tee-Tee," Elise asked.

"Lise, all of you know Tee-Tee is good. I barely get to see her because of you guys," Marisol answered.

At that point, Lace realized that Marisol didn't know about him and The God. "So you just gonna pack up and leave, choosing some nigga over your daughter?"

"I'm not choosing anyone over my daughter. Don't be stupid Lawson, I'm coming back in a few weeks!"

At least that's what The God led her to believe, and once she said Georgia, Lace knew what was up. He had been waiting to hear from The God and Hitz, but they never called back. "You know what Marisol, I'm done with you. Go down there. I don't give a fuck! Stay. Tisha doesn't need you and I definitely don't need you. You're worthless!"

"Yeah whatever Lawson, like Chanel is God's gift to the world! Fuck everybody else as long as Lawson is happy."

Lace just sucked his teeth and walked out. He had business to attend to, and if she wanted to run behind some man, then so be it. She was grown and his daughter was well taken care of.

The next day, Marisol boarded the Greyhound bus to Georgia with a half pound of weed and an ounce of crack. Her heart was pounding so hard, that she swore people could see it through her blouse. As she sat in her seat and the bus began to move, she began to have second thoughts, that maybe Lawson was right. What was she doing? She allowed this man to manipulate her and was now risking her life to transport drugs down south. He loved her though. She felt he proved his love, took care of her, paid her rent, and brought her everything she wanted. Yes, she was sure. He had to love her because she loved him. She was doing what she had to do to be there for her man, and these were the things she knew she should've done for Lace. Now he was in love with that black bitch Chanel and so happy, and this was what she deserved. Happiness. She was going to do whatever needed to be done, to show him she loved him.

*****

While Tisha was with his mother and sisters, Lace decided to do something he normally wouldn't and bagged up the brick Ebony gave him. He sat in the kitchen with the digital scale, breaking everything down to twenty-eight gram packages. Over the past few months, Lace hooked up with a single mother that lived in the 221st Street building. Monica was struggling with her bills, so they worked out a business arrangement for her services, which included her apartment as a stash house and her bagging up the dimes. Lace paid her rent and gave her pocket money too. So after packaging the ounces, he'd take them to Monica so she could earn hers.

"Why do you wear gloves when you bag up," CoCo asked.

With a smile, Lace answered, "Why do you ask so many questions?"

She wanted to say, her other boyfriends never told her anything and that they never used gloves, but figured that wasn't the right answer. "I mean it. If I don't ask how would I know?"

"You right. Well coke is funny, because it can get into your pores. I don't know how true it is, but I've heard of dudes getting addicted to their products by touching it."

"C'mon," CoCo replied laughing.

"I'm serious!"

"Oh," she replied with her smile quickly vanishing. "Are you still gonna look out for Cornell?"

Now Lace's facial expression changed. "CoCo, he fucked up!"

"I know, but Lawson you never told him what he was supposed to do."

"I know that, but he should've known!"

"He's not a drug dealer," she replied. "Truthfully Lawson, no disrespect, but it is because of him you really blew up!"

He just looked at her. She did have a point, one he would probably never admit to.

"So you think I should still just leave him on as a partner," he couldn't help but ask with an attitude and she couldn't help but notice it.

"No, oh no, not at all, but you could still help him out a little. You know he is going through a lot now, that's all."

"Like I'm not Chanel?"

"I know baby, but his boys abandoned him and Sin left with the baby. His problems and your problems are a lot different Lawson." Lace didn't bother to answer and just finished packaging his work. CoCo didn't bother to push the issue because she knew Lace was a good man, and would do what he thought was right. He got up and began to place the zip locked ounces in a shopping bag. "Why you never let me bag up for you?"

"Please, CoCo. I'll be back in a minute!"

"Are you fucking Monica?"

"Are you crazy? What's wrong with you?"

"You're paying her rent, and besides you'll help her, but won't help my brother!"

"Yo, I'm gone I'll be back." Lace jumped in his whip and rode out. He had so much on his mind, but he wasn't the only one.

CoCo was on her own and she had no friends, mostly because of her brother. Even her best friend was gone. With no words and not even a good bye, she just vanished. CoCo was just lonely. She threw on a pair of jeans and a sweater with her Gucci flip flops. She had a little cash around the house, so she counted out two grand. Most of the time when she went out she was with Lace. He always gave her money but she never had to spend it, so she had a nice little stash. She hopped in the Range and headed to Webster. CoCo tried to avoid the old neighborhood for a while because of the snake man, which was the name the children had given the old, raggedy face man that wandered the neighborhood, but still she needed to just see her old apartment.

As she took the elevator up, unconsciously she'd pressed nine, forgetting for a moment her best friend was gone. So once the elevator hit the ninth floor she pushed seven and headed back down. She stood in front of the door, hesitant to walk inside and afraid of the ghosts she'd unleash by entering the apartment. Maybe she would just call Elise, and see what she and Tee-Tee were doing. Yes that's what she would do, after she got a whiff of her dearly departed mother. Even after Mrs. Winston passed away, CoCo didn't change a thing. She still used the same household cleaners her mother used from air fresheners to even candles, just to have something other than faded photos and memories. The apartment was dark, but the aroma of fresh marijuana lingered in the air.

She turned on the light switch and there was Blast passed out on the sofa and the house was a mess. Food wrappers, empty beer bottles, and a half bottle of Wray and Nephew over proof rum lay at his feet. This was all Blast did since Sin vanished, sat around drinking as if spirits could chase his ghost away. Without waking him, she began to clean up the living room. It was only 7:30 p.m. and he was in a drunken sleep, snoring and drooling.

He reminded her so much of their father, who died years before their mother. He was a hard working man, but a violent drunk who would get drunk and beat on their mother. When Blast was nine, he ran to his mother's aide one night, and Mr. Winston beat the little boy until he was bloody. CoCo often blamed their abusive father for the man Blast grew up to be.

In a little under a half an hour, CoCo managed to clean up the living room for the most part. Now all it needed was a good dusting and a vacuuming. As the garbage bag full of beer bottles rattled, Blast stirred. "Sincerely," he called out in a drunken slur.

"No, Cornell it's me."

"Chanel," he said with a smile, the same way their dad used to call her and in almost the same exact voice. It was frightening, because as much as Blast hated their father, he had become the same man. "When did you get here?"

"A little while ago," she answered.

"Here," he said patting the sofa cushion next to him. "Sit down!" She did as he asked. "I'm glad you came by, I was bored," he said.

"Yeah me too, and this place is a mess!"

"Yeah, mom would've flipped!"

They both laughed. "Daddy would've flipped," she said as it brought about a small chuckle.

"She ain't coming back Chanel." She knew exactly who he was talking about, but there was nothing she could say. "It's all my fault. I was such an ass to her." She rubbed his shoulder. "Chanel I'd give anything just to have her back. All of this, the cars, the jewelry, everything, just for her to be home. I'd be so different!"

"It's your anger Cornell, but you got it honestly with the things daddy did to you. You didn't deserve it."

"It's like he haunts me Chanel. Not just in my dreams either. It's like I can't escape him!"

CoCo took a deep breath. "Maybe you need to just get away from everything!"

"I can't. Suppose she comes back and I'm not here," he asked.

Coco knew he didn't have to worry about Sin coming back. Wherever she was, she was gone for good.

★ ★ ★ ★ 213

"You know my baby is six months old now? I bet she looks just like mommy."

CoCo smiled at that thought.

"I'm scared Chanel…"

"Of what," she asked in shock. She couldn't picture her brother, the man called Blast, the fearless leader of the notorious Do Dem Boys, afraid of anything.

"Everything! Everyone I love leaves me. I don't know what I'd do or where I'd be if you weren't here."

She hugged him. "I'll always be here Cornell and we'll always have each other!"

Her cell phone ringing, broke up the moment. It was Lace and just seeing his number made her light up. "Hello," she answered in her sweet voice.

"Where you at," Lace asked.

"With my brother."

Lace sucked his teeth. "Why'd you leave, I told you I was coming right back?"

"I didn't think you meant right back."

"I'm hungry mommy, wanna go eat?"

"Yeah, what," CoCo replied.

"Let's go by Sizzler in Bay Plaza," he answered.

"Sounds good to me! I'll be there in about twenty minutes."

"Alright, love you."

She was about to say it too, but caught herself. Blast would have flipped to here her say those words, "Me too, see you in a few," she said before she hung up.

Blast was pissed. She was off and running, and he knew it.

"So you alright," she asked him.

"Yeah, I guess. I'll walk you out in case the snake man is out there." Everyone talked about the snake man and Blast knew his sister was scared to death of him. They took the elevator down and Blast walked her to her Range.

"You hungry? We're going to Sizzler in Bay Plaza. I could bring you a doggie bag," she said with a smile.

"No" he answered flatly. He couldn't help but feel a little envious about his sister's happiness.

"Oh, I almost forgot," she said digging through her pocket book. "Lawson wanted me to give you this." She handed him the two grand.

He quickly counted it.

She once again saw her father in his eyes. "Two gee's? What the fuck is this Chanel," he swallowed.

"What Cornell?"

"Fuck him, that piece of shit!"

"Cornell, please. He'll give you more. He said it was the first of the month and just wanted to make sure your bills were paid!"

"Whatever!" Blast turned and walked away. She called to him, but he just continued on his way to the back parking. She didn't bother to chase after him, so she pulled off.

'*Bay Plaza*,' Blast thought to himself. Alright, he knew what he would have to do.

Marisol had been in Georgia a week and was already in an apartment, for only four hundred and seventy-five dollars a month. Now he wanted her to do something she wasn't sure she could handle, but Sha made it clear that if she didn't do it, he would get one of these country women that really loved their men to do it. He put her on the spot and she had to prove her love. Marisol thought she had done that by leaving everything, including her child and job, to come to Georgia to support him. It obviously wasn't enough, because here she was going through the visitor's search, heart pounding and palms sweaty, nervous as hell, with a half ounce of weed and three grams of crack in her vagina.

She calmed down just a little as she made it through and sat at the table to wait for Sha. When he walked out, she couldn't help but to smile from ear to ear. Marisol stood up with her arms open and didn't realize how much she really cared about him until she saw him in that orange jumpsuit. She was determined she would do whatever was necessary to get him out of there. "Oh baby, I've missed you so much!"

"Yeah, I missed you too. You got everything," Sha said coldly.

"Yes," she said disappointedly as she sat down.

Sha sat down too. He saw she was upset and knew he had come too far to blow this now. "I'm sorry baby," he began. "It's just I need this. I need this all to go right so I can get home to you!"

She understood. The God began to run through the bullshit just to satisfy her need for affection. They only had an hour for the visit, so he couldn't waste too much time lolly gagging with her. With twenty minutes left, he had to move quickly. With her left hand she reached under her skirt, and pushing her panties to the side, dug with her index finger and thumb into her vagina, pulling out the lubricated balloon which contained what he told her to bring. He told her how important it was for the package to be as greasy as possible. She had used so much Vaseline, that it felt as if it would slide right out of her.

The God grabbed the package with his right hand, quickly grabbed her left hand, and sucked the moisture from her fingers. The act quickly caused her to get wet. "Oh God please, I can't take that," she said with a smile. He smiled, really ignoring her, as he did what he had to do. Before coming out for the visit, he tore a hole in the seat of the jumper and now he pushed the oiled down package into his rectum. He was glad the visit was just about over, because it was too uncomfortable. They called his name and upon his departure, he passionately kissed Marisol while promising to call her that night as they went separate ways.

The entire plan was mapped out. Since it was Marisol's first time, he only had her bring a little of both, just so she could see how easy it was. Now it was time for The God to hustle. Jail prices were ridiculous. The weed would go for twenty-five dollars a gram, while the crack was two hundred and fifty dollars a gram, and the transactions were simple. Gutta spread the word that the drugs were available, and for that he'd get twenty dollars a gram and some weed to smoke. Payments were done like this, if a man wanted to purchase, he'd have his people on the street go to a Western Union or Money Gram and deposit the money order to Marisol. Once done, they would give Sha the tracking number and The God would have it verified by Marisol. Once she collected, Mookie would deliver the product. Everyone in jail wanted to get high to relieve their stress, and in three days Marisol was on her way up to see Sha with more. They made eight hundred dollars in three days, so this time she brought an ounce of weed and six grams coke.

*****

Another month passed, and Lace still hadn't mentioned doing anything for Blast. CoCo watched him count over fifty thousand dollars. He put about half in a shopping bag and the other half in a safe that he kept in a set of dummy speakers in their bedroom. As usual, he had runs to make, but promised that after he stopped by his mom's to see little Tisha they'd go out.

"Lawson," she said. Her voice was flat, which made him think she was about to start an argument.

"What Chanel?"

She exhaled before speaking. "Did you think about what we talked about last month?"

"And what did we talk about last month?"

"You know, helping out Cornell…"

Lace laughed. "Helping Blast? You know what? He helped me, so it's the least I could do," Lace said as he dug in his pocket. He counted out five hundred dollars. "Here give this to 'em. Tell 'em I'll give him some more later, and I'll see you when I get back."

Before she could say anything, he was gone. Five hundred dollars? Cornell had a fit when she gave him two grand and said it was from Lace. He'd really flip over five hundred. She went to her panty drawer where she had almost ten grand saved up. *'I'll save again,'* she thought to herself. She'd give the ten to her brother and say it was from Lace. Just then the doorbell rang, causing her to jump. Startled, she slammed the drawer shut and raced to the front door. Without looking through the peep hole she opened the door, and her heart skipped a beat. This was impossible.

"Hey sis!"

"Cornell, what are you doing here?"

"I came to check out my big sister!"

"Oh my God, come," she said pulling him in. "How did…"

"I know where you live? C'mon Chanel, this is me," he said as his face grew real serious. "You know I know everything," he finished.

★ ★ ★ ★ 218

She swallowed the knot in her throat.

"So, where is Lace?"

"He just..."

"Left," Blast interrupted her again. "I know, I watched him leave. So answer this Chanel, why didn't you two want me to know where you lived," he asked looking around.

"It wasn't that, it's..."

"He must have a lot of money stashed around here," he replied with a smile, as he sat down on the sofa feeling under the pillows.

Oh Cornell, I have something for you. Lace left a couple of dollars for me to give you. Wait here, I'll be right back." She was nervous as hell as she ran to the bedroom. She went back to her panty drawer and began to count out the money.

"This is a nice room!" She jumped seeing her brother walk into the bedroom and begin to look around. He opened the closet and looked under the bed. She knew what he was looking for, a safe.

"Here! Here's ten grand. He said he'd give you more later," she said, praying he'd take the money and leave.

"No he didn't. Don't worry, I won't let him catch me here." He now looked under the mattress. "But trust me Chanel, you should be more afraid of me than him."

Again she swallowed.

"Don't worry, I'll let myself out, but I'll be back soon," he said with a smile.

Three days later, after taking Tisha to Chuckie Cheese in New Jersey, CoCo and Lace came home to find their apartment had been burglarized. The sofa had been cut to pieces and the closets ravaged. Kitchen cabinets, the refrigerator, and the stove were all pulled out, and their bedroom and the bathroom was destroyed.

Luckily the dummy speakers were left untouched and the safe was safe.

"Dammit, who the fuck would do this?"

"I know who it was…"

"What? Who?"

"Cornell."

"How? Didn't I tell you not to tell him or anyone where we lived?"

"Yes, and I didn't, but the other day right after you left he rang the bell."

Lace was pissed, because Blast must've followed one of them home, and he couldn't blame CoCo for that. Still they had to move. Although Blast didn't find what he was looking for, Lace refused to give him another chance. It was fucked up, but it had to be done. Lace gave Coco an ultimatum, that if they were going to stay together, she had to cut all ties to her brother. She didn't want to, but she had no choice. The next day they got new cellular phones, and they stayed at his mother's house for two weeks, until they found a new apartment. Nette still didn't like her brother dealing with CoCo and she tried to convince Lace that CoCo may have had something to do with Blast breaking in, but he didn't believe it. Had Coco set it up, Blast would've gotten the safe. Lace found an apartment in a house on 234th and Carpenter Avenue in the Bronx, and the first of the month they moved in. CoCo now understood the importance of why no one could know where they lived.

*****

It was the anniversary of the day Lace got shot, and it was almost he and CoCo's one year anniversary. Mrs. Anderson couldn't understand why anyone would be celebrating almost being killed, but Lace took the five women in his life out. They were his mother, sisters, daughter, and Coco, and this was the night he proposed to CoCo. She couldn't believe it. Lace spent nine grand on a ring that had a rock the size of a crunch berry. Elise and Mrs. Anderson loved it, but Nette was pissed. Mrs. Anderson made a joke about Nette just being jealous, that if she'd stop being mad at the world, some foolish man would ask her to marry him.

"I... I... don't know what to say," CoCo stuttered.

"You're supposed to say yes Chanel, damn!"

"Elise watch your mouth girl."

"Sorry mom," Elise quickly answered.

"Are you sure Lawson," CoCo asked. "I mean, I don't want you to think or…"

"Just answer 'em," Nette said rolling her eyes.

"Mind your business, Nette," Elise started, "Answer 'em!"

"Yes, Lawson!"

The entire table applauded except Nette, and even Tisha seeing the excitement clapped, not really understanding what was going on. Lace ordered a bottle of champagne, and when the owner heard what just occurred, the bottle was on the house. Once everything settled down, Nette asked to speak to Lace outside.

The two stood outside and Nette lit a cigarette. "Is this why I came outside, a cigarette break," he asked.

"What the fuck is wrong with you," Nette asked.

"What are you talking about?"

"You're going to marry this bum bitch?"

"Watch your mouth Nette!"

"I don't believe you Lawson. Chanel ain't nothing but a money hungry, trifling skank!"

"Nette, you said the same thing about Marisol…"

"Lawson, I hated Marisol, but I'd rather it be her than Chanel."

"Why because she's from the projects just like us? What she doesn't deserve me because I'm no longer in the projects? She doesn't deserve to be loved because she's from the projects?"

Nette sucked her teeth before answering. "No Lawson it doesn't have shit to do with that."

"Then what Lynette?"

"I don't trust her, I just don't like her!"

"Shit Lynette, you don't like nobody and that's your problem. If you spent some time worrying about your own shit rather than everyone else's, you might be happy!"

"That's fucked up Lawson!"

"Is it, or is it the truth?"

"I'm not out here to argue with you, I just want you to listen to me."

"For what Lynette? For fucking what? When was the last time you had a fucking man? You're so worried about what everybody else is doing your turning into a lonely, miserable little bitch. Now listen to me, I'm going inside to enjoy the rest of my night. Now either you can come inside and enjoy it with me or you can jump in your truck, the truck that I brought, not your man, and go the fuck home!"

Without hearing her answer, Lace turned and headed back into BBQ's. CoCo couldn't explain how happy she was, because a year ago she was hating her life, and now here she was with a huge rock on her finger. She tried to hide her sadness with a huge smile, but to Lace it was see through. He leaned over and whispered in her ear, "What's wrong?" She smiled at him. He knew her so well, in such a short amount of time. Although they'd known each other for over two decades, they had never been intimate and now here he was able to see her true feelings.

"I just wish Sincerely was here."

He knew she considered Sin like a sister and for years. Sin had been the only family, besides Blast that she had. "Chanel this your family now," he replied. She bit her bottom lip to try and fight the tears, but it didn't work.

"Welcome to my family baby," Mrs. Anderson said.

Yes, it was official. She would be Mrs. Chanel Anderson.

*****

For two months, Gutta and The God controlled the detention center's drug flow and built what they jokingly called their empire. In that short time, The God managed to stash over twenty-five grand, and in a day Marisol would be back in GA with the third shipment. She proved to be a valuable asset and his mule for real. He began to wonder why Lace never put shortie to work. She'd gone up to New York to pick up two pounds of weed and five ounces of crack. The God couldn't wait, because this was the move to get him out of jail. It was a regular day. Gutta, The God, and the rest of the team were sitting at a bench, playing chess during the one hour recreation. The God was the best chess player in the jail block, and one by one they lined up to get a game.

Mook wasn't paying any attention to the board game, as he watched the area. "Oh shit," Mook called out, getting everyone's attention.

"What's up fool," Gutta asked.

"There go that busta Dapper," Mook said pointing in the direction of the man.

"Oh shit," Gutta repeated.

"Is it a problem," The God asked.

"Nah that's peoples. I'll be back," Gutta said walking off towards Dapper.

The God stayed focused on the challenger he had in front of him. Dapper, Gutta, and Mook showed love, giving pounds and bro hugs.

"Fool, what you done did," Mook asked.

"Mane, done let them boys run up on me in the whip wit the strap in the glove compartment!"

"Damn fool what they talkin'," Gutta asked.

"Nothing yet. I know they got me, 'bout stressed like a mofo."

"Better come light some of this New Yalk bud," Mook offered.

"New Yalk bud?"

"Yeah fool, we got it crunk in this mug. Done connected wit my man over here. C'mon let me introduce you to my potner," Gutta said escorting Dapper to the chess table. "Yo God, this my man Dapper, Dapper this The God Sha Asiatic."

"Peace Black Man," The God answered extending his hand.

Dapper accepted it, but looked at The God funny. The God didn't notice, as he still kept his attention on the chess board. Dapper recognized him right away. Besides, weren't too many New York cats in the detention center. Dapper decided to sit back, because when the time was right, he'd drop the bomb on Mook.

The first package was an ounce of weed, which would make about seven hundred dollars and five grams which would make about fifteen hundred. Although Dapper was in a different wing of the jail, Mook kept him posted about the dealings, whenever they got to see each other in the yard or in the mess hall. Dapper had been there about three weeks, when he decided to put Mook on.

See when cats are locked up, they're out of sight and out of mind, and certain things they'd hear, but behind the brick bars and fences, some things they couldn't find out, until a real street cat got knocked.

The God and Gutta stayed on the tier during chow so Mook strolled by himself, and this was what Dapper was waiting for. When Dapper saw Mook, he waved him over to the table. "Aye fool what's good," Mook asked.

"Just kickin' it mane. What's good with you," Dapper asked. They kicked some idle bullshit for a minute and then Dapper hit Mook. "What you know about that cat Sha," Dapper asked.

"The God? Fool that nigga real mane! He done came and broke bread for real!"

"Word, so when was the last time you holla'd at yo' kin folk?"

"Who you talkin bout," Mook asked.

"Pork Chop," Dapper replied.

"Mane, that fool? I wrote him 'bout three letters and ain't heard one word from that busta yet."

"I know why," Dapper said, looking around as if he were delivering a top secret message, as he told Mook about Pork chop and The God.

"What," Mook yelled causing others to look in their direction.

"Aye mane, relax fool. Be easy, this situation is easy to handle!"

"Tell me what's up," Mook said eagerly.

One thing Dapper needed to know was The God's next pick up, which was Thursday afternoon. Another thing, Gutta couldn't know anything about what was going on. Dapper had grown up with a lot of the CO's in the detention center and spoke to most of them. He had a plan that would eliminate their adversary and open doors for him and Mook to take control of the drug ring, with the possibility of getting rid of Gutta also.

Thursday morning started off just as any other day, Marisol got up and made herself an omelet with green peppers, onions, and pork sausage. She laughed, as she devoured the swine, because Daniel would have had a fit if he knew she was eating pork. He had to love her as much as she loved him, although he beefed about what she ate, what she wore, and even what she watched on television. He cared about her so much, that he'd put all his faith in her, and at that moment she was sitting on forty-five grand of his money, twenty-seven of which she helped him make, doing the same thing she had to do today. She spent all night wrapping two ounces of weed as tightly as she could in saran wrap. In total, there were two ounces of weed and fourteen grams of crack rocks.

As she stood in front of the mirror, it amazed her how much she could get inside of her small coochie. It also amazed her, how wet her private got when stuffing the package inside of her. She giggled at the thought of her man getting out of jail and being inside her as she wiped the juices from her thigh. As she put on her tight fitting Moschino sport dress, which Lace brought her, she thought about how she missed Lace and Latisha. It had been over two months since she spoke to her little girl. Lace was taking good care of her, but he was also taking care of that bum bitch Chanel as well. The thought of CoCo quickly erased all good thoughts of Lace. She had business to take care of. Fully dressed, she grabbed her Prada hand bag and headed out the door. It was a half hour ride to the detention center. No more dusty road buses, she now had an '05 Dodge Caliber to ride.

"Daniel Garns, Gary Booth," the C.O. called out.

"Yo, God they calling you and Gutta," the little flunky ran to the day room to let Sha and Gutta know.

"Damn its only 10 o'clock," Sha said looking at his watch. "This bitch here mad early," he said as he was expecting the visit.

"Why they calling me? Suzie ain't coming til tomorrow," Gutta replied as they both got up to walk to the C.O. bubble.

"Yo, what's up, that's my VI," The God asked.

"No, Garns. You and Booth step outside," the cop said over the intercom.

"What the fuck man," Gutta said, as the electronic doors buzzed, then hummed as they opened.

Both men walked out the doors and then out stepped the Suge Knight look alike C.O. He always wore black gloves, as if it made him look tough. His size made The God want to get at him, but there was no way he'd give The God a fair one.

"What the fuck is up Harris," Gutta asked.

"A pee-pee test," C.O. Harris said in his deep voice.

"What," The God said.

"Yep. You boys are the next contestants on who's got a dirty dick," Harris said as if it were a joke.

As they headed to the lab, both Gutta and Sha knew they were headed to the hole. Sha looked at Gutta, who just shrugged his shoulders, because he couldn't understand what was going on. Gutta paid C.O. Thompson good money to make sure they were never called for a urinalysis. As they walked through the doors Suge Knight told them to have a seat. They did as they were told, but just then Thompson walked out. Gutta gave him a look, like *'what's up.'*

Since officers were around that didn't know about their business arrangements, Thompson had to be professional. "You guys know the deal, you got two hours to piss. If you can't piss in two hours, that's the same as having a dirty." Thompson turned, seeing Harris still standing there and he couldn't say what he wanted to say, so he flipped through the paper work. "Ah suspicion," he uttered letting Gutta know it wasn't a random test, and Gutta and Sha both knew they'd been set up.

Harris laughed, "I guess you guys had a party and didn't invite somebody, 'cause somebody is mad at you two. So, who is first?"

Neither man moved.

Marisol was getting pissed because it was after 12 and she'd been sitting there over an hour and a half. She watched men and women come in after her get searched and go in, and she was ready to flip, but she had too much shit on her so she didn't want to make a scene. She was ready to get up and leave as now it was after 1 p.m. She finally got up.

"Ah, Ms. Rivera," the officer finally called her as soon as she headed toward the exit doors.

"Yes," she answered with an attitude.

"Follow me," an officer told her.

"It's about time," Marisol replied following the C.O., but something was wrong. This wasn't the right way. The C.O didn't take her through the usual visitor's search, and as they walked through the steel, automatic doors, they slammed shut and the auto lock engaged. As the lock snapped shut Marisol's heart jumped when she looked back. Something told her to get out of there, but it was obviously too late.

"Where... Where are we going," she stuttered.

"Just follow me!"

"This is not the visitor's search room..." Just as Marisol spoke, the C.O. stopped in front of a door marked Warden Johnson. When

Marisol saw the stenciled Warden Johnson, her throat became instantly dry and her palms got sweaty. All she could think was something terrible happened to Daniel. The C.O. knocked on the door, and shortly after the door opened.

"Please, Ms. Rivera," the officer said gesturing for her to enter first.

As she began to walk in, she asked, "What's going on? Did something happen to Daniel?" Then she saw the man in a cheap suit sitting behind the desk, which had to be Warden Johnson. There were also three Georgia State Sheriffs, one of which was a woman. "What's going on here," Marisol asked with the feeling in her stomach telling her it was definitely bad.

"Ms. Rivera, I'm Warden Johnson. Regardless of what you may believe or may have been told I run this jail, and certain things I will not, I repeat will not tolerate!"

"Warden Johnson, please what's going on! Is Daniel alright," Marisol asked not thinking of herself. All she could think was The God did something or something had been done to him.

Warden Johnson stood up, walked around to the front of his desk, and sat on top of it. With a smile he began to talk, "Ms. Rivera, right now Mr. Garns is the least of your worries! We have reason to believe you've been smuggling in drugs for Mr. Garns!"

"What... What, why, how?" Marisol was so nervous she couldn't even form her sentence.

"How? Ms. Rivera, are you admitting to your guilt," Johnson asked.

"Well, no... no of course not," she stammered.

Now Johnson stood up. "Well Ms. Rivera, if your innocent you'd have no disapproval with having Sheriff Marlon searching you," Johnson said pointing to the female trooper.

"Of course," Marisol agreed because there was no way for the female cop to find the package deep inside her sacred cave. It was as safe as a buried treasure.

"Follow me miss," the officer said gesturing for Marisol to enter the bathroom.

With no fear, Marisol entered the windowless facility and right away handed the female officer her jacket, her purse, and then her shoes. After all those items were thoroughly searched, Officer Marlon put on a pair of latex gloves. This made Marisol nervous somewhat.

"Please ma'am, slowly remove your dress and do not shake it. Just hand it to me."

"Excuse me?"

"Take off your dress…"

Nervously, Marisol did as she was told with sweaty, shaky palms. She pulled her fifteen thousand dollar sports dress over her head. It was not only her hands, but also her forehead that began to sweat profusely. Marlon, a very perceptive officer, could see the woman was becoming more and more disoriented. Once finished searching the dress, Marlon delayed her next request for a moment just to make matters a little worse for Marisol. "Now, remove your bra." Tears began to form in Marisol's eyes as she undid her brassiere and handed it to the officer, with her right arm covering her breast. Marlon tossed the bra on the floor with the rest of Marisol's belongings. "Remove your panties." Marisol no longer had tears forming in her eyes as she was now completely crying. As she slid one leg at a time through the legs of her thong panties, she handed them to her.

Marlon just threw them on the floor. "Please turn around and place your hands on the wall." Again, Marisol did as the officer told her. Marlon placed her palm flat on Marisol's lower back. "Do not move Ms. Rivera! If you move, I will take it as you're resisting and I will be forced to use force. Do you understand?"

"Yes," Marisol answered through her sobs.

"Now show me the bottoms of your feet, one at a time." Marisol complied. Marlon ran her gloved hands under Marisol's breast and underarms. "Turn around," Marlon ordered.

All Marisol hoped was that this ordeal was over.

"Open your mouth, and with both index fingers run the tips along your gums." Marisol did as told. "Alright," Marlon said.

"Can I get dressed," she now asked.

"No, now I want you to turn around and squat."

The sobs were now silent, and as she turned her back to the officer she kneeled down shivering, while the officer ran her hand under and up to her vagina. She held her breath, as the officer stuck her two gloved fingers inside of her.

"Stand up."

'*Thank God*,' Marisol thought to herself as she stood up and was about to turn around.

"Don't move," Marlon said pushing her back into the wall. "Put your hands on the wall and spread your legs!" Marlon kicked Marisol's ankles to spread her legs more. Marisol grunted because the boots against her bare flesh hurt badly, but not as bad as Marlon shoving her four fingers inside of her.

She had it.

"Marisol Rivera, you're under arrest!"

Chapter 9

Lace and CoCo moved over a month and a half ago now, and although he changed both of their cell phones the house phone remained the same. Too many people of importance had that number, and there were too many people to remember to call and give a new number to. It was 9:30 p.m. He, CoCo, and Tisha laid in the bed watching 'Finding Nemo', when the phone rang. Lace rolled over to answer. "Hello?"

"Lawson, Mad-dee is on the other line," Nette replied.

"Marisol," he said as CoCo's attention was not focused on him.

"Lawson," Marisol began, "I'm locked up!"

"Locked up," he repeated. "For what," he asked.

She told what happened to her.

"Why didn't you call me?"

"I tried, but there is a block on the phone," she cried.

"A block," he repeated, looking at CoCo.

She just turned away.

Lace sucked his teeth, because now he knew why he hadn't heard from Hitz or The God. "What's your bail," he asked.

"A hundred thousand cash or fifty thousand bond, but even the bond is cash."

"Listen, I got you. I'll have the block off the phone in the morning."

"Lawson, I love you. Thank you!"

"I love you too." When he said that, CoCo got up and stomped out of the bedroom. "Just hold your head, I'll have you out of there before the end of the week."

"Thank you, but what about Daniel?"

"What," Nette yelled on the other line.

"Chill Nette," Lace replied,

"Fuck that, her dumb ass goes down there and get locked up chasing some dick, and now she expects you to get him out too?"

"Nette shut the fuck up please! Marisol, call me tomorrow. I'll let you know what's going on!"

Lace hung up and he was pissed that CoCo put the block on the phone. "What the fuck is your problem," he asked.

"Nothing," she answered slamming the cabinet shut.

"Why the fuck would you put a block on my phone?"

"Your phone, Lawson?"

"Yes, I pay the fuckin' bills here and you had no right!"

"Oh, so I have no right but you can run and play Superman for any and every fuckin' body!"

"What the fuck are you talkin' about?"

"You know what I'm talkin' about Lawson. You love her?"

"She's my daughter's mother," he yelled.

Just as loudly she replied, "She left you. Now I'm carrying your baby and you're all that I have. Just think about that and I won't leave!"

Lace was at a loss for words. She was carrying his baby, but he had to help Marisol. "I gotta help her CoCo, you know that!"

"You do what you have to do." CoCo turned and went back to the bedroom. She was having his second child, but he wasn't sure what the right thing to do was.

Georgia was a lot different from New York. Lace gave Marisol's mother fifty thousand and paid for a plane ticket down south for her. Before leaving, Mrs. Rivera had to get five signatures to prove where the money came from. Once she got everyone to sign the paperwork, she flew down south, but she still had to wait for Marisol's court date to bail her out, which was another week away. So, Lace ended up sending her another five grand for food, motel, and get around money. Her court date came and Lace kept his cell phone on his hip, anxiously awaiting the call. The love was no longer there for Marisol, but she was there from the beginning. They grew up together, they were friends, and he took care of his friends.

The phone barely rang once. He snatched it from his waist and hit the call button. "Hello," he answered.

"Lawson?" It was Mrs. Rivera. "Adios, they don't let her go!"

"What? What happened?"

She explained that the district attorney talked the judge into revoking her bail, with the reasoning that since she was from New York she was a flight risk. Also, while Marisol was in custody they raided her apartment and found marijuana and coke, so they were now charging her with trafficking across state lines. "Why Lawson, why did you let her leave?"

It wasn't his fault, but he was forced to take the blame. They'd just wait a few months later, to find that Marisol was sentenced to six and a half years. Hitz was sentenced to eight years, The God eight, and all his charges ran concurrently.

*****

Another three months passed and Blast hadn't seen or heard from his sister. She chose that bitch ass motherfucker over him. In that little bit of time, he lost their mother's apartment and was now in Sin's old one bedroom. He was doing so bad that he resorted to two bit stick ups. It was easy to snatch up these young hustlers for two or three hundred dollars, but once again his face was hot on the streets and was back to parking his whip in the back of the parking lot. He kicked in Coco and Lace's apartment on Mundy Lane but they moved. He asked but no one saw her, and she even changed her cell number. On 221st there was a set of different cats, so he was growing desperate.

*****

Nette was living the life off her little brother's money. Now, while he ran around like a chicken with its head cut off trying to bail Marisol's dumb ass out of jail, Nette partied like a rock star. She attended any and every party, and always dressed to kill. She had two grand in her Fendi purse as she shopped for an outfit. Friday's party was going to be huge because every baller in the Bronx would be in attendance. Nette was sick of being alone and sleeping by herself every night, and Friday she would get her a man. She was so tired of everyone ridiculing her about not having a man, and even her mother began to tease her about being gay. She wasn't gay, she loved men! It was sad that even her little sister constantly had young men calling her mother's house who were dying to be with her.

Nette on the other hand hadn't had a man in over two years and honestly didn't know why. She didn't want the hassle of dealing with a drug dealer, because sooner or later, either jail or some other tragedy occurred. The good men were either married or gay, and if she didn't find a man that wasn't taken it was usually wham, bam, thank you, or maybe we could do this again sometime. She was definitely tired of those situations because she deserved so much more. Thanks to her brother, she had a nice one bedroom apartment and a 2001 Expedition, so she had a few things going for herself. Let's not forget to mention that she was fine, and her nails, hair, and toe game were always up to par. All this was complimented by nice, firm breasts and a fat apple bottom ass. Why was she single?

She began to think that maybe she needed to stop hanging in the Bronx and needed to go and party out in New Jersey or Connecticut, or maybe she needed to stop expecting so much from a man. She shot down so many men that approached her on the bus or train, and had been so rude. It was her. One of those men could have been the one, but she'd been so materialistic, she just shunned away their attention and attempts. Lace was right, she was miserable and because of her misery, she wanted everyone else to be miserable too. As of today it was different because she was making her New Year's resolution early. She had almost a week until Christmas and knew just how to start her new Lynette. She sat behind the wheel of her truck and dialed the house number. It rang about three times before she answered.

"Hello?"

"Hey Chanel, what's up girl?"

It caught CoCo off guard, so she didn't know how to answer. "Lynette?"

"Yeah, what's up?"

"Uh, nothin'. Your brother is not here."

"Girl, I ain't call to speak to his dumbass. I just wanted to see how you was doin'."

"Uh, good I guess!"

"What you been up to," Nette now asked.

"Are you alright Lynette?"

"Yes, and please I'm your family CoCo. Call me Nette."

Coco and Nette spoke for a while with Nette getting personal and telling her exactly what she'd been thinking all day. Nette expressed how she'd been an asshole to CoCo and realized she didn't deserve how she treated her in the past. Nette at least hoped they could be friends. CoCo also opened up some, telling Nette how she needed a friend and they decided to be friends from that day forward. Nette didn't want to take the two hour ride by herself and CoCo admitted she didn't feel like driving out to Connecticut when asked, so the partying idea for tonight was deaded.

*****

Lace was far from a fool, so to stop his team from getting stuck up, he hooked up with a few of the Yardies in the neighborhood. He demoted Noodles and Rich, but to them they were promoted, because now their jobs were to bag up the work and distribute packs to the new crew of hustlers downstairs. Rich and Noodles sat in Monica's house all night smoking and drinking. It cost more money out of Lace's pockets to pay three more men, but his new pitchers wouldn't be robbed that easily. Besides, the block was pulling in close to twenty grand a week, so ten grand a week on workers wasn't hurting too much.

For the past week or so, Coco and Nette were inseparable, which was a good thing to Lace because with his plans, he needed the two to be close. CoCo would soon be family. It was Christmas Eve and a little after 2:30 pm. Lace had forty-four grand for Mark, but of course he had to give it to Ebony. Mark would be in town for the New Years, but wanted the visit to be on the low. The size of Ebony's belly told Lace that Mark was in town several times.

"What are you looking at Lace," Ebony asked.

Lace nodded and gestured to her stomach. "Is that my little cousin," he now asked.

"What this," Ebony said, rubbing her stomach.

"Yeah!"

"Please… Lace you should know your cousin, he would never mix business with pleasure!"

The last words echoed in his head, 'business and pleasure', but they weren't Ebony's words. It was as if he forgot everything they taught him over the years. The haunting words sent chills down his spine. It'd been over a year and a half since he'd been shot, Maurice was locked up in the feds, Mark constantly disappeared, and he hooked up with Blast of all people. The God and his baby's mother were locked up down south. He looked at Ebony.

"What did you say?"

"Nothing," she answered, as she finished weighing out the next two bricks for Lace.

Maybe it was his conscious or maybe it was the ghost of hustlers before him. He had over two hundred grand stashed and another child on the way. Maybe it was time to get out the game. Henny did. Shit, Henny was working and found some chick that he settled down with.

It would take about thirty days to finish these last two bricks. "Yo Eb, this is it!"

"What," she replied.

 238

"The game is over. I might as well get out while I'm ahead!"

"I understand," she started as she rubbed her belly. "Your cousin is really takin' care of me, but I'm not sure if this is the life I want to bring my child into. But what else can I do," she finished,

Lace realized that he never thought about that. "Maybe that's a road we'll have to cross when we get there," he replied.

"Maybe your right Lace, but until then, I've grown accustomed to a certain lifestyle and I'm not sure if I could live any other way!"

With two bricks in the trunk, Lace headed cross town to see momma love. They sat in the living room for a while. "So what's wrong baby," she asked and it caused Lace to smile.

"I guess you can tell huh?"

"You're my only boy. Of course I can see when something is bothering you. So what is it?"

"I'm just tired," he replied.

"So go home and get some rest."

"Not that kind of tired mom…"

"Oh, I see the streets getting to you huh?"

Lace just nodded.

"You know Lawson, I never approved of what you doing, but I always prayed for you. This world isn't easy, especially for a black man, and once you choose certain paths you narrow your own options. You see life is simple baby, but we choose to make it harder on ourselves." She sat up in her chair. "Don't get me wrong it was hard, lord knows it was, especially when your daddy died. It was definitely a struggle being a single black woman with three kids to raise. But you see you and your sisters made it easy for me to see what I had to do. There were times I resented every last one of you…"

"Why would you say that," Lace interrupted.

"Ha," Mrs. Anderson laughed as she began. "What you think I didn't want a life? Shit, I was eighteen when I got pregnant with Nette and a year later you came. You think I didn't wanna party? Boy yo momma was a bad bitch, s'cuse my language, but I wanted to party, dance, smoke reefa, and drink!"

"You?"

"Yes me boy! What you thought I was born a nun? Anyway, your father led by example, and like any other parents, he wanted his children to have everything he didn't." Now she sat back and smiled at the memories. "When we moved to Webster, it was more than just the projects to us, it was a beginning. We were gonna show everybody that two teenagers could make a family and that we didn't need help. Your father worked, put me through school, and showed me that hard work would give us everything we needed, but you see that's where priorities got screwed up. Over the years, what you needed wasn't important anymore. It was all about what you wanted because you all had everything you needed, family, a place to live, and a good hot meal every night but you wanted more. What you wanted couldn't be found on the path of righteousness. It says in the Bible, and no I'm not getting religious on you, but it says it's easier for a camel to walk through the eye of a needle, than for a rich man to enter the gates of heaven."

She sat back up and continued. "Heaven is not in the sky Lawson. Heaven is here and now, and I'm damn near there, because every night I lay my head down and I know that two of my children are safe when I close my eyes. Heaven is back there right now sleeping in my bed and any minute now she'll be up asking for peanut butter and jelly, and it's gonna be heaven making it for her. At this moment Lawson, and you know I love you with all my heart. You are the only hell in my life because every night that I lay in that bed and close my eyes I know that Nette, Elise, and Tisha are safe. Still I toss and turn because I'm haunted by the ghost that you bring to my dreams because I don't know if you are safe. Now, I'm telling you if you're tired get off that road. Hell, it may be paved with good intention, but I'm also telling you to really think about that baby girl in my bed and the baby in Chanel's stomach. They need you and I pray that like your father, you realize what you need to do." Lace just sat there at a loss for words. She got up as she was finished with her statement and just walked out of the living room. Mrs. Anderson went to her bedroom and closed the door.

Lace got up and headed to 221st to drop off the work. After this, he was sure he was done, because it needed to be over. He knew what the right thing was, and that was for him to just walk away from the game.

*****

Christmas Eve and once again Nette was out by herself. No matter what she promised, she couldn't get CoCo out of the house. Nette was a regular at Act III Night Club on 238th and Nerid Avenue. It was the hottest night club in the Bronx and played reggae all night. She sipped Canai white wines all night and now she had to piss. She had offers from men all night as usual, and although she promised to be less picky, she hadn't heard an original line yet. While in the ladies room, she realized she was out of cigarettes, and the Italian bozo that owned the club charged ten dollars a pack, which she refused to pay. She'd rather pay the six dollars and seventy-five cents at the corner store. Stretch, the head bouncer, was one of the many men promising to give her the world just to spend one night with him. He probably promised every woman in the place the same thing.

Nette hadn't realized how drunk she was until she hit the cold winter air. She quickly rushed to the store and got her Newports because she needed a smoke right away. Nette packed her pack and opened it. "Shit," she said out loud because the Arab didn't give her any matches. She figured she would just run to her truck which was parked outside of the club's parking lot on the White Plains Road side. Nette hated parking in the lot because nine times out of ten, some shit would jump off and she wouldn't be able to get away quick enough. As she walked to the truck, she bumped into a couple of regulars who were also outside smoking and bummed a light. It was cold as hell. Maybe she'd smoke in her truck and call it a night.

Nette didn't get ten yards to her Ford, when a horn blew from across the street. She looked to see a pearl white Lexus. '*Not bad she thought*,' as the driver waved her over. She joked silently to herself, '*watch him be Shabba Ranks ugly!*' Still the Lexus was worth seeing who was inside. Nette crossed and went around the front, tilting her head to see the driver but couldn't. She stood at the driver side window and then it slowly rolled down, so that she could finally see the driver. She sucked her teeth but smiled as she leaned in. "Hey what's up nigga? Merry Christmas! What you doin' up here?" She didn't see him reaching, and by the time she saw his hand it was too late.

Bang Bang! Her body fell backwards into a dirty, slushy snow bank on the sidewalk. As the Lexus sped off, people began to run over to Nette's lifeless body. She laid there in the filthy snow and her blood quickly changed from red, to a black and gray sooted color.

Mrs. Anderson couldn't do it and Elise held her as they sat on the cold metal bench in the morgue. Lace stood at the window with Chanel's arm around his waist and tears falling from both of their eyes. As the examiner pulled back the sheet, it was CoCo that nodded to ID the body of Lynette Anderson. Lace just bit his bottom lip. His oldest sister was murdered on Christmas 2008, no witnesses and no suspects. Lace had been to Act III several times and he knew there had to be people outside of the club, but no one would ever come out and give a statement. The holiday season was definitely gloomy.

Christmas wasn't a holiday, it was a hell day. That week Mrs. Anderson couldn't even get out of bed. Lace was busy interrogating the night club. The owner offered to pay for the funeral, but Lace didn't want the Italian's money. He wanted the man's life, but was smart enough to know it was stupid to start that war. So, while he ran around, Elise and CoCo handled all the arrangements. The day of the funeral came too quickly, but Mrs. Anderson was up and vibrant, as if she'd slept away all her pain and misery. She vowed that the day would not be a day of mourning, but a celebration of her daughter's life.

As the service went on, Lace was amazed at how many people showed up. It was really hard to believe, because Nette always said she had no friends. During the eulogies, Lace continuously looked back at the doors, and CoCo knew what was troubling him. "He'll show up baby," she said rubbing his shoulder. Still Lace couldn't hide his emotion, because although they constantly fought, he loved his sister more than anything. Lace was a little disappointed that Ebony showed up, but Mark didn't. Elise was speaking, and when Lace turned he saw both of them. The smile on his face brought relief and suspicion to CoCo. "What's wrong with you," she asked, glad to see him finally smiling.

"Look in the back."

She did as Lace told her. She never meant it to be rude and no one took it that way. Even Mrs. Anderson stood and smiled, seeing Henny carrying the little girl in his arms. CoCo ran up and hugged them both, then led her best friend to the front pew with the rest of the family, which was what Henry and Sin were, family.

The services were over at the cemetery and after they went back to the church where a huge dinner had been prepared. Just as Mrs. Anderson demanded, there were no tears of sorrow, just laughter and tears of joy as they remembered Lynette. Still, most of the focus was on Henny, Sincerely, and the ten month old little girl that couldn't be removed from Henny. There was no doubt who the child's father was. Camille was the spitting image of the two, although she looked more like she was CoCo's sister.

Sin and CoCo shared tears, as they spoke on the last year of their lives. As Henny explained to Lace what was going on in his, Lace also told of his epiphany that it was time to get out the game. It was time to rid himself of the love of the streets, the lies of the people, and the loyalty to the devil. After all was done, Lace and CoCo drove Elise and his mother home. Henny and Sin followed them back to their apartment. It amazed CoCo how beautiful her niece was, and how Camille and Henny adored each other, but it also hurt her to see so much of her brother in the child. Sin showed so much excitement to hear that CoCo was pregnant. Before leaving they made two promises, one that they would stay in touch now that CoCo knew the truth and two, for everyone's good that

Blast could never know the truth. So after kisses, pounds, and hugs, Sin and Henny headed home to upstate New York.

The ride home was peaceful and it felt like such a weight had been taken off Sin's shoulders. CoCo saw her niece, and now everyone knew she was alright. As Henny continuously checked the rearview mirror to see if the responsibility he had taken on as his own daughter was sleeping well, he caught a glimpse of the huge smile on Sin's face. "I see you're feeling good," he replied.

"I mean under the circumstances you know. We all loved Nette, even though I knew you two were screwing behind my back!"

"What," Henny uttered in shock.

"Oh, you just think I'm blind, death, and dumb because I said nothing? I know you loved her."

"It was a different kind of love, Sin…"

"Whatever. Truthfully, whatever ya'll had was between ya'll."

She was quiet for a moment and her smile was gone, as she thought about the love Henny and Nette shared. Now, Henny was hers again and she was his, plus he took responsibility of another man's child, which proved the love he had for her. Still Henny just drove quietly. What could he say? For years Nette had been the only woman he had cheated on Sin with. Feelings were definitely involved. If it hadn't been Sin, it would've been Nette, but life chose for him.

"You're beautiful when you're mad."

She couldn't help but smile at his comment. "I hate to say it, but everything worked out regardless of how it all started," she replied. He didn't understand what she meant, and she felt she might've said a little too much, as he stared at her.

"What? The way what started," he asked.

"Nothing," she said hoping he wouldn't dig.

"Sincerely, the way what started," his voice expressed his seriousness.

Sin exhaled. "CoCo really loves Lace!"

"How what started Sin," he repeated.

She bit her bottom lip.

"Sin, don't play with me. What's going on?"

Still she said nothing.

"Sin," he yelled. "What the fuck are you talking about?" he quickly looked back to make sure Camille was still sleeping.

"It was all a set up…"

"What?"

"It was a set up. Blast shot Lawson."

10:30 p.m. and a half an hour from home, Henny pulled to the shoulder of the thru-way and slammed the gearshift into park. He looked at her but she looked away. "Sin look at me." She did. "Tell me what happened!"

She told him everything leaving out only one detail, that she gave Blast the idea to use CoCo to get to Lace. It didn't take long for Henny to put it all together. "Henry," she called, but he was deep into thought.

"Ceily," he now said out loud.

"What?"

"You called my phone and talked to Carol!" She said nothing. "Sin, you called my phone?"

"Yes Henry I called. I didn't want anything to happen to you."

"He killed Carol," he said shaking his head, as he punched the dashboard.

She was innocent. Carol had nothing to do with any of them, and now he knew for sure it was Blast that had murdered her.

Henny slammed the car into drive. Sin tried to talk to him, but he begged her for silence. He just headed north going home. Blast killing Carol was the only thing on his mind. He ran out on her that night and left her. Blast murdered her in part of some sick plan, and now CoCo sat in a beautiful apartment, driving a Range Rover, living the life.

Carol didn't deserve to die and CoCo didn't deserve to live like a queen. Henny was coming up on a highway u-turn that was illegal to use. He dipped across the lanes and the jerk of the vehicle caused Sin to grab for the dashboard. As Henny made the u-turn, he checked on Camille who was still asleep in the back seat.

"What are you doing," Sin asked in horror.

"CoCo's gonna tell Lace the fuckin' truth!"

Sin felt horrible. What had she done? For the first time she could ever remember in life, both she and CoCo were happy and both had real relationships. CoCo was in love, and now they were headed back to the Bronx to put an end to her happiness. This was all Sin's fault.

*****

Lace laid in bed quietly as they watched re-runs of Seinfeld. CoCo didn't want to disturb him because he had been through so much. Regardless of their constant arguing, Lace and Nette had been best friends so he and Elise took today hard.

"You hungry," CoCo asked. Lace just shook his head. "Lawson you haven't eaten anything all day. I'd feel better if you ate something."

"I just don't have an appetite," he answered.

"Lawson, do you want me to call your mother," she said jokingly.

Finally getting a smile out of him he answered, "No Mrs. Anderson!"

Now she smiled. "So can I warm something up for my husband?"

"Yeah go head, I'll eat for you!"

"Umm," CoCo moaned and again Lace smiled.

"I said I'd eat for you. I didn't say nothing about eating you!"

"We'll see about that," CoCo answered getting up putting on her silk robe.

Once in the kitchen, she didn't know what to fix him to eat. It was a choice between Wednesday's oxtails and Monday's stewed chicken. Whatever it was, she'd definitely take him an ice cold Becks. Lace hated microwaved food, so CoCo put the pot of oxtails on the stove over a low fire. She poured herself a glass of White Zinfandel and sat at the table with a copy of the latest consumer report magazine. After flipping through the entire magazine she got up to stir the pot, but just then the doorbell rang. "Shit who could that be," she said to herself, turning off the pot. She pulled her robe closed and went to answer the door. Knowing better than to just open the door, she looked through the window first. "Henny," she said out loud, then opening the door with a smile.

Without any words, Henny walked in with little Camille in his arms. Sin followed. "Is everything alright," CoCo asked watching Henny and her niece. She could see the anger in his eyes, so she turned to Sin, whose eyes told her everything. "Sin," was all she could say. Her shoulders were sagging and her eyes quickly formed water.

"What's good, everything alright?" They all turned to see Lace standing there in his boxers and t-shirt, but no one said a word. He saw the tears in CoCo's eyes. "What's up," Lace asked again.

"Tell 'em Chanel," Henny replied with anger still written all over his face.

"Tell me what," Lace said looking at Henny and then at Coco. "Tell me what CoCo?"

"Sincerely, how could you do this to me," CoCo said with the tears now flowing like a faucet.

"What the fuck is going on," Lace yelled.

"You not gonna tell 'em Chanel? I'll tell 'em" Henny said.

"Tell me what?"

"This was all a fuckin' set up," Henny yelled.

"What," Lace replied, still confused.

"Chanel tell him!"

In a low but sincere voice Sin said, "I never thought I'd love."

"Tell me what the fuck is going on," Lace repeated with his voice beginning to crack, as if he were on the verge of tears.

"We didn't want to do it. Sin knows I didn't have a choice!"

"What is she talking about," Lace asked, looking from Sin to Henny.

"That night in the club. Lace we were all there," Sin answered with her head down.

Lace understood now. He shook his head, as he remembered the night he was shot. "I gave you everything Chanel!"

"I know Lawson and I love you so much. I made a mistake!"

"A mistake? Chanel you tried to kill me!"

"It wasn't me! I swear I had no choice. Please tell him Sincerely, please" CoCo pled but Sin said nothing.

"I trusted you Chanel, I even tried to love you, and all this time my sister was right. You're just a snake like your brother!"

"Lawson please," she pled.

"Just get your shit and get the fuck out of my house!"

"Henry, Sin please talk to him…"

"I'm sorry CoCo, but you should have been told the truth," Sin said.

Lace just turned and walked out of the living room.

"I'm sorry too Chanel, but he needed to know the truth," Henny added as he and Sin headed for the door.

The bedroom door was locked. CoCo knocked and begged Lace to open the door and talk to her, but her pleas went unanswered. With her back against the wall, she slid down to the floor crying uncontrollably. In her thoughts she wanted to be mad with Sin but she couldn't, because her anger could only be focused on one person, Blast. Finally the door opened and she jumped to her feet.

"Lawson, I…"

"No need Chanel," he interrupted her. He had bags in his hand. "Here are your clothes. Well, most of them. I'm keeping all the jewelry and you can have your car. Here are your car keys," he said as he led her to the door.

"Lawson, I swear I love you!"

"Yeah, I thought I did too. It was fun while it lasted, goodbye!" With that, Lace closed the door.

In tears, CoCo made her way to the Range Rover and was headed back to Webster. She'd have to face the man who ruined her life since they were kids, but now she knew for a fact that she hated Blast.

*****

3 Weeks Later...

It seemed as if Lace lost more than just his girl or his baby mother. With Coco out of the house, it was as if he'd lost his best friend. Even time with Tisha didn't fill the emptiness because she would ask over and over, "Daddy where's Tanel?" She always had problems pronouncing her C's, which always came out sounding like T's, since she lost her front teeth. Still, Lace knew their relationship wasn't completely over since she was carrying his second child. CoCo knew as well as he did that his main focus was getting out of the game, and the entire situation came about over the drug game. Blast almost killed him and now the man's sister was carrying his baby. It was all frightening.

He explained to his crew that after this last flip he was through and would give entire control of the block to Noodles and Rich. Ebony also understood. She gave Mark the news that his first cousin had been killed. Mark sent cards and flowers to Mrs. Anderson with no return address. Ebony explained that with Maurice in the feds, Mark couldn't afford prison and his life was very secretive. His family didn't know half the things he had going on, like for example he had four children by three different women which he supported, as well as two women that claimed to be the mothers of Maurice's children. Hearing these things blew Lace's mind, to know that Mark had children that none of them ever saw or heard of.

Mark was dealing with so much money and he never knew if and when someone would get jealous and use his weaknesses to get at him, but there was a bigger weakness than children. Most times, it was the men closest to a man that decided it was time for kidnaping, extortion, or robbery. Homicide was the best way to move, which was something discreet that Maurice could never do.

"Honestly Lace," Ebony began, "tell me where Mark lived."

Lace was quiet, as he thought about her question. He knew several spots that Mark crashed, but had no idea where his cousin laid his head or called home. "You see this paranoia didn't just start when Maurice got knocked. Mark has been this way for years, and as much as he loves you, he knows no one can be trusted! But he trusts you," Lace replied.

Ebony smiled, while rubbing her plump seven month pregnant stomach. "The funny thing Lace is that Mark trusts me with his money but he'd never trust me with his life."

For years, Lace looked up to Maurice and believed him to be the man. Whenever Mark was preaching to Moe and Lace, Moe would just fan the advice off and Lace never paid any attention to his sermons. If he only listened to a quarter of what Mark tried to show him he wouldn't be in this situation now.

*****

Henny pulled up, and although he couldn't tell what kind of car he was driving, it was actually too big to be a car. Maybe it was a truck. He jumped out. "Yo Hen Rock," the voice called out. Henny turned to see Star standing there. "What's up my nigga," Star added. As Henny got out the vehicle, he walked around to open the door for Sin. As Henny walked around, he realized he had no idea where they were. He opened the door as Star told him to hurry, but it wasn't Sin who stepped out of whatever he was driving, it was Nette.

"You know I've always loved you right," she asked.

"Yeah, I know!"

"So why'd you let this happen to us?"

"What" he asked, but then there was a scream. Star turned to see Tior holding a gun pointed at his head.

"Henry... Henry!" She shook him.

"What, what," he said as he woke expecting to see Nette, but it was Sin. '*Thank God*,' he thought to himself.

"Are you alright," she asked. He rubbed his forehead which was soaking wet with sweat. "You must've had another nightmare," she replied.

For the past two weeks, he'd been having these dreams of Nette, Star, Tior and Blast. In each dream either he or Nette had been killed, and it was as if Tior and Blast were haunting him. "I'm alright," he answered as he sat up.

"Your mom and pops again," she asked.

"Yeah," he nodded.

He never told her what he'd really been dreaming about these last few days, and he didn't know why.

"You want anything," she asked.

"Yeah, I want these ghosts out my head!"

"Well, I'm gonna go get you something to drink," she said getting out of the bed. She walked out of their bedroom. First she stopped to check on Camille, who she found was fast asleep.

Sin made her way to the kitchen and got him a cold glass of orange juice. When she got back, he also was fast asleep, so she sat on the edge of the bed just watching him. She felt so horrible, because she created this misery for all of them. CoCo, whom she couldn't muster up the courage to talk to, called her several times over the past three weeks, but Sin ignored her calls letting her get the voice mail. She felt like shit because Henny made it worse every night, because for days he'd moaned and screamed Nette and Star's names in his sleep. She allowed him to lie to her about his dreams, but still there was one name from his nightmares that puzzled her, Tior, The Wild Appache. Why would he be having nightmares about that Guyanese bastard? He has been dead almost two years now, but maybe that was what the ghost had in common. Nette, Star, and Tior were all dead and ghosts of the Bx. All she could do was pray that he'd be alright.

*****

It surprised her that Blast hadn't been pissed that she was home, but then again misery loved company. He was so happy not to be by himself, that he hadn't even pressured her about how and where to get Lace. He was even anxious about her baby being born, which would be in about five months. She didn't realize how much she missed the projects and how much they missed her. Everyday different people stopped by to see her, and she was glad they came because the snake skinned, old man had her terrified of going outside. He was always out there staring at her with that gray, slimy dead eye. Just looking at him made her feel nauseous. Blast left earlier that morning, which was usual for the past few days. After showering and getting dressed she tried calling Sin, but only got the voice mail. If only Sin knew they were now living in her apartment.

All she wanted to tell her was thank you because for two years she had been trying to tell Lace the truth, but just didn't know how. Once their baby was born, CoCo honestly felt they'd be back together. Even if she had to beg, Lace was the best thing to happen to her life and she was ready and willing to fight for him if necessary. She wasn't expecting anyone, so the knock at the door sort of startled her. She waddled to the door, and still trained by Lace checked the peephole. It was Shamika. Coco smiled as she opened the door. "Hey Mika!"

"What's up girl?"

"Ain't nothin', just sittin' around here. My fat ass eating everything that ain't movin'," Coco answered as she led Shamika into the living room.

"So how'd you know I was up here," CoCo asked.

"Shit, girl I knocked on your door for about ten minutes and that nosey ass Mrs. Cross answered her door!"

They both laughed because Mrs. Cross had to be the nosiest person in Webster Projects.

"She told me ya'll moved up here. So where is your sexy ass brother?"

"Girl please," CoCo answered.

They sat around just talking for about an hour and of course CoCo lied about why she was back in the PJs. She said she was feeling sorry for her brother and just came to spend a few days with him because once she had the baby, there was no telling when she'd be back on this side of town. They went on about baby names and her fast ass daughter, but CoCo couldn't help but think her daughter got it honestly.

Blast walked in and Shamika smiled from ear to ear. "Hey Cornell," she said blushing.

"Mika, what's up?"

"You!"

Now Blast blushed. "Chanel how you feeling," He asked. Blast was always so concerned about her condition.

"I'm good, just hungry," she said with a smile. Blast smiled because she was always hungry.

"I'm hungry too," Shamika said biting her bottom lip.

"I think we're hungry for different things," CoCo replied causing both Blast and Shamika to laugh. That's when Blast pulled the Wendy's bag from behind his back. CoCo jumped up with a smile grabbing the bag, sat down, and began stuffing her mouth with french fries. Now the three of them began to talk while he rolled a blunt for him and Shamika.

With the food and weed gone, they sat there. Coco was full for a moment, and Shamika and Blast were high. They were quiet until Shamika spoke. "It's fucked up what happened to Lynette," she said. Both Blast and CoCo were quiet for their own reasons, CoCo because she was afraid Shamika would say the wrong thing. "It was a nice funeral though," Shamika now added.

CoCo changed the topic. "I wanna know who the hell that fucked up old man is!"

"What man," Shamika asked. Blast explained to her who Coco was talking about. "Oh God, I'm glad I ain't seen 'em," Shamika replied.

"For real girl, he's disgusting. He just has this way of looking at you that makes your skin crawl, his eyes…," before CoCo could finish, Shamika interrupted her.

"Speaking of eyes, Blast your daughter is so beautiful," Shamika said.

Blast was in shock. He just looked from CoCo to Shamika. "What the fuck are you talking about," he asked.

"Nothing Cornell, she's just high," CoCo said. Shamika knew as well as anyone else, the drama between Blast and Henny.

"What you mean my daughter? Chanel what is she talking about?"

Before CoCo could speak again, Shamika started, "Your daughter, she's so pretty!"

"Where did you see her," Blast asked.

"Oh Coco ain't tell you? Sin and Henny brought…"

CoCo barely let out a yelp as Blast gripped her so tightly around her neck.

"What the fuck is wrong with you," Shamika yelled out.

"You fuckin' bitch," Blast yelled as he began to snatch the breath from his sister. "You knew all along," he added as tears ran down his cheeks.

"Get off of her," Shamika screamed as she ran up behind Blast.

Unable to breathe, CoCo felt the hot liquid run from between her legs. She began to claw at Blast's hands, but he wouldn't let go. Her eyes were now bloodshot.

Shamika began punching Blast in the back of his head. "Stop you fuckin' asshole," she screamed.

With one hand, he turned and pushed her away. He was so powerful the one hand knocked her to the floor as he continued to choke the life from his own flesh and blood. "I told you Chanel… I told you I'd kill you if you betrayed me for them niggas!" Tears ran freely from his eyes, as they seemed to be forced from hers.

Shamika jumped up and snatched the phone off the receiver. Blast saw her from the corner of his eye. He let go of CoCo's neck and she just gasped, being too weak and unable to move. Blast snatched the leg of the broken coffee table.

"Nine one one," Shamika spoke into the phone, but she didn't see it coming. Crash! She fell into the wall, dropping the phone and leaving its cord dangling. Smash, smash, smash. He bashed her over and over with the leg of the table, until she was a bloody motionless mess. He turned to see his sister had managed to turn over, and was now on her hands and knees. Blast rushed to her with the slab of bloody wood still in his hand.

"Why, Chanel Why," he cried barely audible.

She begged as blood poured from between her legs. "My... M... baby," she muttered.

"What," he cried out. "Your baby... Bitch!" He swung the leg of the table and connected with her forehead. Again he repeatedly swung the wooden slab with each word. "What... about... my... baby?" He dropped his club with the last word. "Get up," he told her, but she didn't move. "Dammit Chanel get the fuck up," he cried but still she didn't respond. "Chanel," he cried out louder while dropping to his knees in her blood. "Please Chanel," he now begged, lifting her small, lifeless body, hugging her to him. "I'm sorry, baby I'm sorry please," he pled with her dead body.

Chapter 10

Lace didn't know what to think when he opened the door and saw the NYPD. First he'd been praying it was CoCo, but now he was praying it wasn't a sale indictment. As they helped him into the back seat of the Crown Victoria he began to think about everything Ebony told him Mark said. He couldn't help but speculate that one of the crew, or even The God or Hitz, gave him up. They said they only wanted to ask him a couple of questions. What the fuck kind of questions could they have for him, better yet what kind of answers did they expect to get from him? He'd been sitting in a room with just a desk and four chairs. There were no windows, and of course he checked the door, which was locked from the outside.

He sat there for over two hours and still had no idea why he was there. Finally the door opened and three detectives walked in. Two of them sat down in front of Lace. "Lawson Anderson, my name is Detective Cherry, this is my partner Norman, and that's Ray," Cherry said gesturing to the officer standing by the door.

"Alright, now that your through with the introductions, why am I here," Lace asked.

"Relax buddy," Ray spoke from his position by the door. "We'll ask all the questions," he added.

Lace figured that was his tough guy routine.

"Mr. Anderson, where were you yesterday afternoon between the hours of 2 and 4 p.m.?"

Lace knew exactly where he was during those hours, but still decided to take his time answering. "Um, I believe I was at the zoo with my daughter, why?"

Norman nodded, as he checked the paperwork in front of him. "That's what his mother said," he replied.

"My mother," Lace repeated. "You questioned my mother?"

"Yeah," Ray answered, still by the door.

"How do yo think we found you Mr. Anderson," Cherry replied.

Lace never thought about that. "What's this about," Lace asked.

"Do you know this woman," Norman asked, pushing the photo in front of Lace. Lace looked at the photo, then he looked at the police. "Who is that Mr. Anderson," Norman asked.

"Chanel Winston…"

"And what's your relationship with Ms. Winston?"

"She's having my baby," Lace answered.

"So she's not your woman," Ray now asked.

"We broke up…"

"So when was the last time you saw her?"

"Maybe four or five days ago, why?"

Ray spoke first. "Didn't I tell you we'll ask the questions?"

"Mr. Anderson, who's this," Norman asked, as he pushed another photo in front of Lace.

"Who is this Mr. Anderson," Cherry now asked.

"Shamika Knight…"

"Where do you know her from," Norman asked.

"We all grew up in the projects together. What's goin' on," Lace said, now getting a little anxious.

"Did you know Ms. Winston was pregnant," Ray asked.

"Yes…"

"Did you want her to keep the baby," Norman asked.

"Of course I knew she was pregnant, and yes I wanted it…"

"So why'd you put her out," Ray asked.

Lace sucked his teeth. "That's our personal business. Now why am I here?"

"Mr. Anderson, we found Ms. Anderson and Ms. Knight dead yesterday in the apartment of…," Norman paused to look through his paperwork, "of a Ms. Sincerely White. Do you know Ms. White?"

"Dead," Lace repeated, because that was all he heard. "What do you mean dead?"

"We found them murdered. It seems as if someone bludgeoned both women with the leg of a broken coffee table."

Lace broke down crying for Coco and his unborn child. They explained that during the death of Chanel, she gave birth, but his son was also dead at the scene. Someone made an anonymous call but the assholes hadn't arrived in time to save the baby, which suffocated on the placenta. Once the detectives saw how distraught he was over the death of his child, they let him go. He only was asked, that if he found out anything to let them know, which they seriously doubted he would.

Lace lost so much over the past two years, which included his sister, Marisol, his newborn child, and CoCo. Every man is faced with adversity and problems, but its how a man deals with these things that define who he is. Pain is an emotion that most do not know how to cope with, and Lace was one of those men. The problems were one thing and adversity was something he overcame many times, but the pain was too severe. If Blast or anyone else wanted him, he'd put himself out there, but they better come blasting because he refused to get caught out there slipping. He would never get caught out there without the hammer, and he'd be the bait if need be.

Four bottles of Henny and an ounce of sour diesel weed later, Lace drove out to 221st Street with the system blasting. Cory, Noodles, Cream, and Rich came out. "What's the deal Lace," Rich asked.

"Nothing son. We ballin' right? So let's enjoy it!" It was easy to see the man was already drunk, but that was just the beginning. Everyone was chilling in front of the building and still all drugs were sold in the lobby. It was a block party, but after the third day Rich and Noodles began to feel some kind of way. After all the talk about Lace quitting his new routine had them worried. Maybe he changed his mind on the block. After three days in a row of getting everyone drunk and high, to them he was enjoying the life just a little too much. It was time for the men to solidify their come up.

It was Friday night. No one knew CoCo's funeral was Saturday morning. Lace celebrated all day and by 1:30 a.m. he was stumbling drunk. Noodles saw his chance.

"Yo Cory, we'll be back in about an hour!" Cory nodded.

"Where ya'll goin'," Lace asked with his words slurred.

"We goin' to get something to eat. You riding," Rich asked.

"Yeah man. I ain't, ain't drivin'," he mumbled.

"Hell no nigga, get in the back," Noodles told Lace. He climbed into the back seat of the Jeep Cherokee. "Were we goin to eat," Noodles asked as he pulled off.

"White Castle on Boston Road," Rich offered. Lace said nothing in the back seat, semi-conscious.

"That's what's up," Noodles replied as they headed for Boston Road.

After getting the food from the drive thru window, Noodles drove north towards the border of Mount Vernon and the Bronx. He parked on a dark back road, in the junkyard areas. They laughed and joked but their intention was to leave Lace right where they were, literally. Noodles had the bowing knife under his seat. They doubted the drunk man would be a problem for both of them, so the plan was to pull him out, slit his throat, and leave him for dead on the deserted back streets. Both were just waiting for the other to give the word.

After a bout of laughter about Monica, the car was quiet, truthfully a little too quiet for Lace. He felt strange and something was wrong because he could hear Ebony in his head. *'Most times it's the men closest to you that decide it is time for kidnapping, extortion, or robbery homicide.'* As those words echoed in his head, he began to sober up a little, and then his own words echoed. *"I refuse to get caught out here slipping."* That's just what he was doing, slipping. He eased up and gained his focus, but as he looked out of the dark tints, he realized that wherever they were, it was too damn dark. His heart began to pound, maybe he was just being paranoid, but it was paranoia that made Mark the man he was, and wherever he might've been at the moment, Lace knew one thing for sure, that Mark was somewhere safe.

"Shit," he yelled out.

"What's up," Rich asked.

"I think I'm gonna throw up!"

"Oh shit nigga," Noodles yelled with a smile, as Lace watched him in the rearview mirror. "Get out! Don't toss your cookies in my whip," Noodles added.

Lace saw Rich's nod. It hurt Lace to think it was true, because he and Rich came up in this together, but he could hear Ebony's words again. *'He trusts me with his money, but he would never trust me with his life.'* One thing for certain was that Lace was prepared. He slowly opened the door, still playing the drunk role to the t, although his thoughts sobered him up. He stumbled out the car and left the door open.

"We gonna get this nigga now," Noodles whispered as he pulled the Rambo knife from under the seat. Lace placed his left hand on the wall and his right on the handle of the gun while he bent over as if preparing to lose his White Castle. As Rich's door opened, Lace could feel a tear forming in the corner of his eye. Now, he heard both doors open.

"Yo, Lace you alright," Rich asked.

"Yeah, Yeah I... I... just needed a little air," Lace answered slowly pulling the nine from his waist. His back was to them so they couldn't see his actions, but as he heard the footsteps approaching, he could hear the thoughts echoing through his mind. *'The ones closest, refuse to get caught slipping, trust no one with your life.'*

"Yo, Lace you good man," Noodles asked.

He could hear his voice only a few feet away from him, but he didn't answer.

"Yo, Lace," Rich called out, now a little closer.

Lace knew he wasn't a killer, so maybe he should just let these men, his men, take his life and be done with it all. Then he saw Latisha with her smile and her beautiful snagga tooth smile. It made him smile, so now he wasn't ready to die. It hadn't been his time two years ago and it wasn't his time now. "Yah, I'm good," he said with his voice steady, no slurring, no drunken stutter, just anger. He turned with the nine millimeter in hand. Noodles just stopped short with the knife in his hand. Rich was stuck in wide eyed shock.

"This was how you were gonna do me Rich, huh? After all the shit I did for you, you was just gonna leave me to die on some dirty stinkin' side street?"

"Yo Lace, it's not even like... like that," Rich stuttered, causing Lace to smile.

"A couple of dollars would make you put a knife in my back Rich? Fuck Noodles, but me and you built everything by ourselves... you, me and Hitz!"

"What about Hitz? You left him and The God to rot," Noodles yelled.

"Lower your voice son, it's just us out here. Ain't nobody here to save you, you know that! That's why you bought me out here to die." Lace paused thinking about Hitz and The God. He did wrong by Hitz and he knew it, but The God, that was something totally different.

"The God, Noodles... From the jump ya'll whole intention was this and you know it. Still, I broke bread! I trusted you and showed you love, but money knows no loyalty, only lies. I trusted you with my money and I almost trusted you with my life Rich. A year ago, Noodles and I couldn't have done this. It wasn't that I didn't have the heart. It was that I didn't have the anger, but now fuck you."

Bang! Noodles fell to the ground as the shot erupted in his chest and the knife flew to Rich's feet. "Yo Lace man," Rich began to cry. "I don't know what I was thinking man. I fucked up!"

"Yeah," Lace said calmly nodding his head. "You fucked up!"

"Give me a chance man, I'll make it up," Rich begged.

"You can't. You lack love and loyalty, and I could never believe your lies."

"Yo," Rich pled as he got down on his knees. "Please Lace," he begged.

"Would you have shown me any mercy, or did ya'll drive out here just to murder me in cold blood?"

Rich didn't answer.

"If I would've got down on my knees and begged you to think about my daughter, would you have changed your mind and just let me walk away...? Answer me," Lace yelled, but still Rich said nothing. "Tell me the truth Rich and I'll set you free!"

"No," Rich answered, barely in a whisper.

"I didn't think so!"

At point blank range, Lace put the barrel of the gun to Rich's head and pulled the trigger twice. Rich's body slumped over. Lace stood over Noodles and hit him once in the head also. He then jumped in the Jeep and quickly pulled off. Before jumping on the Bruckner Expressway he stopped, wiped off the gun, and threw it in the East River.

His stomach felt horrible, as if he had to vomit. He just wanted to get home so he didn't stop. At first it was just a deep cough, but then ugh! He threw up on the passenger seat. One wasn't enough, as it was coming in violent spasms. He pulled over and fell to his knees, but it wasn't the alcohol. It was the effects of the event that just took place. He never killed anyone before and had no idea it would have been so easy, but now he was bent over on his hands and knees spilling his guts. Whoop Whoop! The lights flashed and that was the police. "Shit!"

Blast couldn't believe what he did, in allowing his anger to control him. Now he lost the only person in the world he had, the only one to ever love him besides his mother. Not only was he broke, but he had no where to go. For the past week, he'd been hiding out in his mom's old apartment, and he knew it would only be a matter of time before they'd rent it out, so he had to make a move. He doubted the police would be looking for him, because who would expect him to have murdered his own sister. He was back to his old antics where he would hide out all day in his old apartment and then hit the streets at night looking for a come up. In the past week, he caught a couple of small hustlers uptown and stacked a little five grand. Five more and he'd bounce. Maybe he would head south and try to start over where no one knew him.

He rode up to 221st Street and was surprised when he saw no familiar faces. He was leery about hopping out on some cats not knowing who they were or what they were about. If he had Do Dem Boys with him, it would be different, but by himself it was plain stupid to jump out one deep on three men. He sat there for over an hour watching the men operate, and he couldn't deny the operation was tight. Noodles and Rich were nowhere in sight and they made sure no transactions were seen. Everything was taken care of inside the building. The only way he would be able to rob them was to get inside the hallway, but he had no idea what they'd have inside for protection. He looked at his watch. It was almost 3 a.m. "Fuck it," he said to himself as he put the Lex in gear. He thought he would have a better chance catching one of them young cats on 3rd Ave or Washington.

*****

"Come on Elise, you said your moms ain't home..."

"OH! You must think I'm one of them chicken heads you use to fuckin' with!"

"What you talkin' 'bout? I'm tryin' to show you it's all about you!"

"So you think 'cause you took me out a few times, that I'm supposed to just give you some pussy?"

"Why you gotta talk like that? You too sweet to talk so dirty."

Elise smiled, "My brother warned me about smoove talkin' dudes like you…"

"I think your brother is your problem," he replied.

"Why would you say that?"

"He's got you spoiled," he answered.

"Now I'm spoiled because I don't need a man? My brother gives me whatever I need!"

"No, you're spoiled because you don't realize when there's another man willing to give you what you need…"

She didn't have a response for his comment, but she couldn't just leave it at that. "I can't lie, I'm feeling you. I'm just scared."

"I understand that. I'm not pressuring you. I'm trying to be with you, but you won't let your guard down to allow me in your heart. I just want to love you!"

Elise had many guys try to holler at her, but she never felt for any of them like she did Micheal because he was different. For months they'd been dating. He was from the same neighborhood and she saw him a few times growing up, but once her mother moved, she didn't really visit the old neighborhood much. She met Micheal at a party at the New Savoy, a club. Her brother would have flipped if he knew she'd been there, especially after the death of Nette. However, Elise couldn't lie. Micheal helped her a lot through those hard times. Maybe he did deserve a taste. Lace always told her to let a man earn it, and Micheal did.

"We can't go to my mother's house," Elise said shyly. Micheal had been to the house a few times and even met her mother, but she had too much of Lace's money stashed in the house to have someone walking around freely.

"Don't take this the wrong way, but I know a nice hotel in Westchester. It's the Marriot, not no cheap shit either!" Agreeing, Elise put her truck in gear, and before they pulled off Micheal rolled down his window and shouted to his boys. Elise made the u-turn on 3rd Avenue and headed north.

*****

It was after 3:30 a.m., Henny jumped up in shock to see that Sin was sitting up watching him. She saw that he was crying and wiped the tears away from his eyes. "You were crying in your sleep," she said quietly. Henny decided to tell her the truth that he continued to have dreams about Nette and Carol. He apologized for not telling her the truth about the nightmares, which they really were. She accepted his apology, as he continued to talk about them.

In each dream, Blast approached him with a gun, but the shot always missed him and hit either Carol or Nette. The dream tonight was totally different because in this one he woke up in Sin's grandmother's apartment, but he was in bed with CoCo. When he said that, Sin scrunched up her face. Blast woke him up with the gun pointed at him and was yelling about CoCo knowing where Sin was. When CoCo said she didn't, Blast cocked back the gun and shot her. Henny jumped up, but could do nothing, but then the gun was pointed at him. "I couldn't do nothing Sin. He killed his own sister and I couldn't do anything!"

Sin rubbed his shoulders, "It was just a dream baby."

Henny nodded in acknowledgement, but they just seemed so real. He had never been religious or spiritual, but he felt as if the dreams were trying to tell him something.

"Why were you crying," she now asked.

Henny smiled, and that was something she hadn't seen in months. "It's stupid!"

"No, it's not. Tell me."

"I was scared, so I ran out the apartment. Blast was right behind me as I ran into the elevator. I was just scared."

She smiled because she knew his phobia of elevators. "That's not silly!"

"It is! I'm almost thirty years old and I'm still scared of elevators. Let's go downstairs, I'm hungry."

They headed downstairs. "I want you to call CoCo tomorrow," Henny said.

"Why?"

"Sin, that's your best friend!"

"Well Lace is your best friend and you haven't called him."

Henny couldn't argue. He felt just as bad as Sin did about having to tell Lace the truth. Still CoCo had been the only one Sin had, especially once he left her. He felt Sin owed CoCo more than to just ignore her. "We'll both call tomorrow."

Tomorrow came faster than both of them hoped. They both tried to call but neither got an answer. CoCo's cell phone was disconnected and Lace's phone went straight through to voicemail. They both promised to call back later.

*****

Lace woke up in a holding cell with a pounding headache. He remembered seeing the police pull up behind him the night before, but didn't remember being arrested. His heart began pounding as he called the C.O. over to ask what he was being charged with. The young woman chuckled as she began to speak.

"You were that drunk huh?"

"Yeah," Lace answered nodding.

"Well the arresting officer was just going to write you a ticket, but you were in no condition to let go, so he brought you in. So, now you have to wait to see the judge. Just be glad it's not a DUI, because you were pulled over on the shoulder. It will be something minor," she added as she walked away.

Lace was so glad it was his drunkenness and not the bodies, so he just laid back against the wall. He'd be seeing the judge soon and just thanked God he threw the gun away. This was definitely no good for him. No more drug game and definitely no more drinking. By 2:30 p.m. Saturday afternoon he was released. He missed CoCo's funeral, so he took a cab over to 221st. Cory and them weren't out there, but he left a message with Monica for them. They were on their own. Monica was sad that Lace was leaving and she offered him some going away pussy, stating that she always had a thing for him, but he declined. He had a few things to do.

*****

On the other side of town, Detective Mason sat at his desk right across from his partner Hobbs. Mason looked through files of paperwork dealing with cold cases, while Hobbs tossed a baseball in the air, catching it in his old baseball glove. Opening a file marked 49th house, he found something that was interesting. He quickly jumped up startling Hobbs, causing him to drop his baseball. "What the hell is wrong with you," Hobbs called out. Mason didn't answer; he just pulled open two of the file cabinets. He was a little pissed off, that in the times of internet his station house was still in the stone ages. He dug through the cabinet and pulled out two files. "Mason what the fuck are you doing," Hobbs asked again.

"Hold on," Mason started. "I think I might have something," he said while setting down three open files in front of him.

Hobbs sat up at attention. Once Mason found what he was looking for in the first file, he dug through his desk trying to find his old note pad. "What," Hobbs repeated as his partner flipped through his old, yellowing pad.

"Listen to this," Mason started finding the page written in his pad. "June 14th, 2007, Lawson Anderson is shot five times in front of his apartment. You remember that?"

"Of course, the little cousin of Maurice Brown. And…?"

"Well, on Monday June 17th, we go check him out and we see Henry Charles…"

"Yeah, the kid's best friend. What are you getting at?"

"Well, right here," Mason said pushing the second file in front of Hobbs.

He quickly sat up studying the paperwork marked December 2007. "Carol Kennedy, alright," Hobbs responded, but not fully comprehending.

"Look who ID'd the body," Mason said sitting back in his chair.

"Henry Charles and Sarah Kennedy of Orangetown, New York. That's Rockland County."

"Well hear this, on June 17th leaving the hospital we see Cornell and Chanel Winston entering Anderson's hospital room. Now look at this," Mason said pushing the third file in front of Hobbs marked April 8th 2009.

"This was a few days ago," Hobbs replied.

"You thinking what I'm thinking," Mason asked.

"Is the address still the same on that file?"

"Let's go see."

Both men jumped up. It was too much of a coincidence, so they threw on their jackets and headed uptown to question Lawson Anderson. Something was going on, and now they had reasons to believe that these cold cases were about to warm up.

*****

By 1 pm, Lace had all his property and was released with a fifteen hundred dollar citation. As soon as he got out of the precinct, he checked his messages and found that Henny called him several times. He was hesitant to call his right hand man, so he stopped a cab, jumped in, and headed home. He needed a shower bad as hell and was also starving. So after washing up and getting dressed he went into the kitchen, but looking in the fridge and the cabinets and seeing nothing but cereal depressed him. He missed CoCo so much. Knowing that he missed her funeral caused a tear to form, but he wiped it from his cheek. His child and the second woman he honestly loved were gone, but she had been a lie. Her love and loyalty had all been a lie, but regardless of how it all started, he knew she loved him.

After pouring a box of cereal in a big mixing bowl, he found out the milk was spoiled, and nothing was going right. He sat on the sofa looking at his cell phone and when he picked it up, he dialed Henny's house. After three rings, she answered, "Hello." Just hearing her voice hurt Lace. "Sin?"

"Yeah who is this? Lace?"

"Yeah."

"How you doin' baby?"

"Honestly Sin, I don't know." She felt like Lace's misery was her fault and badly wished that she never opened her mouth.

"Lace, I'm so sorry. I never wanted to hurt you or CoCo!"

"I know Sin, what's done is done."

Those words pained her, because she believed Lace and CoCo deserved love. "Lace, I know how you must feel, but I swear to you CoCo didn't want anything to do with that. Cornell made her do it, and we were both terrified of him!"

The line was silent because Lace had nothing to say.

"Lace…? Lace?"

"Yeah?"

"She loves you, I know she does. Please, for me and for your child that she's carrying give her a chance." Lace laughed, but it was only to not cry. Hearing the laugh upset Sin because he had to believe CoCo loved him "Lace, are you laughing?"

"CoCo's dead."

"What?"

"She is dead Sin. They found her, the baby, and Tamika dead in your old apartment a week ago," Instantly Sin began to cry, and hearing her was about to make Lace break down.

"Lace that shit ain't funny, tell me you're playing!" Lace couldn't even speak because his throat was so dry. "Lace talk to me!"

"Sin she's dead!" Beep. Lace forced the words out his parched throat and they hurt. He looked at the phone and the battery was dying. "Sin all da ib…" The phone went dead. He just dropped it and ran to the kitchen for some water.

"Lace…? Lace…? Hello?" She didn't hear what he said but she had to call Henny before she did anything.

*****

The old woman downstairs told the detectives that Lawson moved and almost a year ago Marisol moved down south. Hobbs and Mason drove around the corner to the block they knew Lace to hustle on, 225th and Bronxwood. It was funny to Hobbs that the so called gangster he'd grown up with had some kind of morals. These new millennium thugs were heartless and he didn't mean that in a good way. It barely took a little threat for the young boys to talk. After a few tugs and shoves they told that Lace moved down to 221st street, so that was the detectives' next stop.

These boys were a lot tougher on this end of the block, and with the pushing and the threats they became more rebellious. They didn't know anyone by the name, never saw him, and were sticking to their stories. Pushing the yardie boys around got them no where, so they got back in their car and heard the call over radio that a coroner was needed in the Eastchester section of the Bronx. With nothing else to do, they rode over, just to see what was going on. They arrived at the scene to find two young black males murdered, and according to the M.E. they'd been dead less than twenty-four hours. Mason and Hobbs walked up to the detectives in charge and introduced themselves.

Detective Sharpe brought them up to speed, but as they talked, a call came over the radio for Sharpe. It appeared that earlier that morning, a young man named Lawson Anderson was pulled over driving the deceased's vehicle. "What was he pulled over for," Hobbs asked, with a grin on his face, sensing they had what they needed.

Sharpe looked at him strangely trying to understand the joke. "Is this a joke Detective," Sharpe asked.

"Not at all," Hobbs started, still smiling, "but would you believe we were just looking for Lawson Anderson to ask him a few questions about two other homicides?"

"Public intoxication, but he was released earlier today."

"Do they have an address on Anderson," Mason asked.

After getting the info, Hobbs and Mason were on their way.

*****

The phone rang and Hard White looked at the time. He knew just who it was, because somehow even time couldn't stop The God. He found a way to still drive the white boy mad from the pen. With seven years to do, he had a plan that Hard White couldn't refuse, that would not only put another ten to twenty grand a week in the white boy's pocket, but would also take care of Sha while he was down and make sure he had a nice sized nest egg to come home to. White wasted no time accepting the collect call. "Yo Peace God!"

Sha still hated hearing this white boy speaking like he was a part of this earth, but he needed the Caucasoid. "Yeah, you heard anything from them fools," The God asked.

"Nah God, I been waitin but nothing yet. I did put my lil man on to shortie though!"

"Shit," The God cursed in the background because he couldn't talk too much over the tapped lines. "Yeah I tried him first, but got no answer. C-Rock already told me everything was a go, but I want you to make sure they handled that business, even if you have to handle it yourself, understood?"

"Of course, God." White knew The God spared him, so he would handle whatever he needed done. He had no choice, because if he didn't, the God would just send them four building boys after him, and he doubted his boys would go against The God's.

"Alright, I'll call you Thursday at 3 p.m."

"I'll be here." As soon as Hard hung up he dialed the followers.

"Yeah Daddy I'm right behind him now…"

"Where ya'll at?"

"On the Major Deagan."

"You hear me baby? As soon as you get a chance, finish that!"

"No doubt daddy, pop bottles all night!" Click, the line went dead.

*****

The phone was ringing and he knew it was Sin, but he couldn't deal with her at that moment. He was hungry and there wasn't shit in the house to eat, so he headed out the house to the one place he knew he could always get a good meal, his mom's house. It took him about twenty minutes to get there, and as he walked up the stairs he pulled out his keys. He doubted his moms was there because her Volvo 70 C wasn't parked outside, but Elise's truck was there, so he knew she'd fix him something to eat. He walked in the apartment. It was odd not seeing Nette's lazy ass on the sofa watching soap operas. Even Nette accepted the fact that CoCo was family now, but that no longer mattered, because she was gone.

He opened Elise's bedroom door. "What the fuck," he yelled.

"Lawson, close my door!"

"Who the fuck are you," Lace yelled.

"Lawson will you get out!"

"No, put on some clothes. And who are you," Lawson again asked, as the naked boy jumped off his naked sister, trying but having a hard time getting on his pants.

"I'm... I'm Mike. You know me, I'm Darren's little brother," Mike answered.

"Little Most from 3rd?"

Most just nodded.

"Lawson, will you get out," Elise yelled again while hiding herself with her sheet.

"My little sister is fuckin' unbelievable." Lace wasn't mad. Besides, Elise was grown now and Darren was good peoples, so his little brother was alright with him. "Yo get dressed hoe so you can make me something to eat," Lace said laughing, as he closed the door.

Elise quickly put on a sweat suit. She was embarrassed, but at least it wasn't her mother.

"You hungry," she asked Most.

"Yeah." he answered.

She walked out the room and Most picked up his cell phone. As Elise warmed up some leftovers from the other night, they began to laugh and joke about what happened. A few minutes later, Most joined them in the kitchen.

Henny wasted no time as he left work and headed home. He was pissed, and hearing Sin crying only added to his anger. It was worse when he walked in and saw the tears in her swollen, red eyes. "What did he say?"

"They found her and Tamika dead in my grandmother's apartment."

"Blast did it," Henny yelled as he went to the closet.

"What are you gonna do?"

"I'm gonna kill this nigga. Sin, I'm sick of this motherfucker. He killed Carol, I know he killed Nette, and now CoCo. His own fuckin' sister?"

"How do you know Henry?"

"The same fucking way you know!"

"Henry, he's Camille's father…"

"I'm that little girl's father!"

"Please, Henry I need you. Don't do this, think about your dreams!"

"Yeah, well I'm about to put an end to those nightmares," he said stuffing the desert eagle in his waist line. He then threw on his leather jacket to conceal the weapon.

"Henry, please look at me."

He refused to look at her, because if he did. he knew he would change his mind, and that was something he couldn't allow. He owed this to Carol, Nette, CoCo, and Lace. He walked out the door and as he hopped in the Caravan, he looked back at Sin standing in the doorway shaking her head, as she held Camille in her arms. He took a deep breath, put the car in gear, and pulled off. It was an hour and a half ride to the Bronx. He hit speeds up to one hundred-ten on the thru-way, and at that speed he'd be there in at least an hour. Murder was the only thing on his mind. He dialed Lace's cell number several times but only got his voicemail. It didn't matter, because this would be done. It had to be done. For years, Blast caused them all nothing but misery, but it would all end today.

*****

They sat there for about an hour. Lace was full as he settled into his favorite recliner in his mother's living room and rolled up a blunt. His nerves were so bad that at the moment, he needed the herb to calm him down. After lighting it, he took a few pulls and then handed it to little Most, who took a few drags, and then extended it to Elise. She quickly looked at her brother.

"My little sister is fucking and getting high too? Damn," he said smacking himself in the forehead. They all laughed.

The knock on the door caused them all to jump. Elise quickly began spraying Febreeze as she got up to answer the door. She nearly had a heart attack when she opened the door and saw the two detectives standing there.

"Excuse me ma'am, is Lawson Anderson here?" She started to say no and close the door, but it was too late because Lace was right behind her. "Mr. Anderson, remember me? Detective Hobbs?"

"Yeah," Lace answered nodding his head.

"Well, we'd like you to come with us because we have a few questions to ask you."

Lace wanted to say not again but fear stopped the words, because all he could think of was Noodles and Rich. He was going to jail for the rest of his life. "Am I under arrest or something?"

"No, at least not yet," Mason offered. Lace walked out with them uncuffed and stepped into the back seat. Within minutes he was sitting in an interrogation room again.

With Hobbs and Mason sitting in front of him, they began to question him about Carol, Lynette Chanel, and Tamika. He just answered questions about CoCo and Mika, but couldn't understand why they would ask him about Carol. He answered as best as he could, but he honestly knew nothing about the women's murders, and from his facial expressions and body language, Hobbs believed his words to be true.

Then Hobbs popped the question that made Lace nervous as hell. "Anderson, Richard Green and Melvin Turner were found dead this morning. Do you know these men?" As Hobbs finished, Mason pushed mug shots of both men in front of Lace. He looked at the pictures and decided he should lie, but why? He thought knowing them wasn't a crime. Lace nodded his head avoiding eye contact, which was something he maintained the entire time he was being questioned about the women. Hobbs noted the change.

"When was the last time you saw these men," Mason asked.

"Honestly, we got drunk last night."

Hobbs looked at Mason. "I understand you were arrested early this morning?"

"Yes." Again, Lace was making eye contact.

"For what," Hobbs now asked.

"Public intoxication."

Hobbs smiled, as he fingered some paperwork in front of him. "Lawson," Hobbs spoke. "What were you doing driving Mr. Turner's car?"

Lace put his head down. "Rich and Melvin were going to meet two chicks, so I dropped them off at Oasis Motel, but Melvin let me take his jeep home." The entire time Lace focused on the floor.

Hobbs smiled and just then the door flew open. "Shots fired inside 1240 Webster Avenue," A uniformed officer looked in and told the detectives, and both men jumped up.

"Mr. Anderson, you're free to go right now, but don't go too far. I'm positive this isn't over!" Both detectives headed out the door.

1240 was his old building and all he could think was Blast.

*****

Henny's first thought was to leave the car running, just in case he had to make a speedy exit, but this neighborhood no longer knew him. Years ago he could leave his car wide open with the music blasting and no one would dare touch his ride, but now he might return and find it gone. He cocked the eagle, placed a bullet in the chamber, and then tucked it back safely on his waist. Henny got out of the car and quickly headed towards the doors of 1240. Afraid that someone would see his face and be able to give a description of him, he kept his head down and walked swiftly to the doors. He never saw the lizard get up, but lizard man smiled. It was the first smile he cracked in years.

Henny entered the building. He looked at the elevator, then quickly turned and headed up the stairs. The odor of urine caused him to smile because some things just never changed. He made his way up to the 9th floor slower than he expected and realized that these past few months the family man slowed down. He wasn't in his best shape. As he opened the door, he stopped for a second to catch his breath. He'd never been tired before going up and down those steps and he used to live on the 11th floor. Henny opened the door to the 9th floor apartment 9G and could see where police tape was ripped off. He then tried the door knob. It turned and he quietly opened the door, pulling the desert from his waist. Henny poked his head in, but Blast wasn't in the living room. The carpet was torn up and Henny could see the stairs. It was evident that the old linoleum soaked up the blood underneath the carpet.

Anger made Henny bite his bottom lip because this pig murdered everyone he loved, and now he would die for all the pain and misery he caused. Henny quietly closed the door and crept from room to room with the gun raised, but the apartment was empty. Disappointment made him even more upset. What was he thinking? Blast wouldn't be stupid enough to be hanging around this apartment. He tucked the gun back in his waist and slowly walked back to the front door. Once in the hallway, he quickly made his way to the stairwell and rushed down the stairs, desperate to get out of there. 7th floor. The sign made his heart pound as he stopped to stare at it. Sin told him she tried the house phone but it had been disconnected, but now for some reason his legs wouldn't work. CoCo and Blast lived on this same floor for over seventeen years and it wouldn't hurt to try. He opened the door to the seventh floor and he swore he smelled the aroma of weed.

With his heart pounding and a funny feeling in his gut, he reached for the door knob. Henny swallowed the knot in his throat as he turned the knob. It clicked as it opened and he stuck his head in. The apartment was bare, the walls and floors had been stripped clean, and beer bottles were scattered around the open space, which had been the living room a few months ago. Henny figured this was the kids' late night hang out crib, but nosey ass Ms. Cross had always been the type to call police. She called police on them on a regular basis when they were teenagers. He used to smoke weed and drink beers with CoCo and Sin, and the thought made him smile. He just slowly walked through the kitchen, then the bathroom, and finally the room that had once been Mrs. Winston's. Henny inhaled. It was as if he could still smell Mrs. Winston's perfume. Even when she was diagnosed with cancer, which would take her life later, she never lost her beauty.

CoCo definitely inherited her mother's looks and body. All of the young boys had crushes on Mrs. Winston. As he inhaled, he had the brief scent of bud again. He looked around and listened but heard nothing as he continued to tour the apartment. First, he looked in Blast's old room, as the door was cracked a little. He paused to listen and heard nothing, but he was sure the smell of weed was stronger. He slowly pushed open the door and it squeaked, as it opened. Henny poked his head in and saw a pile of blankets and bags. Someone had recently been there. There were also condom wrappers scattered on the floor, so this had to be kids. He walked further into the room to investigate the bags. He then kneeled down and began to fumble through them.

As he watched from the closet, he was pissed his gun was in the bag next to the window. He was so worried it was the police that he just ran into the closet as if it was a safe hiding spot, and right in front of him was the man, who this entire shit had been about. If he could kill this motherfucker for everyone that died in the past two years, it would've been worth it all, but he didn't even have a knife. They weren't kids anymore and he was sure there would be a different outcome in hand to hand combat. He had to make a move, because in minutes this bastard would be digging through the bag with his gun and his money. Now!

He pushed the door open and it didn't even make a sound. He slowly crept up behind Henny, but as he was just a few feet away the floor creaked. Henny turned just in time to catch the size eleven and a half boot to the cheek. "Arghh," Henny groaned in pain falling over.

"Yeah motherfucker," Blast yelled as he attacked.

The first right caught Henny right to the temple, causing him to see a flash of white light. The blow was followed by another and another and another, with Blast yelling with each one. Henny could understand nothing as Blast pummeled him. It felt as if he was on his way into unconsciousness, but the last blow woke him right up.

"Yeah motherfucker," Blast continued. "A lot has motherfucking changed!" With each word he delivered a blow. Henny's face had been beaten bloody, and weak from the ass whipping he was taking, he slowly reached for his waist. Blast was so excited about finally getting his hands on the man, that as blood flew from his fists, he paid no attention to Henny's movement. Henny had the small cannon in hand and he could barely lift it, but he managed to pull the trigger.

"Arghh," Blast screamed in pain as he fell back with his leg feeling as if it had been smashed by a sledge hammer. Shaking off the beating, Henny staggered to his feet, gun trained on Blast who was rolling back and forth in pain.

"Mother... motherfucker," Henny managed to say, spitting blood with his words. "You killed Carol you faggot," he gasped, then swallowed a mouth full of blood.

"No," Blast screamed. "No I didn't, I swear," he added. Henny knew this was what it would be, the pussy motherfucker begging for his life, but that's not what it was. Blast knew today was his death and there was no way Henny would allow him to leave, but he refused to die without seeing the man's pain.

"You... You fucking liar," Henny managed.

"I swear it wasn't me," Blast said slowly, trying to ease over to the knapsack containing his nine. "I swear it wasn't me Henry."

Henny didn't know if he should believe it or not, but then again why should he care anyway. The man tried to kill his best friend.

"It doesn't matter," Henny said raising the gun chest level with Blast.

"Wait, wait Henry wait." He was almost near the knap sack. "I know who it was," Blast continued, as he pulled the bag to him. "And he told me she cried your name when they cut her up!"

Bang, bang, bang, bang! The four shots ripped Blast apart. Henny quickly wiped the gun clean of his prints and dropped it as the tears ran down his cheeks. This was not the time for an emotional break down; it was time to get out of the BX and away from all the ghosts that wandered there. He quickly made his way to the front of the apartment, opened the door, and stepped into the hallway.

"Henry," he turned to see Mrs. Cross sticking her head out of her door. *"Nosey bitch,"* he couldn't help but think to himself. "Henry Charles is that you?"

What Henny couldn't see was the cordless phone she held in her hand, which she had already used.

He looked towards the stairs. Then he saw the elevator was on its way down, so he pushed the button. He was too out of it to take the stairs, as his head pounded and his swollen lips throbbed.

"Henry Charles," Ms. Cross called again. "What is goin on? The police are on their way, boy. What are you over there doing?"

"Shut up you nosey bitch," he yelled and she slammed her door in fear.

Just then the elevator dinged and its doors slid open. Henny stood there for a moment. His heart beat matched the throbbing pain in his head, and fear hit him as he visioned John John falling down that elevator shaft all those years ago. As he stood there, he could see a young John John standing inside that cold death box smiling at him and urging him to come in. He didn't have time to waste because he needed to get the hell out of there, so he turned again to look at the stairs. The doors of the elevator began to close, and at the last minute he threw his hand in, causing the door to retract. Henny jumped in and he held the walls with his eyes closed, as the car descended. He could hear John John's laugh and he felt like screaming. The ride only took seconds, but it felt like hours. Ding! The first floor destination had been met and his hell ride was over. The doors slid open.

"Oh shit," Henny said, as he saw this raggedy face man standing there with his lip hanging and his nostril flapping. As the man inhaled and exhaled, he then raised his hand. "What the fuck," Henny called out, but it was too late to do anything. As he was tossed back into the elevators wall with force, he bounced off the wall and landed face first. He didn't move, as the lizard face man kicked him. Still no movement, he was dead for sure. The doors began to close and as they hit Henny's head, they slid back open. The blow caused Henny's dead body to jerk. Acid face laughed a gargled, phlemy laugh, because the scene was hilarious to him. He was so amused, that he didn't notice all the commotion behind him, as the door to the tenements was swung open.

"Drop the gun and put your fucking hands in the air!"

Lizard Man obeyed, as he continued to smile, as the doors continued to try and close on the dead man, only to jerk back open. His laugh was haunting, even to the police.

*****

They made it clear that he wasn't under arrest, so after sitting there for twenty minutes by himself, Lace got up. The door was open. He looked up and down the hallway, but no one paid attention to him, so he made his way to the front door of the precinct. In minutes he was out front. He wondered what could've happened at his old building. So much happened the past few months, that he began to think maybe he should just leave New York altogether. He now understood the pressure Henny was under so many years ago. Henny described it as being haunted by the Ghost of the Bx. Love, Lies, and Loyalty.

He looked around as he needed a cab, because he just wanted to go home. Just then, the horn blew and he turned to see the sexy, honey complexion shortie in a short tennis skirt who was waving him over. Lace walked over, not really knowing what to do or say. Mommy was that bad.

"Your name is Lace right," she asked.

"Yeah, who you," he asked as his face showed his suspicion.

She just smiled extending her hand. "I'm Tanya, but they call me Tay-Tay. Your cousin Mark sent me to pick you up."

"Mark," Lace repeated.

"Yes, you do remember your cousin don't you?"

"Yeah," Lace started nodding his head. "But where is he?"

"All I know is he didn't want to meet you in the BX, so I was told to pick you up and bring you out to Bk."

"Bk?"

"Yes, Brooklyn."

"Where is Ebony," Lace asked.

Tay-Tay shrugged her shoulders. "I guess she's with him…," she replied walking around the back of the Toyota Avalon and putting a little extra bounce in her strut. She hadn't been told how good the dude looked.

Lace couldn't help but watch the shapely thighs and ass sway around to the driver side. Tay-Tay slid into the driver seat and shifted to get comfortable as the cold metal rubbed under her thick thighs. Lace looked around, as the passenger side window slid down.

"Are you coming or should I tell Mark I didn't see you," she asked.

Lace looked around one last time. What he was looking for, he had no idea, but whatever it was, he wished it would appear, before he got in the car with this beautiful woman that gave off a dangerous aura.

Mason and Hobbs sat in the 49th with Detectives Cherry and Norman. They questioned the lizard man, as the neighborhood kids called him, for almost an hour, but still he hadn't given them anything. They all sat around the interrogation room watching lizard continuously wipe a nasty, thick slob that refused to stop running from down his chin. "Please mister," Hobbs began, "talk to us. We want to help you. Trust me, none of us give a shit about Mr. Charles. The world is probably a better place without him. Do you understand," Hobbs finished.

The lizard man just looked at him, with what appeared to be a smile, as he wiped his chin with his filthy handkerchief.

"It's useless Hobbs," Cherry spoke. "This asshole is probably deaf and mute. I wouldn't doubt it, look at him," Cherry added.

The smile was gone from lizard man's face. "Luk aht Mee!"

They all turned to see the man, shocked to hear him speak. "So you can talk," Mason stated more to himself than a question.

Slurp! "Yes," Lizard answered, then dapped at his chin.

"Please sir, can you tell us your name," Mason asked.

Lizard smiled again. "Liizarrd Maan!"

"Alright Lizard Man, why'd you murder Henny Charles," Cherry asked.

"Ta May..." Slurp! "Da worl..." Slurp! "Ah bet..." Slurp! "Ta pla..."

"Did he do this to you," Norman now asked.

Lizard just nodded.

"What did he do to you," Hobbs asked.

Now lizard looked down as he shook his head.

Hobbs thought to himself, maybe the memory was too horrible to relive. "Please sir, can you tell us your name," Mason asked.

Lizard now looked up and stared directly into Mason's eyes. His eyes were repulsive, as phlegm built up in the corner. It took all of Mason's strength not to turn away in disgust, but they had Lizard speaking and he refused to lose him now.

Before speaking, Lizard sucked up his slobber again. "M'I Name s T...Or Bar...Ton," slurp.

Right away Hobbs knew who the man was. The Wild Appache, Tior Barton, had been abducted from his grandmother's house two years ago and was presumed dead. To tell what happened to him would be too much because the man had a hard enough time telling them the little he did already. So he was given a pen and he wrote down exactly what he went through.

★ ★ ★ ★ 290

Maurice, Mark Brown, and Henry Charles left him for dead in an abandoned warehouse in Brooklyn. He told how he was beaten, cut up, and how Maurice poured honey all over him then left. Hundreds of rats attacked him, tearing into his flesh from head to toe. He prayed and prayed as the rodents dug into his body. Thank God they began to eat right through the duck tape around his wrist. As they devoured the tape, they also bit through his skin and right down to the bone. Once his hands were free, although gnarled and bloody, through all the pain, he freed his feet and crawled out of that warehouse. Although he looked like this, he was alive, and he had one thought on his mind. The only thing that kept him going was killing the Brown Brothers and Henry Charles.

*****

Tay-Tay pushed her seat back, exposing more of her honey colored thighs than she usually allowed any man to see. "What are we doing here," Lace asked trying to avoid looking at the woman's lace panties by looking at the old run down buildings and warehouses.

"This is where Mark told me to bring you. He said it was safe and he should be here in a few minutes. So, you got a girlfriend," Tay-Tay asked.

Without looking at her, Lace just nodded.

"Damn all the good guys are either taken or dead," she replied. Lace looked at her with a smile, as she pulled her skirt down some and sat up. "Oh, that's him right there," Tay-Tay said pointing out of the passenger side window.

Lace turned to see the black Range Rover pulling up and parking. The tints were so dark that he couldn't tell who or how many people were in the truck. Lace reached for the door's handle.

"Wait," Tay-Tay said, putting her hand on his shoulder. "He's gonna come to us!"

"What," Lace said, looking at her, and then looking out the window at the Range.

Tay-Tay began reaching up under her, because the cold metal was killing her. As she wrapped her hand around the handle, '*he was so cute*', she thought to herself. It was a shame all the good men we're either dead or taken. Bang Bang! Two to the head. This cutie would be one of the dead good ones.

Tay-Tay got out the car and the back door of the Range opened. A light skinned chick in tight jeans carrying a gasoline can hopped out. She began dousing the Toyota with the liquid as Tay-Tay wiped down the steering wheel, dash board, door, and outside of the door. "Give me a cigarette." Tay-Tay pulled out a pack of matches, lit the Newport, and then threw the match into the gas dripping off the car. It quickly went up in flames. Both women walked back to the Range and hopped in the back seat. The dark skinned female that was driving, reached back handing Tay-Tay a cell phone and then quickly pulled off.

Tay-Tay dialed the number and seconds later the other line was answered. "Yo," the man's voice spoke.

"What's up Daddy? It's done!"

"Thank you Keisha…"

"Come on Hard. Baby you know for you, I'll pop bottles all night. So, what's the next plan," Keisha asked.

"Give me a few days. When I hear from The God, I'll put you on." Hard White hung up.

In a few days, Sha Asiatic would be calling him and everything would be in motion. Yes, shit was definitely about to be on and a quarter of the Bronx would belong to him. He smiled as he thought to himself that a year ago The God came to him, White had a plan, and except for The God getting locked up, everything else went exactly according to plan. '*Yes*,' White thought to himself. Yes, he was truly a criminal mastermind.

The Wrong He's Done
A Novel by
Nathan Gadsden

Greatness is only a step away for Damon Masters. Partnership at his firm is within his grasp; all Damon has to do is prove to the firm that he can handle its main client. His wife, Priscilla, has found entreprenuerial success at her boutiques. The only speed bump in life is his annoying mother-in-law, Queen, whose jealous ways wreak havoc on his marriage. When the firms client turns out to be Frank Vanetti, mob boss and racketeer, Damon has to decide whether his life is worth risking for the idea of greatness. In the meantime, Queen has managed to split his household, leaving him to pick up the pieces of his fractured marriage. With the help of his best friend, Antoine, Damon goes on a road trip to meet past loves and reevaluate where life went wrong. But walking away from Vanetti does not mean that Damon is safe from the mob. And best friend Antoine's schemes and manipulations seek to sabotage Damon's trip and further destroy what is left of his marriage. When ex-loves remind Damon of what he had, and all the drama and chaos of his current life become overwhelming, he must decide whether his current life is worth fighting for.

NOW AVAILABLE

KAI

The Loudest Silence

All night? With his best friend? Then wants the fruit to be juicy when he climbs into bed? Would you believe the obvious, that there was something going on, or continue to turn your head since he was the prince charming that saved you from the ghetto? Do you get even for what you know, must be happening, as he whispers to her every night?

What would happen if you glanced in your home window and saw your wife <u>making passionate love</u> to your best friend's husband. Would you point the gun at him or her?

Gaps of inexplicable time lead to drastic assumptions, jail, and even death as the silence is so loud that it could destroy all four lives...

When Silence is the only answer given and the timing is never right, nothing is what it seems nor will it ever be the same again!

NOW AVAILABLE

Publications Presents

The hottest stripper in the DMV, Fancy, is on a mission. While everyone else see's her as a money hungry hoe, she laughs as they have no idea what she is thirsty for...BLOOD. Fancy has protected her baby sister Liv all her life and now its time to punish those who caused her to grow up too fast.

Liv lives in her cushy bubble that her big sister Fancy has created for her over the years but she has her secrets as well. She has secretly been accepting money from her "father" throughout the last couple of months, but she was told that her father died.

When lies come to light, Fancy and Liv have to decide where their loyalty lies and who has really been Deceitfully Wicked.

Deceitfully **WICKED**

Xtasy

PUBLICATIONS PRESENTS

NICOLE'S FACE WAS SWEET AND INNOCENT,
BUT NIKKI'S REVENGE WAS UNSTOPPABLE...

A NOVEL BY
AMANDA LEE

In Deranged, Nikki achieved her goal of capturing
Jeremy for Nicole, but fell short as Cowboy spoiled their
plans. One year later, Nikki refuses to fail and no longer
needs Nicole or her assistance. In Deranged 2, Nicole's
face was sweet but Nikki s revenge was unstoppable as
she moved heaven & earth to be with her man and live
the dream life that they planned together. Once free,
AND she sees he's cheating and living their dream life
with someone else, Jeremy and his family have nowhere
to hide. The question is: Will she finally get what she
wants or will she die trying?

A NOVEL BY

KAI

Daughter OF THE **GAME II**

HIS LOVE WAS DEEP   BUT HIS HATE WOULD BE INFINITE...

The Secret Keeper

COMING FEBRUARY 2012

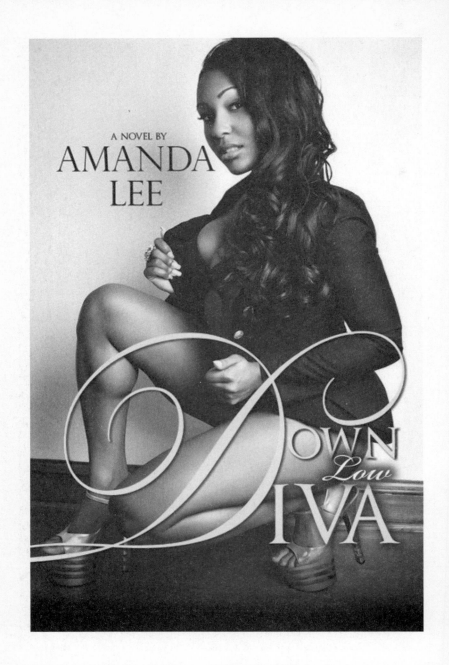

A NOVEL BY

AMANDA LEE

*D*OWN *Low* *D*IVA

COMING FEBRUARY 2012

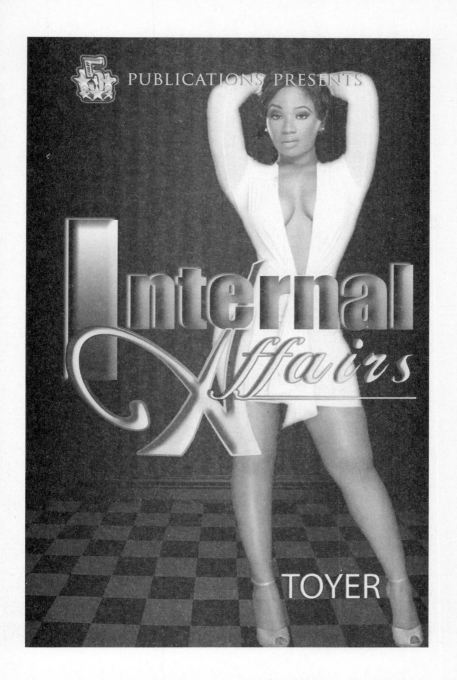

COMING APRIL 2012

ENTER AT YOUR OWN RISK

WELCOME TO A WORLD WHERE A SIMP
CLICK CAN GET YOU SEX, MONEY, AN
EVEN MURDERED...

SPRING 2012

COMING FALL 2012